E.D. HACKETT

Hope Hanna Murphy

Story Two of the Block Island Saga

First published by E.D. Hackett 2021

Cover Art by 100Covers.

First edition

ISBN: 9781737467908

This book was professionally typeset on Reedsy.
Find out more at reedsy.com

For my husband Kris, who has always supported my dreams.

Contents

Acknowledgement

Dear Reader,

For my entire life, I have used writing as an outlet to deal with life. The very first story I wrote was about how I lost my first tooth. I was in first grade. The book was bound and hand illustrated. Every now and then I look back at that story and think about the little girl who had high hopes of using the written word to change lives. I dreamed of being a famous author, writing from my cottage overlooking the wild Atlantic in Ireland.

I kept a journal from the age of ten all the way up until motherhood. I wrote journals specifically to my children from the day I found out I was pregnant until the day they were born. I was afraid that if I died in childbirth, they wouldn't know who I was. Those journals, dedicated to them, contained my soul.

I have always been a reader, using books to escape from the boredom and experiences of my childhood. I still read the last chapter before I start a book, in fear that I will die before I can finish.

Ever since I was a child, my desired superpower was to live other people's lives. I believed that the only way to fully understand others was to walk in their shoes, and what better way than to live their lives. Writing books was my answer to fulfilling my superpower.

This novel is a continuation to AN UNFINISHED STORY. Many readers commented that they needed to know what happened to Joanie and Carly, and I must admit, my heart wasn't through telling their story.

This novel would not have been completed without the help of my husband Kris. He helped me develop the plot, pointed out inconsistencies and plot holes, and assisted with cover design. His patience and understanding when life got crazy and tunnel vision related to writing took over my life is something I will never forget. He continued to support me when I was discouraged and encouraged, happy and annoyed, and excited and anxious. Writing a novel is a long process that encompasses every emotion. I am so thankful that I had him by my side to walk with me throughout this journey.

This novel also wouldn't have happened without the support of my writer friends. Early morning writing sprints, guidance, and experience on how to best self-publish a novel guided me on this journey. Without the consistency of their support, I would be lost.

Thank you to my critique partners, beta readers, and editor. "It takes a village" doesn't only apply to raising children. Without my village behind me, this novel wouldn't be completed.

Enjoy this story of Joanie and Carly. My heart still tells me that their story isn't finished.

I would be honored if you checked out my website or joined my newsletter at www.edhackettwrites.com and am always looking for feedback on my writing.

-E.D. (pronounced "Edy") Hackett

Prologue

She had played the scenario out in her mind at least a million times. The outcome was always the same, but her approach was different. She didn't know what would be best. Accusations of abandonment? Sympathy for the difficult choices life forced her to make? Immediate acceptance despite the pain and confusion? She wasn't sure which approach would result in the best outcome.

She was angry. Her entire life was a lie, yet her parents led her to believe that nothing was out of place. They all had a role to play and played it flawlessly. She thought that they wanted what was best for her when they were only looking out for themselves.

People she didn't know filed into the upholstered seats around the floral trellis. This wasn't her day, but it was undoubtedly about her. She painted a smile on her face, anxiously scanning the eyes staring back at her. Some looked familiar, and some looked unknown. The face she searched for was both comforting and strange.

Her eyes scanned the crowd haphazardly until she settled on a man and older woman across the aisle. She was looking in a mirror. Same petite frame, same round eyes, and same crooked smile stared back at her. It was her, just older. Her body filled with heat, and her feet started to sweat. She pulled off her pumps and placed her feet in the cool, dry grass. The blades rubbed her feet and sent shivers up her spine to the base of her neck.

The room began to spin. She couldn't take her eyes off of her. She wondered if she knew she was there or if she thought she would be alone, unnoticed. The bride and groom walked down the aisle, declaring their love. All the buried emotions emerged as a twister, preparing to touch down and wreak havoc on the lives of many.

She gulped down the rest of the wine she sneaked to her seat, hiding the glass behind the chair's leg. Liquid courage traversed throughout her body, and her bravery overpowered her fear. She knew it was risky because the truth could come out, but it needed to be said. She rehearsed it over and over in her mind. Suddenly, she was standing face to face with the ghost of her past, despite her ignorance and naivety.

She screamed out the words in her head, but her mouth remained silent. *Mom, why did you leave me?*

Chapter 1-Eight Months Earlier

Carly pulled on a t-shirt and her favorite cardigan and pulled open the blinds in her bedroom. The sunlight poured through the window and shined a patch of bright light against the floorboards. The warmth of the sun rejuvenated her, and she wondered how she slept the entire morning away.

"John?" she called out, unsure if he was still in the apartment.

"Morning!" he called from the couch, watching television. He looked at her with a grin and patted the seat next to him. "How was work last night?" he asked.

"It was okay. I was off early last night. Even though I don't make as much money, I love coming home before midnight. I feel more human when I go to bed at a normal time. How was your night?" She chipped at her flaking nail polish, scraping at her cuticle bed.

"I think I got home around seven last night and was passed out on the couch by nine," John replied.

Carly nodded. "Yeah, when we were younger, I could handle the late nights, but now, I'm too old!" she exclaimed. "My body is giving out on me." She grinned and leaned into his hard frame.

"Was it busy?" he asked.

"Yeah, it wasn't too bad. We were short-staffed, so my section was two tables larger. By the end of the night, my feet were killing me, but at least I walked away with more money than I expected." John didn't know it, but Carly saved all her extra money for those "just-in-case" moments. Her past with John taught her that she should never be too comfortable.

"Restaurant life is harder in your forties than it is in your twenties. It's just like fishing. Everything takes more effort, and your body takes a beating," John said.

Carly nodded. "When we lived here ten years ago, I was a superstar waitress. I was quick on my feet, I could juggle multiple tables, and I never messed up. Now, if I have more than three tables at a time, I have to write down everything because I can't remember. And my body doesn't rebound the way it used to." She stretched her back, cracking her shoulders in the process.

Today was John's only day off. He and Carly decided that his weekends would be dedicated to them and them alone. John had probably been up since five and would be in bed before the sun set and awake before the sun rose to get back on the lobster boat.

"What do you want to do today?" he asked.

Carly's body felt broken, and she knew John's body felt the same. "Let's go downtown, grab a late lunch or early dinner at the pub, and then watch the sunset over the harbor." The sun set around seven or so, so they would have plenty of time to get back for John to go to sleep. Carly snuggled up against John's warm, muscular body. She traced her fingers the distance of his tattoo, which enveloped his forearm.

"Sounds great," John said, kissing her tenderly.

The sunrise was Carly's favorite time of day. When she ran the inn, she would look outside her window and watch the purples and pinks mix and mingle in the sky. It set her day up for success. Now, she never saw the sun rise. When she wasn't working, sunsets became the next best thing.

Carly and John sat on the bench overlooking the harbor. At night, especially during the summer, live music played around downtown Portland. People walked arm in arm, laughing and chatting about their day. The energy during high tourist season buzzed with excitement and caused Carly to feel alive.

The light from the setting sun reflected off the top of the water, causing the waves to look golden metallic within the ebb and flow of constant movement. The sky filled with activity, and brush strokes of pink and purple wrapped around the deepening grey clouds.

John and Carly sat in silence as they watched the sky transition from day to night. The vehicle engines rolled by, music poured out of the restaurants' open windows, and the waves collided against each other. The various noises created a beautiful symphony of city life.

Carly enjoyed her day with John. She was still exhausted but grateful to have five hours with him. She knew that the following week would be a repeat of this week, and she felt a heaviness weigh down on her shoulders and heart. It didn't seem fair that they were here, again, facing the same struggles they met a decade before. A decade earlier, they didn't make it out of the stress and chaos together.

As soon as the sun disappeared behind the horizon and the cotton candy sky swirled away, John and Carly walked home. Carly knew John's first love was fishing, and he committed tireless hours to his career. His only time to live life was during the winter season when he was unemployed. He had been honest with Carly when she decided to move back in with him, but she didn't realize how empty his work hours would make her feel.

They moved in together six months ago, and it had been incredible. They found a new apartment, decorated it together, binge-watched tv, and alternated between cooking and eating out. They spent all their time together, and Carly found herself close to John again. They sneaked kisses morning, noon, and night. They only wanted to be with each other. It was an incredible six months full of togetherness, unity, and passion.

Now, six months later, reality pressed her down, and the contrast between the high and low was so great, Carly almost wished the high hadn't existed. If she hadn't experienced the closeness and euphoria they created, she wouldn't miss it so much when it dissipated. Carly struggled with accepting that her life would be a constant yo-yo of good and evil, fun and boring, and love and like.

John kissed Carly gently on the mouth, told her he had a great night, and stumbled into bed. Carly looked at her watch. It was only eight, and she didn't have to work until tomorrow afternoon. Carly curled up on the couch with Ruth's blanket covering her legs. Carly traced the knitted design that her mother created. The wool scent reminded Carly of the inn, and she was transported back to her childhood.

She settled on a movie and sank further into the flat, worn cushions on their tiny loveseat. She listened to the muffled snores escape from the bedroom and turned up the volume to drown out the noise.

Chapter 2

J oanie ran around the kitchen, searching through all the drawers, wondering where she put that darn whisk. The sausages were sizzling in the frying pan, the pancakes were browning on the griddle, and the second coffeepot of the day was dripping at snail's speed. There was always that one guest that needed decaf coffee and meatless sausages. Joanie knew she should have sent up a menu the night before, but she imagined that the guests would take what she served without complaint.

Carly visited the previous weekend to discuss the anticipated chaos with Memorial Day tourism. She reviewed the number of guests, the length of their stay, and the inventory needed to make their home away from home memorable. "The goal," Carly said, "is to make them want to come back and stay here. The customer's always right, and even when they're wrong, we have to smile, agree, and fix it."

This was the first busy weekend Joanie experienced since she ran the bed and breakfast with Matt. Matt told her he would help out, but this first breakfast was not one of those times. He was assigned extra shifts at the police station because of the expected influx of tourists.

Joanie looked at the meatless sausages, wondering if they needed to be cooked or just warmed. She grabbed the cardboard box out of the recycling bin and reread the directions. Joanie tossed it back in the container and rolled the sausages back and forth, wondering how many minutes it had been since she turned on the stove.

The chatter of the guests in the formal dining room seeped into the kitchen. There were four reservations this weekend. Two families were attending the same wedding, one couple was visiting for their anniversary, and three friends were looking for an escape from their lives. Carly told Joanie that she had to mingle with the guests, especially at breakfast.

Joanie struggled with small talk and reviewed the list of questions that she wrote down the night before. The questions were not too personal but showed an interest in their story. Carly always told her to end the interaction with, "Can I help you find anything special to do on the island?" So far, Joanie knew that the two families traveled together, the couple was married for ten years, and the friends lived in New York City.

Joanie brought out the fake sausages and pancakes on a platter and carried the decaf coffee in Ruth's antique coffee carafe. Ruth recently passed away and handed the family business to Carly. When Carly moved to Portland, she gave the keys to Matt, who then passed them onto Joanie.

Breakfast looked beautiful, even if Joanie felt like a disaster. She pushed her thick, red hair back with a headband and wiped away the sweat that permeated her neck and forehead. She spread her arms like a bird and flapped them as naturally as she could, creating a chilly breeze against her hot, sticky skin. She felt the sweat settle within her armpits and quickly wiped them with a towel behind the privacy of the swinging door.

Joanie roamed around the dining room, recalled the list of questions, and asked the guests what they thought of Block Island so far. Most had checked in the night before, so Joanie suggested the local art galleries, moped rentals, and spa. The two families attending the wedding were busy from start to finish, so Joanie knew that they probably would not participate in breakfast the following day. Joanie quickly scolded herself and readjusted her expectations that everyone would be present for breakfast. Carly told Joanie on more than one occasion not to make assumptions about the guests because plans often changed instantly.

After she cleared the tables, Joanie looked at the clock and browsed the kitchen. It looked like a tornado touched down within the perimeter of the connected counter tops, leaving piles of dirty dishes, towels, and trash in its wake. Joanie woke up at four-thirty, the earliest she had woken since her original commute to Block Island almost a year before. Joanie's room used to be Carly's bedroom, which used to be Ruth's room before Ruth moved to the nursing home.

Joanie felt strange at first, sleeping in someone else's bed and knowing the history behind the people who had slept in that bed before her. To make her feel more comfortable, she asked Matt to swap the furniture from the carriage house, where Joanie resided before Ruth died, with the live-in apartment attached to the Willowside Inn.

Before Joanie took over the bed and breakfast, Carly went through everything of her mother's and either put it in storage, took it to Portland, or threw it away. All that remained was furniture, household items, and a series of boxes in the basement. Joanie missed the bedroom and living room set that she grew to love from the carriage house and begged Matt to help her make the swap and redecorate.

Not knowing if she was good at it, Joanie embarked on a different career and took over the inn. She had just been fired from the newspaper and had no means to pay her bills. At the time, her relationship with Matt was new and exciting. She didn't know if she loved him, but she knew he made her happy. On a whim, she started over, not entirely convinced it wasn't a mistake.

Joanie looked at the kitchen, taunting her with the amount of time it was going to steal from her day, and questioned again if she made a big mistake agreeing to run the Willowside Inn. Breakfast was a success, but there were moments when she felt like she made amateur mistakes. Joanie pulled herself to her feet from the hard kitchen chair and got to work scrubbing the pots and pans.

Joanie cleaned the kitchen, folded laundry, and vacuumed once breakfast was over. The empty inn allowed Joanie to move about freely, cleaning as efficiently as possible. By three pm, she sat down for the first time since four-thirty that morning. Joanie couldn't remember the last time she did this much manual labor.

Joanie invited Matt over for dinner so they could talk about how her first day went. Joanie looked at herself in the mirror. She had purple-tinted bags under her eyes, her red hair was wild and chaotic, and her black shirt was untucked and wrinkled along the bottom. She pulled out her favorite tank top and jean shorts and headed to the bathroom to freshen up for dinner.

Joanie wet her hair and applied mousse to give her thick hair extra volume. She applied a fresh coat of mascara and a deep rose lipstick to her freshly washed face. She wanted to look sexy without trying too hard. Joanie quickly painted her toenails a matching shade of deep rose and threw on black, strappy sandals. She looked in the mirror, feeling more confident than she had an hour ago, and went outside to enjoy the warm sun while tidying up the flower bed as she waited for Matt.

That night, Joanie and Matt sat at the bistro table in her kitchen. She found the glass-topped, metal-rimmed table at a local yard sale, and it wobbled with every movement. She placed the Walkie Talkie in the charge stand so if the guests needed her in the night, she would be available. Carly never talked about being awoken mid-night to help a guest, but she knew that this was her first night being in charge, and anything could happen.

"How did it go?" Matt asked between bites of sirloin. He prepared a beautiful meal of grilled steak, corn on the cob, and squash and zucchini. The vegetables glistened with butter the way the sun rays shine through dark clouds. Joanie's mouth watered at the sight of golden butter dripping down the corn.

"On a scale of one to ten, I think it was an eight. No major hiccups, but I'm exhausted. If I had to fold one more sheet or towel, I think I would die," Joanie said dramatically. "I put those tents up on the bathroom sink about saving energy and only swapping out towels when they left, and no one took me up on it. All the towels were on the floor like I asked them not to be. The two families left me a mess to clean. They used all the towels and filled two trash cans."

Joanie slowly chewed the tender meat, seasoned and salted to perfection. "Mmmmm. You know the way to a woman's heart," she smiled softly. "Maybe one day you can teach me how to do this. It's fantastic!!"

Matt leaned over and kissed Joanie. "Go ahead, keep it coming. Tell me how wonderful I am," he teased.

A wave of unease came over Joanie, and she froze. *Was he serious?* It felt ingenuine to feed him compliments on command, but Joanie did find him almost perfect. "Well," she cleared her throat and took a sip of red wine, "You are the best thing in my life right now." Matt waited, but Joanie's vulnerability dried up as quickly as a fallen rose petal. Nothing more came.

They kept eye contact, waiting to see who would break the silence first. Joanie and Matt awkwardly grinned at each other, waiting for what felt like an eternity.

"And you," Matt started, "are the best innkeeper I know." They clinked glasses and toasted to the Willowside Inn. The awkwardness passed, and conversation resumed.

"The best innkeeper for now, but Carly was better," Joanie responded. "Hopefully, by the end of summer, I will have my head on straight."

Technically, Carly owned the Willowside Inn because it had to stay in her family, or else she would lose all the money at the sale per her mother's will. Carly was hours away in Maine, trying to recreate the life she lost over a decade ago. Being Carly's cousin, Matt took over the management piece of the inn, like handling expenses and reservations, and Joanie was now the face of the inn, interacting with the guests and making sure they were happy. Somehow, the agreement they had seemed to be working.

"Carly's in Maine. She doesn't want this place. In my eyes, it's ours. We're the face of the inn, and right now, the success of this place is because of our hard work," Matt defended.

Joanie shrugged. He was right. They worked great as a team, and the success of the inn was on their shoulders.

Later that night, Joanie lay in her bed, listening to the crickets chirp outside her window. She set her alarm and tried to fall asleep, but her mind was swirling. Breakfast was the most challenging part of her day because she wasn't a cook, and she didn't enjoy being around strangers. To force down the anxiety, Joanie closed her eyes softly, inhaled deeply, and thought about Matt.

It had been less than one year since they met and only nine months since they started dating, so everything was still new, exciting, and cute. Joanie knew she had to protect her heart because she still didn't know who Matt was, deep inside his core. She didn't know what made him tick because she had never seen him angry. She knew a little about his past but didn't know enough to feel comfortable sharing her darkness that she worked years to contain.

Despite all this, she felt happy when she was with him. Joanie tried to push all the questions out of the crevices of her mind and focused on the charming characteristics about him: his deep voice, the way his dark brown hair rustled in the ocean breeze, the way his eyes crinkled when he laughed, and the way his jeans hung around his hips.

Joanie fell asleep, not thinking about the craziness that would come with tomorrow but about the reassurances that came with Matt. Instead of thinking about him in the long term, she thought about him now, and for right now, she needed him in her life.

Chapter 3

J oanie placed a single beach rose in four tall, thin vases and put them on each bistro table decorating the dining room. Earlier that morning, Joanie walked along the beach near the dunes, looking for four perfect flowers to decorate the inn. Through the slatted fence protecting the weathered dune, she found a light pink rose bush. Joanie looked around, wondering if tampering with the flowers was illegal, and quickly snipped the stems with her scissors before anyone could notice.

It was midweek, and Joanie was waiting for her sister Jackie and Jackie's boyfriend, Chris, to visit. Since Joanie moved to Block Island almost a year earlier, her relationship with her sister slowly grew closer. Jackie had never paid any attention to Joanie before, but now that they were adults and had a shared interest in Block Island, it seemed easier to connect.

Chris and Carly knew each other as children, but only because they were neighbors. Joanie didn't find it unusual Jackie and Chris planned a visit because Chris and Matt shared mutual friends. Chris couldn't stay with his parents because they moved away years ago.

Joanie didn't know Chris well because her younger sister always shut her out. Joanie got tired of being known as "Jackie's big sister," so she stopped trying to get to know Jackie. Their parents always compared the girls to each other, and no matter what Joanie did, she never lived up to her younger sister in their parents' eyes. It wasn't until Joanie moved to Block Island that her relationship with Jackie started to improve.

Joanie sat in the overstuffed chair overlooking the front flower garden and called Matt while waiting for Jackie to arrive.

"Hey, Matt!" Joanie chirped into the telephone. "What time do you think you'll be over tonight?" She fiddled with the chain of her necklace and ran the links back and forth against her neck. She picked up the nervous habit as soon as they decided they were 'boyfriend' and 'girlfriend.'

"I will be there after four. I have some things I have to do around here. After I mow the lawn, I'll be over."

Joanie giggled into the phone like a young schoolgirl. "Don't forget to shower. As much as I love your sexy, sweaty, shaggy hair, I don't know if Jackie would love it if you stink." Her sister seemed to get along well with Matt, but Joanie's insecurities and confidence still wobbled when Jackie was around. Jackie's perfect life made Joanie question if she was good enough. She didn't want Jackie to have any reason to judge her.

Matt laughed, "Babe, I'll do that for you and only you. I'll see you soon." His deep voice made her heart flutter, and she felt a magnetic pull to kiss him seductively, but he wasn't there.

"Later," she responded. Her hands felt clammy, her stomach fluttered, and her breathing quickened.

Joanie checked her phone and read the last text Jackie sent her: **Leaving now! Be there after lunch.**

Joanie hopped on her bike and rode down to the Cohen's bakery to grab some fresh honey and homemade croissants. When the Cohens first came to Block Island, they only produced local honey, but this year, they introduced fresh bread to their menu, and it was decadent!

She made her way to the Cohen's bakery and could smell the specialty flavors wafting through the barn door, which they used as their kitchen. "Hi, Sara!" Joanie greeted.

Sara looked up from kneading the dough and grinned. "Hi! I have your order right over there," she said, nodding toward the corner of the barn. She continued kneading and quietly grunted under her breath as she pushed and prodded rhythmically.

"What are you making?" Joanie asked, walking toward her packed bag. "It smells delicious."

"Cranberry spice bread. I'm trying out a new recipe. If it's a success, I'll

14

add it to the menu," Sara said, slightly out of breath.

"Let me know how it turns out, and we can add it to my weekly order." Joanie waved as she exited the door and threw the bag into her bicycle basket before riding home.

Joanie saw Chris and Jackie rocking back and forth at the inn on the wooden swing next to the bird feeders, holding hands. They didn't see her yet, and Joanie watched them discreetly. Jackie smiled wide, her straight, white teeth glowing against the backdrop of greenery, and threw her head back laughing. Chris pulled Jackie's hand up to his lips and kissed it gingerly. Jackie giggled again and leaned her head against his upper arm, squeezing the inside of his elbow.

Joanie retreated three steps, concealed by the blue hydrangea bush. She continued to watch them. Jackie seemed different. Giddier. Lighter. Happier. Joanie didn't want to interrupt their moment but couldn't stay hidden in the bushes forever. Joanie dropped her bike on purpose, and the metal clanged against the paved walkway.

Jackie turned, smile still in place, and jumped up, eagerly half-skipping to Joanie. She threw her arms around her sister in greeting, and Joanie stiffened, not quite sure what was happening. Chris slowly got up from the swing and stood, watching Jackie, with a grin on his face.

"Joanie!" Jackie exclaimed. She waved her arms in front of her like someone stranded on an island who just saw a rescue helicopter. Jackie clapped and bounced up and down on her feet, screeching incoherent sounds. Joanie returned the smile because she couldn't figure out what was happening, but it must be good. Joanie grabbed Jackie's shoulders and silenced her movement.

"Joanie! I am getting married!" Jackie cried, holding out her left hand. The princess cut diamond glistened in the sun, which was shining against the blue sky. "We want to get married here! You have to help me plan the wedding! It's going to be perfect!"

Dread filled Joanie's stomach, but she couldn't let her sister sense her reluctance. Joanie pulled back her lips as tight as she could and gave her sister a big hug and a tight squeeze, hoping Chris couldn't see the disappointment in her eyes.

Joanie pulled away from Jackie and smiled brightly with raised eyebrows and wide eyes. "Congratulations, little sister!" she exclaimed, hugging Jackie one last time and breathing in deeply.

She wasn't sure where her emotions were coming from, but she felt disappointed that Jackie did it again. Her younger sister engaged before Joanie. It didn't surprise Joanie, but it still stung. Everyone loved Jackie, especially their parents. Joanie was in her fourth decade and only had enough boyfriends to count on half of a hand. Of course, Jackie would marry first. It was how it always was and how it would always be.

They walked into the house, and Joanie continued to smile while her body stiffened. Her shoulders practically touched her ears, and she forced them to relax as she dropped her honey and bread onto the side table. Jackie and Chris amicably chatted about their future and all the great things going for them.

"Do you want some tea?" Joanie asked them both. "I just grabbed some honey and bread from the Cohen's." Her voice betrayed the disappointment she felt, and she reminded herself to kick it up a notch.

"Where can I drop our bags?" Chris asked.

"The inn has an extra room available. Upstairs, third door on the left."

Jackie kissed Chris on the lips in excitement and followed Joanie into the kitchen while Chris disappeared up the stairs. Joanie never expected her sister to get married on the island. That was the last place she pictured Jackie. Block Island was serene and gentle and peaceful. Jackie was exuberant and extravagant and expensive. When they were kids, Jackie dreamed of marrying in Boston, overlooking the lit-up city. In Jackie's daydream, they served champagne and caviar. Her wedding dress filled the room, and no matter what angle the guests were sitting, she was the center of attention. There was no way she could wear a dress like that on Block Island.

"I am so excited!" Jackie cried again, examining the sparkling rock on her finger. She held it up to the window, and prisms danced across the kitchen. Joanie continued to put her groceries away and grabbed a drink of water. "Chris proposed!" she continued, even though Joanie didn't ask for details.

16

"He took me to the Cape, which is the first place we went as a couple, and we went to the beach. He wrote in the sand with sea rocks: Will You Marry Me?" Jackie accentuated the words in mid-air with a quick arm yank for each word. "He took me to the top of the dunes to watch the sunset, and there it was! The sunset was beautiful, and the message was intoxicating. I turned around, and there he was, on one knee!" Jackie's voice rose an octave, and she screeched and bounced on the wooden floors. "Joanie, I cannot stop smiling!"

Joanie stopped and leaned against the counter. "Cheers!" She held up her glass of water and clinked the air in front of her, rolling her eyes when she turned away. "Do you want a drink?" Jackie shook her head, and Joanie pushed the plate of sliced bread, honey, and butter toward her.

Jackie kept talking, but Joanie's sadness drowned out the words. She liked Chris and wanted Jackie to be happy, but she couldn't believe that her baby sister was getting married. It made sense. Jackie was going to be thirty-seven, and they were already living together. "Did you tell Mom and Dad?" Joanie interrupted.

Jackie nodded. "They were thrilled! Mom said she's been planning my wedding since I got out of college. I told her she could help, and I'd consider her suggestions, but I am a grown woman paying for my wedding. I am going to have it my way."

Joanie nodded blankly. Their mother had been planning Jackie's wedding for years, dreaming of her ideal daughter marrying into a lovely family and pushing out grandbabies. Joanie imagined the celebration if her mother had control: designer clothes, expensive food, random people they wanted to impress, and a big announcement in the paper for her to send to all the influential people in her life. It sounded exactly like how Jackie wanted her wedding ten years ago.

"But I thought you and mom wanted the same thing. Big wedding, big dress, fancy food, Boston posh, a night to remember. I swear that is what you talked about when we were in high school."

"Joanie," Jackie began, "I was in high school! Don't you think life has changed for me since then?" Joanie looked at her sister and took in the designer watch, made-up face, highlighted hair, and genuine leather handbag. She didn't say anything, just waited for Jackie to continue. "I'm in my late thirties! All I want is to have a simple wedding with my closest family and friends. That's why we decided to have it here. Chris needs to get back to his roots. We live in Newport and love it, but we don't want to get married in our backyard."

"Makes sense," Joanie said flatly. The silence sat between them as Jackie examined her ring, and Joanie fiddled with the teapot.

Chris bounded into the kitchen with long strides and bold steps. They could hear his tall, bulky frame approach as the floorboards shuddered under the weight of his large feet. He grinned from ear to ear and jubilantly exclaimed, "Thanks for the room!"

"Congratulations, Chris!" Joanie said, mustering up enthusiasm. "So, did you say the wedding was happening here?" Jackie nodded. "Here, here?" Joanie motioned around the kitchen.

"Well, we wanted to talk to you about that," Chris responded.

"Can we use the inn, Joanie?" Jackie crept closer to Joanie, head angled, hands across her heart, begging.

"I have no idea," Joanie responded. "You'll have to ask Carly. It's her house." Joanie couldn't believe they dared to request the bed and breakfast when they barely knew the owner. Sure, Carly and Chris knew each other when they were kids, but there was no established relationship for at least twenty years.

Chris leaned toward Jackie, half whispering as if Joanie couldn't hear, "I'll talk to her."

"When are you thinking of having the wedding?" Joanie asked.

"Next May," Jackie responded. "If we have a year, we can figure out all the details." She leaned into Chris and gave him a quick kiss on the lips.

Joanie fiddled with her glass of water and ran her fingers around the condensation ring shimmering in the sunlight. At least she had one year to get her emotions in check before her baby sister walked down the aisle.

Chapter 4

"Hi, Carly!" Joanie chirped into the phone. "We survived our first few weeks with success. Breakfast alone is a little overwhelming, but I'll eventually get the hang of it."

"Great!" Carly feigned enthusiasm. "Has it been a full house?"

"We've had three to four rooms booked at a time. I'm exhausted! I think I work sixteen-hour days. I didn't realize how much cleaning you did daily!"

Carly nodded even though Joanie couldn't see. "Yeah, it's a lot, but you get a break here or there when the guests check out."

"I noticed. Today is the first day I have time to relax. It's been fun, though. I am enjoying it. How are you?"

"Oh, you know, living the dream. Work is crazy. Late nights, hard work, pretty good money. John started work again, so I'm preparing myself for being alone for the next few months." Joanie wasn't sure if she heard fatigue or sadness in Carly's voice.

"You know, Carly, anytime you can get away, you are welcome to come home for however long you need. I miss seeing you." They saw each other last over Christmas and New Years' when Carly came home to check out Joanie's changes to the inn.

"Thanks, Joanie. Same to you. Come up to Portland when you can." It was a half-hearted invite because leaving the island for more than a day was nearly impossible. Carly lived that life for thirty of her forty years, feeling trapped by her circumstances.

"Will do! Oh, hey!" Joanie interrupted. "My sister and Chris came up. They are getting married."

"Wow! Really?" Carly said. "That's great!"

"Yeah, I guess so. They want to talk to you because they want to get married on your property next spring. I am assuming outside. Chris said it's important that he get married on the island, and his family's property is gone. You're the next best spot!"

Carly wasn't sure how she felt about hosting a wedding. It could be an excellent opportunity to grow the business and get the word out that maybe they aren't just a bed and breakfast but also an event location. Perhaps they could advertise the inn as a group retreat and rent out the property for a weekend at a time.

"Okay," she said. "Tell Chris to call me, and we can talk about the details."

They discussed everything she knew: next May, a small group of their closest family and friends, and nothing overly extravagant. While the girls were talking, Carly felt a quick and heavy tug in her chest to get planning. She saw a planner at the local bookstore, which could be perfect for planning a wedding. She thought about all the business owners she knew on the island and how she could advertise their services on the website to support local businesses.

She welcomed the feeling of being productive, having a purpose again, and getting her creative mind moving. It surprised her because she wanted to get away, but she felt a magnetic pull to sit down and throw all her thoughts on paper.

Carly hung up the phone, filled with motivation to help Jackie have the wedding she always wanted.

***

Over the next few days, Carly struggled to turn her brain off. The ideas, questions, and comments tumbled over each other, and she couldn't focus. Carly brainstormed ideas for the wedding while also brainstorming romantic getaways. Her second one-year anniversary was coming up with John, and Carly wanted to make it memorable.

Carly knew he was busy, but she wanted to show John how much she appreciated him and loved him. She wasn't sure how to do it. His schedule was nearly impossible to predict because the weather changed by the hour.

Throwing a dart at the calendar could be just as fruitful.

Carly imagined booking a weekend away, where they could lay in bed until well after the sun rose, with no plans to tackle. Just being present with each other for twenty-four hours would be enough for Carly to fall in love again. Carly found the exciting memories they shared during winter slowly erase from her mind like a faded polaroid. The bitterness and resentment equally grew.

Ruth was approaching one year gone, and Carly struggled with knowing how much her life had changed since her mother left. Her life crumbled from the constant worrying to the weekly visits to learning that she could never sell the inn. Almost a year ago, Carly desperately needed an escape or a golden ticket to start new, and Joanie was that answer. No, not Joanie, but Matt. He was the long-lost relative that saved her life from living on repeat until the day she died.

She should have felt refreshed and reborn when she moved back to Maine. Unlimited opportunities streaked through her mind, but she felt ashamed for practically giving up the life her parents had built. She could feel her mother's disappointment from the grave the day she left the island for good.

Ruth's death forced Carly to recreate herself out of spite and rebellion, and she fell into John's arms because of the familiarity and comfort in his smile.

That morning, John's side of the bed was empty and cold when Carly awoke. Her day was free, so she pulled out her laptop, searching for romantic and relaxing day trips. Carly needed to take John away from Portland to celebrate their anniversary.

She settled on Sebago Lake, a short hour ride west with a combination of tourism and seclusion. She researched the restaurants, shopping, state parks, and boat rentals and made a quick list on her phone. Not only did she need to coordinate this trip with John's day off quietly, but she also needed to wait for sunny, warm weather.

Carly checked her phone and had a message from Jackie, asking if anyone on the island rented white horses. Carly didn't feel like talking and sent her a quick text: **Hey! I don't know. Is this for the wedding?**

As quickly as Carly hit send, her phone pinged in response: **Yes! I want to**

ride away on a unicorn.

Carly responded with a smiley face. She laughed, imagining Jackie's poufy dress covering the horse, her train dragging in the dirt. Chris was walking behind Jackie, holding a "Just Married" sign with cans attached to his ankles dragging behind him. Carly chuckled at her imagination.

Carly didn't realize she would be adding Wedding Planner to her resume, but she welcomed the challenge and felt a sense of identity growing within her. It helped keep her mind busy and away from her wobbly relationship that was teetering on stilts. She knew she would do a great job creating the most magical, perfect wedding experience, even if it required finding unicorns.

Between researching Sebago Lake and cheap wedding ideas that looked extravagant, Carly needed a nap. She lay on the couch with a bottle of wine, her favorite movie, and Chinese take-out, enjoying the quiet that her relationship with John provided. He still wasn't home when Carly turned off the last light and climbed into bed.

The following day, Carly woke alone in her bed again. She rolled over to John's side, and the cool sheets stimulated her skin. She breathed into his pillow and smelled his shampoo, wondering where he was right now. Carly looked outside and saw sunny skies. It was going to be another long day.

Carly wasn't used to being alone all the time. For the previous ten years, she ran a bed and breakfast bustling with people day in and day out. She never had a moment to herself, and she hated it. Now, sitting in her apartment alone, she wondered if she would ever have a friend to spend time with while John was away.

Making friends at forty was nearly impossible.

Carly scrolled through her social media, looking for social opportunities for 40+ singles. She wasn't single, but she certainly looked like she was. Even if there were opportunities to join a bowling league or a dart league, or a softball team, she would mix with men and women alike. Perhaps a friendship would develop over time, and Carly would feel less alone in a city that once held her heart.

The Portland, Maine Singles group was a place to find social opportunities. Carly scrolled through, looking for something that she could see herself doing.

She needed something during the day because of work.

Book Club? No. Ballroom dancing? Heck no. Cooking classes? Not necessary. Hiking? Yes! Hiking was perfect. She liked to walk and enjoyed being outside. Carly scrolled through the member photos and saw men and women her age and up. A variety of men and women stared back at her. Before Carly could analyze their pictures to judge who she would want to be friends with, she hit join.

Now all she had to do was wait for her membership to be approved, and then she was in! No more moping around the house, wondering if she made a poor decision about her life. There would be no more loneliness when John was away for six months out of the year. Carly felt a glimmer of hope spark.

Carly pulled out her Willowside Inn notebook and jotted down ideas related to the wedding: *Unicorn. Trellis. Italian food. Beachy-themed favors. Beach theme. Sea Glass. Blue, green, pink, and purple sea glass. Blue, green, pink, and purple unicorn. White unicorn.*

The words fell across the paper. They didn't quite make sense, but right now, they didn't have to. Carly had almost a year to put all the pieces together in a beautiful mosaic. She went online and searched for beach-themed weddings and continued to jot down ideas. She had no idea if the unicorn would come to fruition, but she would certainly try.

"Hi, Jackie!" Carly called into the phone, pouring herself a cup of hot coffee. "I was wondering if you made any decisions about your reception. I think we need to secure the caterer now, just in case we have a heatwave that weekend and the island is bustling. When you only have a few choices, weather becomes a defining factor in the day's success."

"I want everything local, so what are my choices again? Chris and I haven't talked about it seriously, but we want it to be light and refreshing." Jackie responded.

"Light and refreshing? I thought you wanted Italian," Carly questioned.

There was a pause on the other end of the phone. "Yeah...but it's spring. No one wants heavy Italian when it's warm outside."

"So, what were you thinking instead?" Carly asked, somewhat relieved because the island had one Italian restaurant.

"We were thinking seafood. Makes sense, right?" Jackie asked. "We are getting married on an island, surrounded by water, with the saltwater smell in the air. We were thinking lobster, crab cakes, and shrimp. Salad and fresh vegetables for the people that don't eat fish."

"Would you want a chicken dish for those that don't eat fish but do eat meat? We can see if there is a light chicken dish, like kebabs with fresh tomatoes, that they can prepare too?" Carly crossed out Italian and wrote seafood above it.

"That would be great!" Jackie said. "And we were thinking of having the plates be in the shape of either sand dollars or giant shells. That could be fun yet elegant, right?"

"Of course! I think we can do that. So, back to the food, how many people do you think you will have? Just so when I talk to the restaurants, they have an idea of how much food they need."

"We wanted a small group, like fifty or less, but Chris and I started listing everyone out, and we are thinking more like one hundred. Don't they say that only seventy-five percent of the people come? So maybe more like seventy-five." Carly jotted that down.

"Perfect. I will call around. Do you want to meet at the island in two weekends to meet with the restaurants and see who would be a good fit? I can make appointments. I'll meet you there, and we can make a reservation once we decide who we want to work with." Two weekends would give her enough time to take off work and enough time for Jackie and Chris to decide. Maybe the deadline would force them to figure out what they want.

She tossed her notebook on the table and got dressed. In three hours, she would be hustling around the restaurant, grabbing drinks and appetizers. She refused to stay in her pajamas until then. Carly browsed the small closet in their room and settled on a long cotton skirt and a black tank top. The farmer's market was closing soon, and Carly needed to get some fresh veggies and fruit.

The breeze ruffled her hair, and the sunshine warmed her chest while she pedaled down to the center of town. Carly's messenger bag rhythmically tapped against her leg as her legs pumped up and down and occasionally braked.

By the time she got to the Farmer's Market, the covered displays were nearly empty. Either it had been a lucrative day, or they were packing up what was left. Carly stopped by the vegetable stall and filled a bag with tomatoes, lettuce, cucumbers, and corn. She paid the man and then sat by the water, popping cherry tomatoes in her mouth.

She noticed a group of people to her left, wearing spandex and windbreakers. A pile of bikes laid at their feet with the occasional helmet tossed between the bicycle frames. The people circled closely together, forming a perfect button. Smiles, laughter, and animation played across their faces. Carly watched them for a few minutes, wondering how they knew each other and if she could somehow inconspicuously join their group and go on a bike ride.

She almost got up enough nerve to invite herself into the group, but her flowery skirt and bag of produce interfered with her follow-through. She made a mental note to look up social groups related to bike riding and wondered if her Huffy Cruiser would fit in with their serious bikes. She watched them gather their things and disperse into the crowded streets, pedaling rhythmically.

Carly desperately wanted to be near people. She checked her phone and saw an email from a person named Michelle. The subject line read "Hiking Club." Carly opened the email, skimmed it, and replied, "Yes!"

She rode home feeling lighter and optimistic about her decision to move to Maine. Perhaps she wasn't destined to be alone. She tried to socialize with her work friends, but they were all in college, single, and loved to party after work. Carly was too old for that. She knew she needed to find friends around her age but didn't know how to work her way into the social scene.

John preferred to keep his circle small and keep them close. Since moving in with him six months before, Carly met the other fishermen, but only because she and John bumped into them one day at the Farmer's Market. It was brief, and Carly couldn't remember who she met.

She wasn't sure how John would feel, knowing that she was going hiking with a group of single middle-aged people. She decided to participate when he was working because their time together was essential to Carly. On the other hand, he was always working, and she needed something to keep her mind clear. Carly never realized how badly she needed social interaction to feel whole.

She reread the email and penciled Hiking Club into her planner for this Thursday. She decided to start with a walking group since she loved the sunrise, was eager to meet new people, and barely owned a pair of sneakers. She pictured herself, immersed with a group of women walking through the quiet city streets that hadn't yet woken from its slumber. She imagined herself wearing yoga pants, an oversized t-shirt, and a baseball hat to keep the sun out of her eyes. She saw herself laughing, smiling, and feeling alive. She couldn't wait!

***

"Hey, Michelle!" Carly waved at the woman who resembled the small photo embedded within her emails. She dropped her mini backpack with her water bottle and long-sleeved shirt on the ground to tie her shoe. The city was quiet, and the sun was rising. The breeze chilled Carly's bare arms, and she shivered as goose-pimples created mountainous terrain across her body.

Michelle approached Carly with a warm smile and crinkled crow's feet. "Nice to meet you! I see you have your water and sneakers. Perfect for today." A group of people slowly filtered in and assembled in Monument Square and Michelle dispersed into the crowd. Carly wondered if they were all walking.

Carly quickly sized up the women, who managed to form individual cliques within the group. A mix of overwhelmed mothers, grandmothers, and overworked corporate climbers was the first group to arrive. Carly decided that she would befriend the first person who smiled at her, but these women, sectioned off in their inner circles, did not appear to notice the new visitor. Carly wondered where the men were hiding.

Michelle clapped her hands over her head. "Good morning! Today we have a four-mile walk planned. I uploaded the route to the website, so check your account if you are unsure where to go or get separated from the group. We will end here. It should take a little over an hour."

Carly stood alone, observing and wondering which conversation she should try and join. It appeared that everyone knew each other. By the time they

CHAPTER 4

started walking, there were about a dozen women and a handful of men.

Carly approached a woman who looked to be about her age, was physically fit, petite, and wore her straight, black hair in a loose ponytail. She looked like she had showered and taken the time to get ready for the walk, and Carly decided she must not have any kids. The woman glanced at Carly while adjusting her bag and threw Carly a smile. The skin around her eyes creased, and the space between her teeth was wide enough to slide a toothpick through, unscathed.

"Hi, I love your sunglasses," Carly complimented. The woman's black sunglasses rested along her shirt collar, slightly pulling down her t-shirt.

"Thanks." The woman removed her sunglasses and put them over her eyes.

"My name is Carly. Today is my first day."

"Sandra. Nice to meet you." She spoke to the air in front of her and started walking, pumping her arms with each stride.

"I thought this was a singles group," Carly started, rushing to keep up with her. "Where are all the men?"

"The men come out for the monthly hikes. Walking is more of a girl thing. So, I take it you're straight?" she asked.

"Yes. I'm not single, but sometimes I feel like I am. I moved here a few months ago to be with my boyfriend, but he works long hours during the summer, so I am looking for anyone to talk to." Carly laughed nervously at the absurdity of her situation. "I'm not searching for love. I'm searching for friends."

"You might find friends here. A lot of the women grew up around here. They've known each other for years, so it might be hard to join their circles."

An awkward silence sat between them. "Do you walk with them?" Carly didn't want to be considered a third wheel or the new kid on the block.

"Nah. I come out here to get exercise. I'm from down south and keep to myself. I could care less about little league, soccer, or who has what teacher. I've been walking with this group for over a year now but still walk alone most days."

Carly picked up on the southern twang with her elongated vowels and

27

decreased rate of speech. Another awkward silence settled between them as Carly questioned if she should continue speedwalking after Sandra or step back and find another person to engage.

"Can I walk with you? I don't know anyone."

Sandra turned and smiled. "Sure. I tend to walk fast, so if you can't keep up, tell me to slow down."

"Where are you from?" Carly asked.

"Tennessee. I moved up here with my husband. Well, husband at the time, ex-husband now. He got a job transfer, so I came with him. Now we're divorced, and I'm still here. He's living with his girlfriend down in Portsmouth. Sometimes I think I should go home to Tennessee, but I'm still here. I've kind of grown partial to the ocean. It relaxes me."

"I love the ocean too."

They made small talk for the rest of the walk, talking about their backgrounds, jobs, and love life. Conversation hovered just below the superficial layer of acquaintances. Sandra kept focusing on the road in front of her, making conversation easy for Carly. Sandra appeared to listen but didn't seem to judge. She was too focused on getting her steps in.

Sandra seemed just as lost as Carly, and they hit it off right away.

By the end of the walk, Carly felt refreshed and rejuvenated. Speaking to another woman who knew nothing about her past life on Block Island created a sense of acceptance and intrigue. Sandra appeared to understand that life was complicated as she nodded and shared details about her past.

"Do you want to get together sometime for coffee? I work nights at a restaurant, and John works day and night. I would love to get together sometime, outside of these walks." Carly prayed Sandra would accept her.

"Sure. That would be great. I tend to make my own hours, so I'm sure we could find a time that worked." Sandra's grin warmed Carly, and they exchanged numbers.

Over the next few weeks, Sandra and Carly met for lunch, walked, and shopped. Carly felt like she was in high school, with little responsibility beyond hanging out and going to school. Soon she and Sandra were inseparable.

Chapter 5

"Mom, please! We will not have a unicorn for the wedding!" Joanie exclaimed into the phone.

"Oh honey, it would be so great! I have a friend who knows a girl who works with this guy, whose parents own a farm, and they rent out their horses for weddings. They have white horses, Joanie, and they have these gorgeous crystal studded horns that they place on the horse's head. Wouldn't that be gorgeous? Chris and Jackie could ride around the island on a unicorn!" Sheila exclaimed into the phone.

Joanie turned on her speakerphone and placed it on the kitchenette counter. She threw a glance to Matt, silently screaming, *You've gotta hear this,* accompanied with an eye roll.

"Mom, no! That doesn't sound anything like what Jackie wants!" Joanie argued.

"It would be so romantic!" Sheila cried. "Your sister always wanted a fairy tale wedding! What's more romantic than riding away on a unicorn?" Joanie looked to Matt for help, and he stifled a snicker as he turned away from her.

"Mom, how about I run it by her and let you know? We are talking about having a wedding on an island. Things might not be as easy as you think." All Joanie wanted was to get her mother off the phone. Her mom had been yakking her ear off since she heard about the engagement two weeks ago, and Joanie had other things to do. "Mom, the wedding is in a year. Let's think about it and see."

Silence responded, and Joanie wondered if her mom got disconnected. "Mom?" she asked, looking at the face of her phone.

"I already spoke to Jackie. She is all about the unicorn," Sheila insisted. "Please let me know within the next month or so. I can't imagine securing a unicorn will be an easy feat."

Joanie couldn't believe this was real. She hung up the phone and wrapped her arms around Matt's muscular torso. "The last time I spoke to her was when she visited me here and told me that the linens were nice, but Egyptian Cotton would have been better."

Matt grinned. "Hey," he turned toward her to look into her eyes. "Does she know about us?"

Joanie pursed her lips, smiled, and raised her eyebrows. "Not yet," she hesitated. "I can only handle one topic where she knows best. She'll find out." Joanie kissed his lips. "At the wedding," she added.

Matt pulled her down next to him. "As the manager of this establishment, I will be sure to provide Egyptian Cotton sheets to her room."

Joanie giggled.

"The customer's always right, and we can't afford a bad review."

Joanie rolled her eyes at the absurdity of her harshest critic. "The customer is always right, but we will NOT have a unicorn at this wedding. Now I have to do my research to prove to her that we can't have a unicorn. And if Jackie insists, I swear, I'll lose my mind!"

That week, Joanie fell into her weekly schedule of laundry, cooking, cleaning, and gardening. As each day passed, her body ached, and her mind ran with to-do lists. She never made lists and preferred to live life as opportunities arose, but running a business successfully without a plan was nearly impossible.

Joanie tried to check in weekly with Carly. She knew it was Matt's job, but Matt only took this job to help Carly. His real job at the police station was busier than ever. Joanie thought he would be more available, but she found that she was often scrambling to figure out how to run the business by herself.

Matt agreed to run the business side of things, such as finances, technology, and advertising. Joanie was his workhorse. If someone requested organic and locally pasteurized milk, she had to find it. They wanted to present themselves as an elite bed and breakfast because the people who visited expected that comfort level. Every week, Joanie spent hours scouring the island and the mainland for requested luxuries.

On Wednesdays, she scrambled to get the items for the upcoming guests. Carly had taken off Wednesdays to visit her mom before she passed, so the inn had a long-standing rule of no check-ins on Wednesdays. It helped Joanie keep control of her growing list of places to go and things to buy. Matt was working the second shift, so Joanie was on her own this Wednesday.

Joanie didn't have a car, which was a massive problem for these Wednesday trips. When she moved to Block Island permanently, it didn't make sense to have a car. She sold her car to have just enough money to cushion her nest egg if her plan failed miserably.

As the wedding plans unfolded, Jackie called Joanie incessantly. Joanie carefully analyzed Jackie's intentions. Joanie could make or break the most critical day of Jackie's life by refusing to accommodate their wedding location, so Jackie sounded extra sweet whenever they talked.

Jackie agreed to pick up Joanie at the ferry port every Wednesday to drive her around for errands. Joanie used Jackie for her transportation, and Jackie used Joanie for a wedding venue. It was what sisters did, and to the two of them, it was completely acceptable.

Joanie stood on the upper deck and looked out at the island as it slowly decreased in size. The wind whipped through her hair, and the splash of water sprinkled her face. Her stomach knotted like a pretzel, and her heart raced. Joanie tapped her back pocket and felt the outline of her phone. She reached in and pulled out the folded paper with her list of things to find.

It was best to have Jackie accompany Joanie because Jackie dreamed of living the expensive lifestyle all the guests anticipated. On Joanie's list today, she had to find fresh lavender potpourri for one of the bathrooms and loose white jasmine tea for breakfast. Joanie didn't remember Carly going through these hoops last year to please the guests, but Matt accepted the requests, so Joanie was on the hunt.

As the ferry approached the dock, Joanie sat back, waiting for most guests to exit. She was mentally preparing herself for a day of gab, most likely about the wedding. Joanie was not going to bring up the unicorn.

Once all the cars exited the ferry, Joanie meandered down the ramp, visually scanning the crowd of faces for her sister. She saw the thick red hair blowing in the breeze and the freshly applied red lipstick contrasting against Jackie's fair skin. Joanie raised a hand and waved, and Jackie waved both arms over her head in return. Embarrassed by her enthusiasm, Joanie broke eye contact and focused on the ramp in front of her.

"Joanie!" Jackie hollered through the crowd, still waving. Her red lips spread to her ears, and her white teeth flashed against the sun. Joanie gave her a small, loose hug and a nervous smile and thanked her for the ride.

Joanie melted into the leather seats of Jackie's new Lexus. "Wow! Is this new?" Joanie asked, rubbing the center console.

Jackie smiled. "Yeah, Chris and I decided that if we wanted to appear like the successful business people we are, we need to fit the part." Jackie worked at a jewelry store in Newport.

"Oh, did you get a promotion?" Joanie asked.

Jackie nodded. "You are looking at the newest store manager!"

Joanie nodded back, wondering how much they paid. She eyed the black Kate Spade bag sitting at Joanie's feet and the shimmering engagement ring on her finger.

"Congratulations!" Joanie said, preferring not to ask questions because it wasn't her business.

"Where are we going today?" Jackie asked, pulling onto the main road.

"I don't know. I need to get Egyptian sheets, per Mom, fancy loose tea, and fresh lavender to put in the rooms."

"We are going to Newport! I know exactly where to go!" Jackie exclaimed.

Jackie was right; she knew exactly where to go. They parked near the water and walked up and down the cobblestone streets. The sunny, warm weather brought out people of all ages who littered the sidewalks and mingled outside the business doors. Joanie realized that she needed Jackie around to do her job well. She would not have known where to go to get these random items.

Once they had the tea and flowers, Joanie and Jackie sat down for lunch. The ambiance was fun, with modern art along the walls, electronica music quietly playing, and a menu full of sophistication and chef show-offs. Jackie ordered the deconstructed Monte Carlo with pureed cauliflower, and Joanie ordered braised leeks with mozzarella. She had no idea what her plate would look like but imagined a variation of chicken parmigiana. She didn't know if she had leeks before or what they looked like, beyond the description within the menu.

"Wow, Jackie, this menu is unbelievable," Joanie started.

"Yeah, this is a new restaurant. Chris and I always wanted to try it out, but we never got here. On the weekends, you have to make reservations. It's great that we're able to get in for lunch!"

Joanie sensed her sister's pride in obtaining reservations and smiled. "Next time, I will treat you to lunch," *at a pizza place*, she finished in her head. After a few sips of their infused blackberry lemonade, Joanie asked the dreaded question. "How are things going with the wedding?"

Jackie's eyes lit up like a Christmas tree at the word wedding. Joanie inwardly cringed because she knowingly but unintentionally unleashed the beast.

"It's going great! We talked with Carly a few days ago, and she agreed to let us use her land. We're going to get married outside, and I'm picturing flowers everywhere! There will be a red runner with a trellis of flowers outlining the runner. I'm picturing a tiara of flowers in my hair and not too many people. Less than fifty. Besides work, Chris and I don't have many friends. It will mostly be family, a few friends that we have kept in touch with over the years, and that's it. It's going to be quaint and romantic and magical." Jackie took a breath and took another sip of her drink.

"What's the date again?" Joanie asked, wondering how long she would have to anticipate this torture.

"We moved the date up to the end of April. We don't want it to be too hot, and Carly said it had to be before the summer season kicked off. I like April. It's a time of rebirth when things start blooming. I like that it's right before my birthday too. I would rather say I got married closer to thirty-five than forty."

Joanie nodded. She wondered how Jackie hadn't gotten married right out of college. She always had boyfriends and was always surrounded by people who loved her bubbly, cheery self. It killed her mother that both girls were still unwed and there were no grandbabies to dote over. According to Ruth, they were both almost past their prime.

"It's going to be fun!" Joanie commented, hoping the sarcasm didn't penetrate her words.

The food came out, and Joanie ogled at the presentation. *Bed and breakfast goals*, she thought. She was tempted to take a picture and use it to experiment at home but decided it would be tacky and probably embarrass Jackie. Instead, Joanie resorted to Pinterest and quickly wrote down the dishes' names on her to-do list.

Decadence exploded in Joanie's mouth with every bite. She ate her entire plate and noticed that Jackie had a handful of forkfuls scattered around the edges. Joanie wiped her mouth with her blue cloth napkin. She questioned if eating all her food was a compliment or an insult to the chef. Maybe he wanted the food to be so filling that she couldn't eat another bite. Perhaps he wanted it to be so delicious the guests couldn't peel themselves away from the meal.

Jackie graciously grabbed the checkbook and paid. Joanie dropped a few bills on the table for the tip, and the girls headed out to the mall to grab fancy sheets.

By the time Joanie got home, she was exhausted. She had two guests arriving tomorrow and still needed to get the room ready. She decorated the bathrooms with dried flowers, filled the tea urn with fancy tea, and switched out the sheets, silently grumbling about the laundry that never went away.

Joanie called Matt to say good night, fell into her bed and woke before the crack of dawn to the buzzing of her alarm clock to do it all again. She somehow survived another week.

Chapter 6

"Have you ever done DNA TODAY?" Sandra asked. They sat on her cramped balcony on the second floor of a three-family house. The sun made Carly's skin hot and tingly. She rubbed more sunscreen on her shoulders.

"No, why, have you?" DNA TODAY was the newest DNA kit on the market. It claimed to be more sensitive than the other products.

"I haven't, but I was always curious about it since I was adopted."

Carly nodded at her friend. "I didn't know you were adopted!" she replied, sipping her iced tea.

"Yeah, I was adopted when I was three months old. I love my family, which is why I never did a DNA test, but I have always been curious about my birth parents," Sandra confessed.

"How old are you?" Carly asked.

"Forty-three," Sandra responded.

"Are your parents alive?" Carly probed.

"My mother is alive. She still lives in Tennessee. My dad died last year." Carly nodded again, tears clouding her eyes. Reminders of Ruth's death still squashed Carly to the pavement at the most unexpected times.

"My mom died last year too," Carly confided. No wonder they hit it off so well.

"Oh." Sandra looked uncomfortable. "Sorry," she added.

"Same to you." After a quiet moment, Carly broke the silence. "What made you think of DNA TODAY?"

"Oh, I got an email for a buy one get one sale. I bought it, but I'm too chicken to do it by myself. Would you do it with me?"

"Sure! That sounds fun. My parents always told me I was German. I would love to know for sure."

"I don't have the kits yet. Supposedly they shipped already."

Carly nodded and rose out of the low beach chair to get a refill of iced tea. She walked into Sandra's apartment and noticed a framed picture on the end table of a tween-aged boy with blue and purple lasers striking the background. Carly had a school picture just like that from when she was a kid.

Sandra divorced her husband two years before and had no children. That picture was straight from the late 1990s, based on the bushy haircut, thick striped shirt, and laser beams. Carly was curious.

"Hey, Sandra!" Carly called out onto the balcony. "Who's this little boy? The one with the laser background? I think I had that same school picture when I was a kid."

Sandra walked in from the balcony. "Oh, that's Tim. He's my twin brother. He died when I was 14. He was my best friend." The heavy words lingered in the air between them.

Carly gently placed the photo back into the exact spot she found it, paying close attention to not disturb the dust that outlined its place on the table. "I'm sorry," she said.

Sandra waved her hand. "It's fine. It was a long time ago. I like having his photo around so that when I feel the need to talk to him, I have a picture handy to direct my words to."

"What happened?" Carly asked.

"We lived outside of Nashville at the time, and he was riding his bike with his friends. I don't know what happened because he was always so careful, but he ended up getting hit by a car. His friends said the car came out of nowhere and was going fast. We didn't have cell phones then. By the time the police called my parents, he was already gone."

Carly awkwardly hugged her new friend. Sandra's rigid shoulders stiffened further at the touch. Sandra pushed Carly away and brushed at invisible hair hanging in front of her face.

"I was supposed to be with him that day. We were inseparable, but I had a big test the next day, so I decided to stay home. That was the worst day of my entire life. I don't know if I ever really dealt with it. Maybe that's why I never had kids, or maybe why my marriage failed. I don't know."

Suddenly the air hung with a sadness that had not been there a few moments earlier. Carly scolded herself for being nosey and waited for Sandra to look at her eyes before speaking. "I can't fully relate, but anytime you want to talk, I am here." Carly smiled slowly and sadly, and Sandra returned the smile.

The girls moved outside and fell into a simple conversation about Portland, work, and eventually love.

"Yeah, it's weird, you know?" Carly started. "When I moved back in with John, I don't know what I expected. I imagined us spending every waking hour together, laughing, joking, having fun, and being stronger and more connected than we ever had before. It's been eight months, and I feel like I live with a stranger or live alone. He works so much and is so dedicated to his job that I only see him one day a week. We rarely have the entire day together." Carly looked down at her folded hands in her lap. "I don't know if I made a huge mistake."

"Do you miss home?" Sandra asked.

"I do. I didn't expect I would because I was miserable when I was there. I felt trapped and alone and stuffed into this box that my parents created. But now, I feel trapped and alone and stuck at a crossroads with zero direction. I didn't expect to feel the same way when I had such high hopes for a change."

Sandra nodded, looking out toward the houses across the street. "If you were completely independent with no one influencing your decisions, what would you do? Would you stay, or would you go home?"

Carly scrunched up her nose. She asked herself that same question many times before. She pursed her lips, unsure of her feelings. "I don't know. I probably would go home. I'm too old to be an outsider, forced to make new friends."

Sandra laughed.

"No offense! I am so happy we connected. You have been the thread I have been hanging onto this whole summer, but it's hard to start over and make friends."

"I get it. No apologies," Sandra replied.

"But yeah, it's tough. I miss how busy I was at home. At least then, I didn't have time to focus on being single. Here I am, obsessing over why my relationship is at a dead-end when it never really failed. I mean, I moved back to Rhode Island, and John stayed. At that time, there was no infidelity, no drug abuse, nothing that screamed break up. It just happened. And here we are again pretending everything is normal when in reality, the disconnection feels infinitely worse because we live in the same apartment. I don't get it."

Carly continued talking, unable to prevent her heart from spilling out of her mouth. It felt good to have a friend, and it felt good for Carly to get everything off her chest to a person who had no opinion on her relationship.

The girls hung out for a few more hours before Carly peeled herself away to go home and get ready for work. Another day, another dollar. Another late night. Another evening of dealing with people's complaints. She knew she would walk away with a few hundred dollars and that instant gratification kept Carly focused and grounded on giving her the means to figure out what she wanted for her life.

"Thanks for having me over!" Carly said politely.

"Anytime," Sandra replied with a warm smile. "You are welcome any time."

The following week, Carly researched her surprise trip to Sebago Lake with John. She booked an overnight for the next two consecutive days John had available. It was a Tuesday and Wednesday, which Carly thought was perfect. She wouldn't have to take off work herself. It was also a week before her mother's death anniversary, and she welcomed the distraction with John.

Carly couldn't wait to get John alone. They were already six weeks into the summer, and Carly felt like she was losing him more and more every day. She tried not to think about it and just continued working, walking, and taking care of the house, but she was lonely and missed the man she fell in love with so many years ago.

Jackie's wedding plans were slowly ramping up like a roller coaster train inching toward the top. Everyone anticipated the sudden drop and increase in speed, and the list of to-dos exponentially grew. Carly hated roller coasters.

Jackie texted or called almost daily, with one question or other. How are the unicorn plans coming along? Will there be enough room outside to sit seventy-five people comfortably? What if it rains? Should they have a plan B? Carly always answered Jackie's texts, but she didn't always have complete answers. Instead of spending time with her boyfriend, she was spending time planning a wedding. It felt bittersweet because it wasn't even her wedding.

Carly and Sandra walked around the city five mornings a week. When the other walkers found out Carly wasn't single, she sensed a thickness among her interactions with the other walkers that hadn't been there before. Carly separated herself a bit and relied on Sandra to keep her company on the long walks.

"Sebago Lake?" Sandra asked early one morning.

"Yes! It's going to be great. I rented out a little, cozy, romantic one-room cottage right on the lake. From the pictures, it appears to be private, with trees all around. It has a back deck overlooking the water. I think it will be a great jumping-off point if we want to go out and do something but will also be perfect if we want to stay in."

"Does John know?" Sandra asked.

"No, I'm keeping it a surprise. It's a few weeks before our official anniversary, so I don't think he'll be expecting it." Sandra had not met John, but she knew all about him. John didn't know about Sandra, except that they walked together. He never showed an interest in learning more, so Carly never shared details about her friendship with him.

"Does he like surprises?" Sandra asked.

Carly thought about it. "Well," she began, "he surprised me when my mom died, so maybe?" They were hustling through Old Port, their arms pumping and breaths rhythmically increasing in speed and volume. "I don't know. Maybe I should tell him," Carly added.

"Nah, surprises are fun! Pack his bags for him, so when he gets home or gets up, all you have to do is hop in the car and go. It'll be a perfect weekend! Girl, I wish you luck. I hope it's everything you hope it to be."

They continued in silence.

Heat traveled through Carly's neck and redness splattered her cheeks.

Thoughts of lying in bed, naked, with chocolate-covered strawberries, soft music playing about love and sex, and John, caressing her body like he was sculpting the next masterpiece for the Louvre, ran through her mind like a love scene from a rom-com movie.

"Hey!" Sandra exclaimed.

Carly turned, snapped out of her fantasy. "What's up?" she asked.

"I got the DNA kits. Do you want to do it when we get back?"

Carly shrugged. "Sure. Sounds great! Today will be the perfect day to see what my background is!"

The girls trekked through the city and back to Sandra's apartment. Carly was jealous that she had easy access to all the book shops and cafes that littered the city.

Sandra gave Carly another bottle of water and ripped open the DNA package, searching for the directions.

"What are you expecting your results to be?" Carly asked.

"I think I am Italian and French, but who knows, right? My birth parents had a closed adoption, so I have no info." Sandra passed the test tube to Carly. "Here. It says to spit in this."

Carly grabbed the directions to read herself since this was the only shot she had to get it right. She spat in the cylinder repeatedly until it was packed. Tiny spit bubbles rose to the top and spilled out the sides as she secured the lid closed.

"What about you?" Sandra asked.

"My parents always told me that they were German, but I don't know. I feel like my skin is a different tone than theirs. My hair is lighter. I'm probably all English." Carly shrugged.

The girls returned the tubes full of spit into the bag, placed them in the box, downloaded the app, and put them in the mailbox for the mailman to take away. Carly's life changed the moment the mailbox closed.

Chapter 7

J ackie and Sheila drove Joanie crazy. Joanie understood the importance of this event, but the number of texts, phone calls, and drop-ins started to affect Joanie's ability to focus on the inn and her boyfriend.

"My mother won't stop texting," Joanie said, looking at her phone for the hundredth time that day. Her screen screamed at her: **Call me!**

Joanie placed her phone face down on the counter, watching it dance and hearing it buzz as more texts came in.

"Matt! I can't do it!" Joanie cried, half-joking and in half despair. She rubbed her face into his t-shirt, hugging him tightly.

Matt grabbed her phone, silenced it, and placed it in the bathroom with the door closed. "Problem solved."

Joanie held his hand and led him to the couch, where she snuggled into him. Lately, she couldn't get close enough.

"What do you want to do today?" she asked. Wednesday was her day off, and her to-do list was nonexistent. She was too tired to think about the inn. It was now mid-summer, and they somehow survived the revolving door of guests thus far. Her routine was established, but her motivation was waning. The wedding plans crushed her soul and sucked the life out of her.

"Well," Matt started, "I have a surprise for you." Joanie sat up straighter, playing with the rings on her fingers, rolling them back and forth, waiting in anticipation.

"What is it?" Joanie asked. She continued before Matt could respond, "I hate surprises, but I love you. Is it something for today? You know, I don't have any plans at all today."

"Well, I want to spend all day with you, and I know you have stuff you have to do around the inn. So, I will take you somewhere, for a few hours, where we can be alone, and enjoy each other's company. And I promise when we get back, I'll stay with you at the inn until the chores are done, so you don't have to stress. I promise. What do you say? Are you ready?"

Joanie felt herself go tingly inside. Alone with Matt on a beautiful day in one of the most beautiful places Joanie ever experienced? She was living a dream. It sounded perfect.

She gave him a deep, lingering kiss and whispered, "Let's go." She led him up from the couch and grabbed her bag.

They rode their bikes down the hill, through town, and across the island. Matt led the way. He promised that she wouldn't be too tired from the excursion, but Joanie started to wonder. It was almost August, and the town streets overflowed with cars, bikes, and people. Maneuvering through the maze of narrow streets was tough, and Joanie could feel the beads of sweat forming on her forehead and neck. She couldn't remember if she put on deodorant but knew she forgot to put on perfume.

Joanie saw North Lighthouse in the distance. The granite structure rose from the horizon, and Joanie slowed down, following Matt's lead. "The lighthouse?" she called to him.

"Not the lighthouse. Better than the lighthouse!" Matt shouted over his shoulder.

They left their bikes near the edge of the parking lot and walked down to the beach. Dunes rose from their left, and the ocean lapped on their right. They continued past the lighthouse, walking on sea rocks wedged into the sand.

Joanie and Matt had been here before. Joanie was unsure what the big surprise was, but she followed Matt further away from the main road.

Around the bend, they approached a red and black checkered blanket laid out near the edge of the dunes. The rocky beach near the tide turned to soft sand where they were standing.

"Surprise," Matt said, dropping his backpack on the blanket. Joanie kicked off her shoes, and the warm sand tickled her freshly painted toes.

Joanie gave him another kiss. "Beautiful!" she said. They sat on the blanket, and Matt pulled out two sandwiches from their favorite deli, two bottles of soda, and a bag of chips.

"You know, the surprise isn't the picnic, although it is nice. The surprise is the family of seals, right over there." He pointed toward the horizon, and Joanie saw a group of seals sunning themselves on the beach.

"Wow!" she exclaimed. "That is so cool! I have never been this close to seals before!"

"I thought it would be fun to do something different today. After we eat, we can walk a little closer. I wouldn't recommend getting too close, but it's neat to see them in their natural habitat."

They ate in silence, looking out toward the ocean and listening to the waves lap against the rocks. Joanie and Matt sat tucked away in the dunes, invisible to most people walking the beach. The sunbeams beat down on Joanie's face, and the birds flying overhead created a wave of peace within her.

"Thank you, Matt," Joanie said. "This was just what I needed. I have been so stressed out with this wedding. I needed to get away from everyone. Actually, I needed to get away from my phone."

They packed their belongings and walked the beach, collecting flat, smooth rocks to leave their mark on the ocean coast. Joanie and Matt sat on the soft sand, with the sunning seals in the background, and created a stone stack to mark the spot and the memory of their date.

"You know," Matt said, "these stacks are dangerous for the ecosystem." He kissed Joanie on her forehead as she bent down to place another flat stone on their formation.

"Really?" Joanie looked around and saw a dozen stacks of various shapes and sizes.

"Yeah, it disrupts the natural habitat. Some animals use the stones for their home, and when we move them, they are exposed. Also, studies show that by moving the stones, we speed up erosion within the environment. We have an officer who comes down here twice a week to walk the beach and knock down the stacks."

Joanie quickly flicked the pile and watched it fall with a thud. "I had no idea!" She grabbed Matt's hand and pulled him toward the water's edge.

"I love spending time with you," Joanie said, avoiding eye contact. "You have made this year so much fun! It's been nice having a friend." Joanie giggled and looked into Matt's bright eyes. "You are my only friend here."

"I love being your friend. Let's stay friends. And more than friends." He fiddled with her fingers, and a small smile rose in the corners of Matt's mouth.

Joanie felt a flutter of joy bounce in her belly and push up against her heart. In response, she kissed him, grabbed his hand, and walked them toward their bikes.

They rode down the windy, narrow roads back into town and up the hill to the bed and breakfast. Joanie dropped her gear while standing in the doorway and refilled her water bottle.

Her phone was still buzzing on the kitchen counter like an active beehive. Four missed calls from Sheila, three from Jackie, and seventeen text notifications from Jackie, Sheila, and Carly. "Is it wrong if I ignore them all? We had such a great day!" Joanie whined. "I don't want them to ruin it." She held down the power button until all noises ceased. "The rest of the day is for you. And the inn, but you said you would help, so the rest of the day is still for you. And only you."

Joanie wrapped her arms around Matt and held him close. His cool skin rubbed against her cheek, and she tasted the salt on his lips. Joanie felt refreshed, rejuvenated, and at peace. Her life certainly wasn't what she planned, but she couldn't have prepared it better.

***

The next day, Joanie made the mistake of turning on her phone. It was practically nighttime, the sun barely peeking over the hill, and breakfast called. Before Joanie showered, she read all the texts and listened to all the voicemails. Carly wanted to talk about the reservations for August, Sheila wanted an update on the unicorn hunt, and Jackie found perfect party favors she wanted to make herself. Jackie also wanted Joanie to go dress shopping with her, which was a massive surprise since Jackie always complained about Joanie's tom-boyish figure and oversized clothes.

Joanie realized that Jackie's inner circle was small, even though she made everyone believe she was the girl to envy. Joanie didn't want to go dress shopping. She was tired of wedding drama and didn't know if she could pretend to be excited for every gaudy dress Jackie tried.

Joanie wanted to ask Jackie who the Maid of Honor was because wasn't all this prep work that person's job? She was worried that Jackie would say her, and Joanie did not want to make her life any more complicated beyond being her sister's gopher to make the wedding happen.

She texted Jackie, saying she would get back to her in a few days, and texted Carly, saying she was free to talk. She texted her mom, saying she would get back to her after she spoke with Jackie. Joanie was exhausted before she even got out of the shower. She knew Matt was also up, getting ready for his shift, and she sent him a heart and kiss emoji. He quickly responded with a heart-eye emoji, and Joanie smiled.

They made a more profound connection at the beach, and Joanie inferred commitment from Matt's words. She hoped she wasn't setting herself up for heartbreak and toyed with the idea of opening more of herself to him, regardless of the repercussions.

She owed it to him to share the more vulnerable side of herself and open up. She felt a level of seriousness blow over them yesterday, like a breeze blowing through her hair. She sensed the shift, but it wasn't yet interfering with her life or knocking her down. She was afraid to share her deepest secrets with him.

Commitment scared Joanie, but she needed to have an honest conversation with Matt. They were approaching one year of dating, and although one year during high school meant incidental connection, one year at forty was quite serious.

Joanie learned early on that expectations led to disappointment, so she guarded her heart like a museum that held the crowned jewels from centuries past. People could look beyond the plexiglass but couldn't touch it. Joanie struggled to accept that Matt could break apart the wall around her heart, but she knew it was bound to happen.

Chapter 8

arly stuffed John's oversized sweatshirt into her overnight bag. She grabbed their toothbrushes and toothpaste and shoved them into her toiletry bag. Her heart beat against her chest as fast as an 80's pop song. She hadn't yet told John about their night away at Sebago Lake.

John was due home from the bank any minute. Carly packed their bags and placed them by the door. She felt weird packing for him, but things had been so disconnected, she didn't want to give him reason to say no. Deep down inside, she questioned if this approach of trickery would backfire.

Their relationship lacked pizazz and excitement, especially over the past two weeks. Carly's uncertainty in this romantic night away could be another light shining on the fractures in their relationship. Carly planned this trip out of desperation and refused to admit that her certainty in John was wavering.

She confided in no one for fear that saying her true feelings aloud would somehow cause her reservations to come true. She was most disappointed in herself for believing that giving up her entire life for a man was the secret to her happiness.

Carly scanned the small apartment one last time and placed the overnight bag on the couch. She threw on her happiest face and waited anxiously by the door. Her stomach twisted and turned and pushed and pulled in all directions. Her heart thudded rhythmically in her ears in anticipation. She was unsure how John would react when Carly told him she was pulling him away from his only days off this week to participate in her fairy tale story about how she saved their relationship.

She didn't know if John felt the same level of disconnection or if he was just going through the motions of life to survive. There was a chance he didn't even notice her unhappiness, and Carly wondered if it was as bad as her overactive imagination created.

The door opened, and John walked in, his body upright with a smile on his face. "Hey!" he said to Carly. She froze at the sound of the door despite pacing back and forth in front of the window. She didn't understand why she was so nervous.

"Hey!" She picked up the bag and raised it. "I have a surprise for you!" John looked at the bag and back to Carly's smiling face.

"Oh yeah? What is it?" His keys clunked on the table, and he slid out of his boots.

"We're going away! I booked a cottage for a night at Sebago Lake. You know how we have always wanted to go there!" Carly wasn't sure if they ever talked about Sebago Lake, but they had talked about getting away. She quickly wiped the sweat off her brow.

"Oh yeah?" John asked. "When?"

"Tonight. Today. Right now," Carly rambled. "I packed our bags, and we are ready to go! We will be back tomorrow. I checked with your work to make sure you had two days off, and it all worked out! Think of it as an anniversary getaway." Carly couldn't stop talking even though John's face contorted as she spoke. His eyes squinted, his eyebrows furrowed, and he bit half of his bottom lip like he was biting back a rebuttal.

"Today?" he asked. "I can't go anywhere tonight."

Carly's heart dropped to her feet, her heart rate quickened, and her palms seeped with sweat. She had double-checked everything. Why would he turn down his girlfriend, whom he lived with when offered a night away to deepen their relationship?

"Oh," she muttered. "Okay." She turned and walked to the bedroom, feeling one lonely tear seep out the corner of her eye. The face-to-face rejection tormented her, and she had no escape within their cramped apartment to lick her wounds alone.

"I just," John started. "I have that Poker Tournament tonight with the guys. I can't bail on them. It's our first tournament. I thought I told you!" he called through the closed bedroom door. Carly didn't respond.

Foolishness filled Carly's being. How could she have been so stupid? Stupidity quickly turned to anger and rage. She grabbed her phone and promptly texted Sandra: **John bailed on our night away. Are you up for a trip to Sebago Lake? We don't have to spend the night. We can go for the day. Or we can come back tomorrow. We can play it by ear. LMK.**

She grabbed her backpack and pulled her clothes and toiletries out of the canvas tote she had purposely packed for herself and John. With as much composure as she could muster, she walked out of the bedroom with her head held high.

"Enjoy your night. I will see you later."

As she approached the door, he called, "Wait, where are you going?"

"To Sebago Lake. I'll see you later." And with newfound freedom, mixed with anger and sadness, Carly left the apartment she called home for the past year. No kiss, no eye contact, and no understanding.

She walked downtown, her backpack pressed against her shoulders, and sat by the water, numbed by how quickly her final fix crumbled in her fingers. She sat in the grass, watched the people walk by, and wondered who they were and how they had it all together. She questioned what types of battles they were fighting under their designer bags and newly colored hair.

Her phone buzzed in her pocket, and she quickly grabbed it, hoping it was John. She paid for a romantic night in a cozy cottage and had no way to get there. She didn't have a car and assumed they would take John's car. Instead of seeing John's name and face flash across the screen, she saw Sandra.

I'm in, the text said.

Carly picked up her backpack and walked to Sandra's. If Sandra wanted to come, she would have to drive. The anger in Carly's heart slowly transitioned to melancholy.

Three hours later, the girls pulled up to a small log cabin encased in trees overlooking the lake. The pebbles crunched under their sandals, and newly fallen leaves danced in the air as the girls investigated their new surroundings. The cool, clean air filled Carly's soul as she breathed in deeply.

Silence permeated the car on the drive up to the lake. Carly had a lot to say, but she wasn't sure how honest she could be without sounding like a whiny teenager. In one swift movement, John ripped out her heart and exposed her vulnerabilities. He made her feel foolish because she believed he would choose her over a poker game. He hadn't even told her about the Poker Tournament.

Carly wanted to tell John the plan, to make sure something like this would not happen, but Sandra convinced her that surprises were more fun. Now, all that planning was for nothing. Carly climbed out of the car and approached the quaint, wooden cabin.

"I know the key is somewhere," Carly said, searching through her email, looking for the confirmation. She had previously scoured every rock and ledge around the entrance and could not find the key. An edge of anger tilted her voice, and panic threatened to rise up and out. Every choice felt wrong and juvenile. It was the perfect opportunity for Ruth to cackle "I told you so!" from the grave.

Hot, angry tears slowly dripped down her cheek. Carly moved to the back deck to hide her emotions from Sandra. Carly sensed a breakdown coming, and Sandra moved out of the way without a word. Carly looked up to the blue sky and focused on a squirrel scurrying from branch to branch in the distance. "Come on, Carly, pull yourself together. You are fine. It will be fine," she whispered to herself. She closed her eyes and inhaled and exhaled deeply three times, feeling calmness settle her wobbly legs. She wiped her eyes and searched through her email again, wondering if it went to spam.

"I got it!" Carly called, hoping that her quivering voice didn't expose her rocky confidence. "Over here, the back door!"

Sandra quietly followed, making a point to keep her distance until they were comfortably inside.

The cottage smelled of must and dust and was substantially darker inside than out. Carly walked around and vehemently ripped open the curtains to let rays of light penetrate through the windows. The cottage had a small kitchenette, a pull-out couch, and a queen bed, all within one large room. The bathroom was tucked away in the back, next to a small laundry closet. Carly kept the main door open to let the natural breeze push through the scent of wet woods.

"This is perfect!" Sandra called out. "I love it!" She dropped her overnight bag next to the sofa and moseyed into the kitchen, setting a few bottles of wine, crackers, and hummus on the counter. "Are you hungry? Do you need a drink?"

Carly looked at her watch. It was two in the afternoon, and she hadn't eaten in hours. "Do you want to order out tonight? It doesn't make sense to buy food for one night." Carly crunched into a cracker, her stomach rumbling like a distant thunderstorm.

"Totally. Let's hang out, drink wine, and forget about life." Sandra rinsed two glasses she found in a dirty, drab cabinet. There wasn't any soap under the sink, so instead, she used body wash from her luggage to clean the cup. "Definitely clean!" she said, overfilling a pint glass that said, "Happy Camper" and "Life is Better Around the Campfire" with warm, white wine. "Sorry, it's warm. I'm throwing it in the fridge now."

Carly took a sip and felt the smooth liquid run down her throat and splash into her empty belly. The girls went outside and sat around the patio table, a quietness filling the air around them.

After a few moments, Sandra awkwardly broke the silence. "Do you want to talk?" She didn't look at Carly because she didn't want Carly to feel obligated to share her story.

Carly bitterly took another sip of wine and sat back in the Adirondack chair, willing her body to relax. Her eyes filled with hot tears, and she rapidly blinked them away.

"John was running errands, so I packed for us so I could surprise him when he walked in. He came home. I told him I had a trip planned, and he told me he wanted to play Poker and couldn't bail on his friends. That was it. There was no fighting or yelling. Just emptiness between us. I left, walked down to Old Port, and called you."

"What are you going to do?" Sandra asked.

Carly turned toward her and looked into her eyes. She pursed her lips, feeling her eyes well up again. "I don't know. I know I'm not happy. I regret moving here. I thought it was what I wanted and needed, but I feel lonely and isolated. Fifteen years ago, I was young and social and brave, and I could handle him being gone five months out of the year. Aren't I too old to be dealing with this shit?"

Sandra didn't respond and waited for Carly to continue.

"I feel lost and broken. I think I made a mistake. The man who is supposed to be there to hold me up has completely failed. I am an idiot for thinking it would be different." Sobs escaped between words. "I lived this life. I knew how it would be, yet I was blinded by the hope that we could make something out of our relationship again. John never lied to me. He didn't have to. I knew he would be gone. I thought I was strong enough to let him live his life as he always had. I didn't factor in our years away from each other, but we're both ten years older, with a history between us. Of course, it wouldn't be the same. I was so naïve. I don't know what I was thinking." Carly took another sip of wine to quiet the rage churning in her head and her heart.

Sandra didn't say a word. She stared out into the lake, tracking a motorboat pulling a tube filled with kids. Their laughter crept up to the back deck landing and momentarily broke the silence sitting between the two girls. They sat there, frozen in time, watching everyone else on the lake share pleasant moments with each other.

That evening, the scent of hot cheese and cooked crust filled the cottage. The pizzas slightly cooled from the restaurant to their little house, and the melted cheese solidified in the box. They were on their second bottle of wine, and Carly's mood elevated with the slightly tipped room.

"Thank you for coming with me!" Carly called over to Sandra, who was busy washing plates with body wash. The room was slightly tilted, and she felt the best she had felt all day.

"Girl, I got your back. Anytime you need me." Sandra passed a wet plate to Carly, which had a small reservoir of water sitting in the center. Carly placed a paper towel over the puddle and a piece of pizza on top.

"Really. I needed this."

They had three bottles of wine, and Carly probably consumed at least half of the second all by herself. Sandra placed the third bottle in the back of the fridge, hidden behind the pizza boxes.

The girls devoured the pizza and salads and cleansed their palates with chardonnay. The sun set into the lake's edge, and the orange and yellow hues lit up the sky like a firecracker. "Check out that sunset," Sandra said, nodding toward the window.

"Wow!" Carly jumped off her stool and raced to the door, flinging it open clumsily. She stood there, in awe, staring as the clouds and colors shifted and blended in the evening sky.

"Carly!"

Carly turned, hearing the urgency in Sandra's voice.

"I just got my DNA results! You probably got yours too!"

Carly hadn't looked at her phone all day. She wondered if John texted or called but didn't want to know. If Carly looked and saw missed calls or texts, she would likely respond and wasn't ready. Instead, she threw her phone in the very bottom of her bag to deter her from checking.

"Oh yeah? What does it say?" Carly asked, stumbling back to the counter.

"It says that I am 31% Greek, 29% Italian, 16% Scandinavian, 9% French, 6% English, 6% German, and 3% African. Huh. It looks like I'm a little bit of everything! What about you?" Sandra scrolled through the app to see if she could find any other information. "Carly! There is a tab here for relatives! Should I check? I am so scared. What if it says I have a sister or a brother or a mother? Do I really want to know?" Sandra's rate of speech increased. Carly stared into Sandra's chestnut eyes, which intensely held her gaze until Carly responded.

Carly looked at her friend and saw the desperation, hope, and fear embedded in her eyes. "When you are ready to look, I will be here for you."

Sandra nodded and swallowed loudly. "Okay. I am just going to do it." She took a deep breath. "This is what I wanted, right? To know who I am and where I came from." Sandra gave herself a pep talk before manipulating her phone. She impulsively pressed tabs and buttons, unsure of how to navigate the app.

"I think this is it," Sandra said, eyes oscillating quickly from one end of her phone to the other. Her smile vanished, and her eyes bulged. She nibbled on the inside of her left cheek, tapped her toes on the wooden floor, and deeply inhaled through her nose. "I found it."

After a few moments of silence, Carly asked, "Well? What does it say?" Sandra wiped her hands on her shorts.

"Carly," Sandra faintly said, looking deep into her friend's eyes. "I have a sister." Carly didn't respond but waited for more. "I have a sister. But I had a twin brother, and we were together. How could my mother have given us up, but not my sister?" Her voice seeped with sadness and bitterness at the realization that perhaps she had indeed been discarded and intentionally abandoned.

"You don't know that. A different family could have adopted your sister." Carly wondered which would be a better scenario.

"What do I do?" Sandra asked, frantically searching for guidance. "Do I contact her? There is a button, right here, that says Contact. What do I say?"

"Before you contact her, I think you should process this. Figure out how you feel. You seem emotional right now. You may not get the information you want. I would wait," Carly gently prodded.

Sandra nodded. Her face fell, and she turned abruptly, but Carly could still see a single tear fall down her cheek.

Carly quickly changed the subject. "Should I look? My phone is buried." Carly headed toward the kitchen peninsula to grab her bag, which was stuffed full of planners and notebooks and lists that she made but never completed.

"Here, if you remember your log-in info, you can sign in and check it out on my phone." Sandra passed her phone to Carly.

Carly tried a few times but got a login error message each time and was eventually locked out. "I'll check my phone in the morning. I promise." She handed back Sandra's phone and let go too soon. The phone dropped a few inches to the countertop, face up. "Sorry," she mumbled.

That night, they cozied up on the couch scrolling through the television and streaming services preprogrammed on the smart tv. After thirty minutes, they finally settled on a romantic comedy. Carly didn't share any more information about John, and Sandra didn't ask.

Sandra's sister's name was Bianca, which reminded Carly of Italy.

Sandra checked Bianca's profile and looked at the beautiful woman staring back at her. She had friendly blue eyes, full lips, and thick, dark brown, wavy hair that cascaded past her shoulders. Sandra brought the phone close to her eyes and zoomed into the picture. She covered the top of Bianca's head with her thumb and said, "She looks just like Tim."

Carly leaned over and looked at the photo. "She looks like you."

By the end of the movie, the third bottle of wine was gone. Carly snored under the blanket, and her head awkwardly pressed against the arm of the couch.

The following day, Carly woke with a throbbing headache and a sour stomach. The night before was blurry, and moments of clarity shot through her brain like snapshots ejected from a Polaroid. She felt like death and probably looked like death too. She wished she hadn't succumbed to the wine and hoped she didn't get emotional or sloppy around Sandra. Sandra was the only friend she had; she couldn't afford to lose her because of something stupid she said or did while under the influence.

Sandra was up and showered by the time Carly sat up from the couch. Carly's neck ached when she moved it, and she rubbed it gently, rolling her head from shoulder to shoulder.

"Morning, Sunshine," Sandra said. She gave Carly a cup of coffee. "I ran out this morning and got you a regular. I wasn't sure how you liked it."

Carly graciously took the coffee and felt the rush of cream, sugar, and heat coat her dry, starchy mouth. She was so thirsty. "Can I have a bottle of water, too?" Carly asked, still not able to get up. Her stomach felt unsettled, and she worried that drinking coffee would trigger a reaction.

Sandra grabbed a bottle of water from the fridge and passed it to Carly. "Here you go. Also, I charged your phone for you last night." Sandra unplugged it and tossed it to Carly. Carly tried to catch it, but her reflexes were so slow, it hit her in the shoulder and fell into her lap with a thump.

Carly looked down and saw no messages or notifications. "Well, I guess John could care less to know where I am," she said bitterly.

"He did. When you went to bed, I checked your phone, and you had three texts from him, so I responded saying you would be home tomorrow... meaning today. I hope you don't mind. I know what it's like to worry, and he sounded worried."

Carly nodded, not saying a word. She pulled up her messages and saw three from John, just as Sandra said. He apologized for blowing her off and asked when she was coming home. In the third message, he told her he was worried. Carly closed out the app and placed the phone next to her, rubbing her temples. "Thanks," she said to Sandra.

Sandra sorted through her luggage, taking out a sweatshirt.

"How was your night?" Carly asked, hoping she didn't do anything that jeopardized their friendship.

"It was fun. We had pizza, watched a movie, and you fell asleep on the couch. How do you feel?" Sandra asked.

"I've been better. My head hurts, my stomach hurts, and my body feels weak, but other than that, okay."

"Yeah, you had a lot to drink, but I don't blame you. You're in a tough spot. I'm glad I was able to be here for you."

Carly nodded, not remembering the night and hoping that Sandra was just referring to being there with her love troubles.

"What time is it?" Carly asked.

"Almost eleven. I think we have to check out by twelve, right?"

Carly nodded and willed herself up. "I'm going to shower," she said, stumbling to the bathroom with her phone and overnight bag.

In the bathroom, Carly pulled out her phone and reread the texts, unsure if she should respond. The text messages sounded sincere, but shouldn't John have texted her more? She disappeared for an entire day after a fight, and she had no car. Shouldn't he have been more worried?

Carly texted back that she would be home by dinner. She still didn't know what she would do, but she felt like she needed to develop an exit plan. There was no way they were going to work.

She pulled up her email to see if Joanie or Jackie sent anything and instead saw the DNA results sitting in her inbox. She quickly opened the email and logged into her account, not quite sure what to expect. The pie chart stared back at her: 54% Irish, 36% Great Britain, and 10% German. Carly was surprised at how little German ancestry she carried. She clicked through the tutorial, checking out the app and how to navigate between screens. Carly clicked on Contacts and found a list of people related to her. Scanning through, at the top of the list, she read **Christopher Swanson: First Cousin**.

Carly blinked and widened her eyes. Her mouth dropped open, and her hand flew to her mouth. *What? Not Chris. Jackie's Chris? That didn't make any sense. How was Chris, her first cousin?* There was nothing listed for parents, which made sense because her dad died before DNA testing was a thing, and her mom had been living in a nursing home for years. She didn't recognize anyone under Close Family, leaving an uneasy feeling in her belly. She rationalized that her family used a different DNA app or never took the test.

Carly sat on the closed toilet seat, stunned. Her entire world was in a hazy fog and nothing made sense. *How could Chris be her cousin? They were neighbors.* Snapshots of her childhood flashed through her mind like strobe lights at a dance club.

Nothing seemed out of place or unusual when she thought about the Swansons. *Were her parents related to the Swansons?* Carly wished she could pluck a DNA sample from her parent's grave to add them to her DNA list. Nothing made sense.

Carly's entire world crumbled in less than twenty-four hours. She needed to claw her way to something familiar. Nothing felt safe or comfortable. She didn't even know who she was.

Chapter 9

Sandra cruised down the highway. The hot sun beat through the window and warmed Carly's right arm. She turned her face toward the sun, closed her eyes, and inhaled the breeze coursing through her window. Her hair whipped toward the center of the car, and Carly frantically tried to get it under control. She quickly rolled up the window and turned toward Sandra.

"Thank you for coming with me."

The entire ride home, Carly rehearsed in her head how she would say goodbye to John. Carly knew it was the right thing to do but felt incredibly guilty for being so foolish. Happily ever after was a made-up ending to fairy tales, and she was tired of expecting more out of her relationships.

The two days in Sebago changed her life and questioned her identity. There were so many emotions that Carly couldn't quite label, the muddied haze impeding her ability to function or make decisions.

Carly thought about the DNA results and questioned her findings. No matter how the ping pong ball bounced off her brain, she couldn't make sense of the outcome. The emotional isolation contorted her personality, and resentment and confusion trickled into her attitude, thoughts, and words. Worry deepened her forehead creases, confusion clouded her eyes, and anger sat in the fine lines around her lips.

When she got her results, she feigned illness and asked Sandra if they could head home early. No shopping, no lounging near the lake, just home to return to the sedentary life she tried to escape a few days before. Sandra talked about her sister and the excitement around her DNA results, oblivious to Carly's nonchalance. Carly heard her, but she wasn't listening.

When she got home, John lounged on the couch and watched tv, utterly unaware of Carly's melancholy mood. Leaving him right now was not an option. She went through all her savings over the past winter and knew she had enough to last a few months. All she needed was a car to leave.

Carly sat next to him on the couch and kissed him with a big smile. She told him all about the fun she had with Sandra and how she wished he was there. She even apologized for worrying him when she left.

That evening they made love with a renewed hunger. After, Carly laid with her back to him and cried for another loss in her life. She hated herself for deceiving him until it was convenient for her.John didn't notice. Carly led him to believe whatever he wanted. He snored next to her while she plotted her exit.

For the next two weeks, Carly planned her escape. She needed to find her family. She pretended she was happy because she couldn't risk him finding out and forcing her to leave when she had nowhere to go. She grabbed all the cash she saved and methodically planned how far her money would take her.

Carly was finally ready. She sat on the couch, holding her second full glass of wine. "John, I love you, but I can't do this anymore. We've changed too much and are moving in opposite directions. I can't come back here and live my life the way I did when I was thirty. Too much time has passed. This isn't what I wanted for my life." The wine helped her get her feelings out in one fell swoop.

He looked at her, silent and expressionless. Carly sat with the uncomfortable silence until it became unbearable. "I have to go."

They both stood, and John still said nothing. Carly walked to the door and said she would call him in a few days. He kissed her on the cheek goodbye, and that was it—the end.

She sat under a tree next to Sandra in a nearby park and sobbed, her arms resting on her bent legs. How did her life fall apart so quickly? The silence and lack of fighting broke her heart more than any words he could have hurled. That day, she walked down the stairs, into the outside, swallowing back tears until she was well out of sight. She couldn't show weakness in front of him.

"Do you think it's okay that I never called Joanie?" Carly turned to Sandra.

Sandra shrugged her shoulders, keeping her eyes on the road. "It's your house, right?"

"Yeah, and we have a house in the back that is empty right now. I don't mind staying there for the time being." After a few moments, Carly added, "I probably should have called her." At the time, her heart was so raw from all the events that unfolded. She didn't know how to tell Joanie that her life fell apart, and she was going to upend Joanie's life in the process of fixing her own. Carly knew that the only way she could survive was to return to the inn and take over the business, but that would mean Joanie was out.

Carly rationalized her actions from every angle. She barely knew Joanie, but this was her home. Joanie could move in with Matt if she was determined to stay. Carly couldn't worry about Joanie's feelings because she only had enough energy and space to worry about her own.

"Did you talk to John? What did he say?" Sandra asked, still looking ahead. Carly was grateful that she didn't have to make eye contact and expose her sadness at the mention of John.

"I did." Carly heard her voice crack, and she swallowed the lump forming in her throat. "He doesn't understand why I wasn't happy. He said he was honest with me from the beginning, which he was. But that doesn't mean I fully understood what our life would look like. Or not look like. I feel bad for not trying harder."

Sandra interrupted. "Carly, you are forty years old.Please. You are too old to settle. If you are going to question your life, question it because of you, not because of the partner you settled for."

Carly thought about Sandra's words and steadied into the idea of being responsible for her own choices only. Carly spent too many years of her life making choices to benefit others. When she left the island for John, she thought she was choosing herself. Instead, it was a choice for her old self from fifteen years ago. Her old self transformed and mutated through the harsh and bitter experiences life threw at her.

Carly was going home. They drove to the Port Judith ferry in silence. At one point, Sandra turned up the radio, opened the sunroof, and wriggled back in her chair. It was a long day spent on the road with a relatively new friend who knew little about the inn, Carly's parents, or Carly's DNA results. Life was about to get messy.

Chapter 10

It was mid-afternoon, and Joanie stood in the laundry room, folding the third load that day. The white sheets had been starched and ironed to create a "just out of the package" illusion. Carly taught Joanie this technique her first week. Joanie watched video after video, practicing sheet folding with the expert on the television.

Ironing was by far the most monotonous task of the job, yet Joanie could never seem to get it right. The sheets were too long and wide and almost always ended up on the floor. The creases were never precise.

Joanie remembered her grandmother ironing, but never her mother. Sheila had never taught her how to iron, and the entire experience felt foreign. Joanie didn't even know what the symbols on the iron meant or when she was supposed to push the steamer button. It was all a mess.

She geared herself up for hours of ironing by locking herself in the laundry room. Music from the early 90's burst against the walls. Joanie's hips shook, head bobbed, and lips sang while she worked the iron.

All the guests for the week had already checked in, and breakfast had been a success. Joanie's routine ensured the eggs were hot and ready when she flipped the last pancake. She had become a well-oiled machine of one, and the entire process of setting up to clean up had become a breeze.

Most of the time, she was alone because of Matt's work. By the time he got home from his shift at the police station, he was starving and exhausted. The two of them were usually in bed by eight to function by five in the morning. Since they both needed the bathroom early in the morning and Joanie's apartment only had one, Matt slept at his house unless he had the following day off.

It worked for them. Joanie needed to focus on the inn and the guests and not stress between picking her boyfriend or her job. Plus, it allowed her to miss him, which made the overnight stays more special.

Joanie had just gotten into the groove with the hot iron sizzling when the phone rang. It was the house phone, which had a landline in the laundry room.

"Hello! Willowside Inn, this is Joanie speaking!" Joanie bellowed into the phone with a sing-song melody.

"Hello, Joanie."

Joanie recognized the voice, and her shoulders tightened.

"This is your mother."

"Hi, Mom. Why are you calling on the inn phone?"

"Well, I tried your cell all morning, but there was no response. I am here. Can you let me in?"

Joanie felt her breath drop out of her. "Sure, Mom," she managed. "Be right there."

Joanie tiptoed out of the laundry room, through the kitchen, into the formal dining room, and then to the front door, hoping this was a bad dream.

The looming shadow shined through the opaque windows, which ran alongside the door. *Not a dream*, Joanie thought and smoothed out her white apron.

Why would Sheila be here? Joanie took two deep breaths, closed her eyes to reset herself, and then opened the door with a wide grin. "Mom!" she exclaimed, trying to hide the disbelief in her eyes.

Sheila reached out and embraced Joanie in a tight hug. She pulled back, grabbed Joanie's shoulders, and squeezed. "I've missed you!" she beamed.

Joanie led her into the inn, and they settled on the couch in the parlor. It was usually where the guests waited for further directions about their stay. Joanie was speechless. She sat in the oversized chair across from her mother and waited for Sheila to explain this drop-in visit further.

Her mother busied herself in her pocketbook, clearly looking for something. Joanie wondered if it was chapstick or Kleenex she needed. Sheila pulled out a headband and secured her short, thin hair away from her eyes.

"What brings you to Block Island?" Joanie felt her voice waver and hoped it didn't expose her emotions.

"What do you mean? I'm here to help Jackie," Sheila quickly replied.

"Help Jackie?" Joanie asked. "Help Jackie, how?" Joanie hadn't spoken to Jackie in over a week. She welcomed the break away from the drama and chaos revolving around the wedding.

Sheila sat forward on the edge of the couch, looking at Joanie quizzically. "For the wedding. We need to secure the photographer. Jackie knows how much I love taking pictures, so she wanted my input. Didn't she tell you? She told me she told you!"

"Mom," Joanie ignored the question and closed her eyes. She slightly shook her head. "How did you get here? You live in Florida."

"Oh! I flew to Providence and stayed with Jackie last night. She dropped me off at the ferry this morning. She's coming tomorrow because she couldn't get off work today. I thought I would come today and spend some time with you!" Sheila's intentions seemed clear, but Joanie was not ready for a full day and night with Sheila.

"Mom, I wish you told me. I am working today and tomorrow. I don't know how much time I have for you."

"Joanie, I have been calling all day! You never picked up your phone!" It was true. Joanie locked herself in the laundry room for the day to get the washing done. "I never see you," Sheila looked down at her hands, her shoulders slumped. Joanie wasn't sure if she genuinely felt disappointed at the thought of missing out on one-on-one time with her eldest daughter or if she was manipulating Joanie into canceling her day to accommodate her mother.

"Do you want a drink?" Joanie changed the subject, ignoring the possible malicious intentions of Sheila's behavior.

"I'm parched!" Sheila exclaimed.

On the way into the kitchen, Joanie snuck into the laundry room, turned the music as loud as it would go, grabbed a pillow, placed it over her mouth, and screamed as loud as she could in frustration. If there was one thing Joanie hated, it was unexpected drop-ins by Sheila and Jackie.

Joanie returned to Sheila, who was wandering around the room, exploring the kitchen. "Here, Mom. It's water."

Sheila took a sip. "Is this tap? You know I don't drink tap water."

"Mom, it's filtered. You'll be fine."

After a few moments of silence and a heaviness sitting between them, Joanie broke the silence. "All the guest rooms are currently occupied. Were you planning on staying here?" She tried to pepper her voice with sweetness, but the bitterness tainted her words.

"Yes, I was. I thought Jackie talked to you. If it is too much of an inconvenience, I suppose I can take the ferry back and have Jackie pick me up." A wave of uncertainty washed over Sheila's face.

"No, Mom." Joanie rubbed her eyebrows with her thumb and forefinger. "No. You can stay here. You have your choice of the carriage house, which is the little building behind the inn, or you can crash on my couch. It's your choice. Neither is ideal or overly comfortable, but at least you won't be sleeping outside."

"I'll sleep in the carriage house, so you have your own space." She acted like she was doing Joanie a favor. Joanie fumed underneath her calm, cool composure.

"And did you say that Jackie is coming tomorrow? This is all news to me."

Sheila nodded, a smile plastered across her face, yet her forehead creased and her eyebrows furrowed.

"Okay, you can both crash in the carriage house. Do you know if Chris is coming?"

"No," Sheila said. "It was supposed to be a girls-only event. I can't believe Jackie didn't talk to you."

Joanie believed it. Why would her center-of-the-universe sister care if she inconvenienced Joanie's life? Joanie still had so much to do around the inn, yet now she was expected to entertain her mother. Matt took tomorrow off, and he and Joanie were going out to dinner. She imagined a romantic night, alone. Suddenly, images of her mother peeking in the windows destroyed her fantasy of spending alone time with her boyfriend.

"It's okay, Mom," Joanie consoled. It wasn't Sheila's fault that Jackie was entitled and had no concern for anyone else. "But I need your help. I was in the middle of laundry and ironing, and I have to get it done today."

Sheila followed Joanie into the laundry room, dropped her oversized Kate Spade bag on the floor, and grabbed the iron. "My mother taught me how to iron when I was a little girl. I know I didn't iron when you were young, but it's like riding a bike. You never quite forget how to do it." Joanie passed the iron to Sheila and grabbed another sheet.

Joanie scrolled through the radio stations and found a classic rock song. She turned it up for her mom, and the two of them continued to fold and iron until evening fell and the inn filled with the pleasant chatter of her guests.

After Joanie meticulously folded the last sheet, Joanie and Sheila walked to the carriage house. "This was where I spent last summer. It's not the nicest place, but it's your own space and will be perfect for what you need. Feel free to come over in the morning. I am up at dawn and in the kitchen by five. The back door will be open, so feel free to enter from the back." She continued to walk her mom through the small apartment, pointing out the bathroom, kitchen, and bedroom.

"Thanks, Joanie. Do you want to go out for dinner? It would be nice to spend some time together."

Joanie couldn't remember the last time she went out to dinner without her father or sister tagging along. It may have been the night before Joanie left for college. She was home that summer, sleeping in her bedroom that was a cross between adolescence and adulthood. Her twin-sized bed hugged the corner of the room, with its floral comforter covered in stuffed animals. Makeup and trendy jewelry covered the top of her dresser. She was a child desperate to grow up.

"Sure, Mom. I'll see what I can find. Take a rest, and come on over around six tonight. We'll go into town and grab some food."

Joanie left, feeling relieved that she got out of there as quickly as she did. She had two hours to cancel her plans with Matt and mentally prepare herself for dinner.

***

That night, Joanie sat at the table and listened to her mother jabber nonsensically about the wedding plans. Every time Joanie circled the conversation back to herself and her life, Sheila somehow circumlocuted the conversation back to Jackie, the wedding, and her chance at one day having grandchildren. Joanie considered sharing her relationship with Matt just for shock value but decided to hold that relationship close to her.

He took the news well when Joanie uninvited him to dinner. She explained that her relationship with her mother was complicated, and she had requested dinner alone. Matt kissed Joanie and told her he would be waiting for her. She didn't know how she got so lucky.

Sometimes Joanie didn't feel like a grown-up, even though she was considered middle-aged. She felt uncomfortable in her own body, didn't know how to converse with strangers, and had only a handful of short-term boyfriends throughout her life. She was rapidly falling in love with Matt and didn't know how to handle her emotions.

Sheila stabbed her broccoli and placed the crown in her mouth. "Joanie, this food is delicious! It wasn't what I expected, but the food is great!" They were sitting in a vinyl booth at Louie's Clam Shack. The lights overhead buzzed, and one light flickered. The cook in the back was clanging metal against metal, and the sound ricocheted across the walls.

"This is the chef for Jackie's wedding." Joanie saw a look of concern flash across Sheila's face as she soaked in the drab paint and trash on the floor.

"Don't worry, Mom. It's not here. Louie is catering. He's a friend of Chris's family and is one of the nicest people you will meet. It will be delicious. Please don't worry." Joanie felt a slight edge of satisfaction seep into her belly when a flash of despair crossed her mother's face.

"Well, I am sure it will be excellent," Sheila said, wiping her chin with a paper napkin.

They talked about the next few days and the unknown plans made without Joanie's consent. Jackie was coming in the morning, and they had appointments with two photographers. On the third day, they were leaving. Joanie had to push through for the next thirty-six hours, and then they would be gone. Thirty-six hours of hell, but she could do it.

That night, Joanie furiously texted Jackie, accusing her of purposefully leaving her out of the weekend plans so she couldn't say no.

Jackie denied it all: **Life has been so busy! I swear, I told you!**

Joanie leaned into Matt, against the edge of the couch, and jabbed her fingers into the phone. Matt ignored the frantic, unpredictable text exchange and the emotions contorting Joanie's face until she put her phone face down on the coffee table in a huff.

"Are you okay?" he asked.

"Yeah, just tired. Tomorrow, I have a busy day between breakfast, signing guests in and out, and juggling my family. You don't understand. My mother is extremely overbearing. She thinks she belongs on a pedestal, with her proper mannerisms and can't-do-wrong attitude. My entire life, Jackie was the wonder child, and I was just okay. I'm frustrated they are here. I wasn't mentally ready to entertain them together," Joanie giggled despite her frustration.

Matt stroked her hair as she leaned into his chest. "Parents are tough. Where's your dad?"

"Oh, he stayed in Florida. My dad could care less about this wedding. He would be just as happy if they eloped, but my mother would freak. I think he stayed down there to enjoy the peace and quiet."

Matt didn't say anything.

"I'm so sorry." Joanie suddenly sat up next to Matt and looked him in the eyes. "I am so stupid. I don't know why I'm complaining," she mumbled, glancing at the couch cushion just next to his knee from the corner of her eyes.

"My parents died a long time ago. It's okay. I felt the same way when they were alive, and then suddenly, they were gone. I felt guilty for a long time, knowing that I never appreciated them, but we're all human. Bad things happen. It's okay. I don't mind listening."

Matt's parents died in a tragic car accident years ago. Joanie felt foolish for getting so worked up over such minor problems. It was a wedding. It was one visit. She felt better, getting things off her chest, but she didn't want to push it with Matt's emotional instability.

She got up to grab two glasses of wine and changed the subject. There was too much heaviness in her tiny apartment, and she was fighting to breathe. She absentmindedly found a television show to watch and fell asleep on Matt's lap. It was time to get up before she even made it to her bed.

Chapter 11

Joanie juggled breakfast under the judgment of her family. Sheila came over early to witness the chaos yet refused to assist. Joanie's annoyance grew by the second.

Joanie struggled to fall asleep the night before. Her mind raced with wedding drama and petty arguments about flowers, cakes, and unicorns. Her alarm woke her with a jolt, and she groaned as she rolled out of bed.

The guests slept while Joanie quickly set up the dining room. Her coffee hadn't quite kicked in yet, and her morning routine was hazy.

Sheila followed Joanie from the dining room to the kitchen, dressed in black slacks and a pinstripe blazer. Her sandals had gold adornments across the top of her foot. Her black hair appeared to be freshly blow-dried, and each strand was perfectly in place. Her red lips and mauve cheeks were too much for five in the morning, no matter where you were. Joanie thought it was unnecessary and imperious.

Sheila sat at the kitchen table and asked Joanie for a cup of coffee. Joanie cringed, wanting to tell her mother to get it herself, but she kept her composure and gently placed the mug, creamer, and sugar on the farmhouse table. As Sheila prepared her coffee, Joanie stumbled from room to room, clearly busy and unable to chat.

"So," Sheila called as Joanie exited the kitchen, "your sister should be here around ten or so. Our first appointment is at one. I thought I would take you out to lunch, just us girls." Joanie nodded, grabbing the cutlery to place on the dining room tables. She barely threw a glance toward her mother as she exited the kitchen again.

As Joanie re-entered, her mother took a sip of coffee, eyeing her intently. "You know, I am proud of you for taking this chance. For doing something you never did before. And being brave enough to try something new."

Joanie stopped mid-stride and looked at Sheila. "Thank you, Mom. That means a lot to me." She felt a sense of pride and surprise fill her belly. She was not the most adventurous person, but losing her job laid all her weaknesses on the table. She had no choice but to find the courage inside her to say, "What the hell!" and just do it.

"So, when am I going to meet this boyfriend of yours?" Sheila took another sip of coffee, hiding the smirk behind her thin lips.

"What boyfriend?" Joanie asked, deliberately avoiding the question.

"Your boyfriend," Sheila repeated. "Jackie told me about him. Chris did, too, actually, the night I flew in. He sounds like a nice fellow."

Joanie felt her face turn crimson, and she turned away to hide her blush from her mother. Joanie knew her hot pink neck exposed herself and stuck her head in the fridge, pretending to look for something behind the milk and juices.

"His name is Matt. He's managing the inn. We run the inn together, and yes, he's my boyfriend, but he's also Carly's second cousin. That's how we met. We've been dating almost a year now."

Joanie wanted to brag to her mother about how spectacular he was, how well he treated her, and how patient he was with her, but she and Sheila never had that type of relationship. Joanie learned over the years that minimal information was best because Sheila was full of opinions and never shied away from sharing them.

"When will I meet him?" Sheila repeated.

Joanie expected that the next time she saw her mother, it would be during the wedding, another eight months away. "I don't know."

"How about tonight?" Sheila asked. "We don't have any plans."

Joanie quietly stewed, debating her options. Should she introduce Matt and Sheila now, which might send the wrong message to Matt, or wait until the wedding when the day's craziness would limit the amount of time Sheila could pry into his life?

"Let me talk to him. He's very busy with work, and his rental property, and land. I'll let you know later." Joanie turned to the stove and flipped the sausages and pancakes that were sizzling. Breakfast started in an hour, and they had a busy house scheduled to eat.

Once Joanie cleaned up breakfast, Sheila encouraged Joanie to shower and get ready for the day.

"Mom, I am showered and ready." Joanie looked at her jean skirt, white blouse, and black shoes.

"Honey, you need to dress the part. We are meeting with professional photographers. We need to impress them, so they want to work for us. Wash your hair. Take it out of a ponytail, put your contacts in, and throw on a little makeup. This is for your sister. I think you can put in a little effort for her."

Joanie seethed behind the smiling mask she painted across her face. "Sure, Mom," she said icily. "I'll meet you at the carriage house in an hour." She opened the back door and hurried Sheila outside before Sheila could object. That whole bit about being proud of her was just her way of manipulating the day, Joanie thought.

She made her way to the apartment and texted Matt: **My mother is driving me crazy.** She threw in a shocked emoji for effect, possibly to lighten the comment, or strengthen it, depending on Matt's interpretation. Joanie showered, blow-dried her hair, threw on mascara and lip gloss, and dressed in black linen slacks and a floral, button-down blouse. She draped her red beads around her neck for an added sparkle and hoped her mother was pleased with her choices.

They walked down to the dock and watched the ferry slowly enter the pier. The sun was already warming the cool, fresh air, and Joanie inhaled the scent of salt in the gentle breeze. The cars drove off the plank, single file, traveling at a snail's pace. People filed off the boat in droves, squeezed amongst each other like sardines.

"Jackie! Yoohoo!" Sheila called out, waving her arms frantically. Her straw-like hair bobbed back and forth like one of those cartoon drawings where the entire hairstyle moved in unison.

Jackie calmly stepped onto the sidewalk wearing a flowing yellow sundress.

It cascaded to her ankles and floated above the hot pavement. She wore oversized red sunglasses and an oversized sun hat that cast a shadow around her body. She looked like a movie star. Jackie retracted her body away from Sheila, taking in Joanie's worn, tattered sandals and linen pants that were a tad too big. Always being compared, Sheila cried, "You look beautiful!" and threw her arms around Jackie in a warm, tight embrace.

Joanie watched the two of them and wondered when they got so close and how she got so far removed from their inner circle. Joanie threw her sister a slight wave, still angry that Jackie didn't inform her about the plans. She ignored the tension in her shoulders and smiled. "Where do you want to go for lunch?"

They made their way to a fish and chips place near the ferry dock and ate outside on the outdoor patio. Jackie dominated the conversation. She happily reported that she found her dress, picked out her flowers, and finalized the menu. All she needed was a photographer, and she could breathe again when it was secured, she informed.

Sheila encouraged Jackie to explain how she came to certain decisions or what Chris thought, how much money this was costing, or who would be in the wedding. It was evident that for Sheila, planning her daughter's wedding highlighted motherhood.

Joanie ate in silence, listening to Jackie rehash the wedding details for the umpteenth time. As soon as the check came, Joanie paid and hurried them back to the inn so Jackie could drop her stuff off before meeting the photographer.

"What a great lunch!" Sheila said. "Joanie, you are so lucky to live here, and Jackie, you are so lucky you are getting married here! Both my girls, living the good life, with the ocean in your back pocket." Joanie rolled her eyes as she walked ahead of them. Giddy excitement filled the air between Sheila and Jackie as they continued to gossip and brainstorm wedding ideas.

When they returned to the inn, Joanie opened the carriage house door to let Jackie drop her stuff in the tiny living room. "I hope you don't mind, but you and Mom are bunking here tonight."

Joanie stepped inside, and two dark shadows stood before her. "Whoa!"

Joanie gasped. Her heart raced and pounded against her sternum. "What are you doing here?!" A wide grin pulled across Joanie's lips.

Carly stepped forward and hugged Joanie. "Surprise!" Her voice was meek and unsure. She introduced Sandra to Joanie, and Joanie did the same for Sheila and Jackie. Jackie and Carly hugged, and Sheila stuck out her hand. *Always so formal,* Joanie thought.

The five women stood there, crammed into the tiny cottage. Luggage littered the floor, and pocketbooks haphazardly splayed across the furniture.

"I'm back!" Carly exclaimed.

Joanie stood there, unsure why Carly was standing in the carriage house. Jackie and Sheila looked inquisitively at the unexpected guests. There wasn't enough room for everyone, and the inn was full. Joanie's apartment could squeeze in one more, tightly, and two more if they were on top of each other.

Joanie told Carly that Jackie and Sheila unexpectedly dropped by and planned to crash in the carriage house that night. Still, Carly got priority because it was her house.

"Mom and Jackie, you guys can crash at my place. We'll make it work." Everything in Joanie's mind was a jumbled mess. Questions crashed into each other, not just about Carly's surprising appearance, but also about the wedding, and her family, and how her week unraveled so quickly. "Carly, I'll be back. Give me ten minutes."

Joanie escorted her family out across the lush, green grass. They each carried a small suitcase and entered the apartment. Joanie's apartment was quaint and cute and built for two. The kitchenette was small but functional, and the bedroom and living room sat beside each other.

"One of you can take the bed, and one of you can take the couch. I'll find somewhere else to sleep."

"Oh, Joanie, you don't have to do that!" Sheila crowed.

"I do, Mom. I can't have you sleeping on the floor. That wouldn't be fair." Realistically, Joanie could share a bed with Sheila, but that option was least favorable. She changed the sheets and picked up all the clothes mingling in the corners of the room. She quickly did the dishes and wiped down the bathroom. It wasn't perfect, but at least they weren't sleeping under the stars.

"But where will you sleep?" Sheila asked.

"I don't know. Probably in the carriage house. I'll be fine."

Jackie sat on the couch and anxiously looked at her watch. "We have to go. We have our appointment in twenty minutes."

Joanie looked back and forth, recognizing her excuse to get out of this weekend's wedding bliss. "Why don't you guys go, and I'll stay here. I need to talk to Carly and figure out what's going on. When you get back, you can tell me all about it. And now we have Carly to lean on. I'm sure she'll have an opinion as to which photographer is better."

"Sure. Mom, we have to go!" Jackie said, grabbing her purse. "I don't know my way around."

The two women stumbled out of the house and maneuvered their way into town. Joanie gave them directions but knew that Jackie could get lost in a paper bag and wondered if it was wrong for her to send them unsupervised.

Joanie's feet quickly carried her back across the lawn, behind the old house, and into the carriage house. She didn't even bother to knock because although it was Carly's house, Joanie lived here.

"Hey!" she called at the sight of Sandra and Carly surrounded by bags and boxes. "What's going on?"

"Well," Carly looked down and fumbled with the edge of her shirt. She rubbed the fabric in between her thumb and forefinger until the friction burned her fingertips. "I left John."

Joanie's eyes widened, and she leaned against the doorframe. "What? What happened?" She sat on the edge of the couch, one buttock firmly in place, the other one resting in mid-air. She didn't want to get too close because she was unsure if Carly would crumble with a hug or stand tall like a warrior.

"Nothing happened. That's the problem. There's nothing there. I never saw him. I completely redid my life for him, and he didn't make any adjustments. Instead of us building a life together, I reinserted myself into his life, and it didn't work out. For me, at least. He had no idea I was so unhappy."

Joanie nodded, saddened to hear the news. She thought they had a perfect love story.

"How did you get here?" Joanie asked, knowing Carly didn't have a car and certainly could not have carried all this luggage on the boat.

"I drove her," Sandra quipped. "I took a few days off of work. I drove her to the ferry, and we brought the car over. It's filled with stuff."

Joanie hadn't heard about Sandra before and wondered if Carly told her.

"So, are you back? For good?" Joanie hoped the desperation in her voice didn't shine through. If Carly took back the inn, she didn't know what she would do. She loved this chapter in her life and refused to return to a tedious nine-to-five job. Memories of business casual, paperwork, and deadlines clouded her thoughts.

"Yeah, I'm back for now. I'm sorry. I should have called. It happened so fast, and when Sandra said she could help me, I couldn't say no. I was so heartbroken, and I didn't want to tell you over the phone. I didn't realize you would have guests."

Joanie rolled her eyes. "They're not guests. They're intruders. They showed up unannounced and assumed I would parade them around for all their appointments. Trust me. It's not a problem. They are going to sleep in the apartment. Maybe I can crash with Matt. It's fine."

They settled into an easy conversation about the inn and how business had been so far this summer. Carly apologized for not being as active in the inn's management as discussed, and Joanie waved her off. Matt had been her rock through this whole experience, and things got done with just a few hiccups.

The three girls headed into town to show Sandra the beauty they both called home. For the first time in a long time, Carly felt okay. She knew that the feeling wouldn't last.

Chapter 12

That night at dinner, Joanie, Carly, Sandra, Jackie, and Sheila sat around the patio table in the backyard eating burgers and dogs. Carly had not shared her secret with anyone, and it was burning a hole in her belly. Whenever she thought about Chris being her cousin, her stomach grew queasy, and her head grew dizzy and light.

"Carly." She felt a tap on her arm. Sheila held out the macaroni salad bowl and smiled expectantly.

"Oh! Sorry," Carly took the bowl and tuned into the conversation going on around her. A cacophony interrupted her thoughts. Jackie and Sheila chatted, dogs barked in the distance, silverware clinked against the dishes, and the music from the house in the background meshed together and distorted her memories. Carly felt like she was living amongst the static of an old television. All she wanted was to readjust the rabbit ears so she could focus.

"So, what brings you back to the island?" Sheila asked, taking a delicate bite of her hamburger.

Carly hadn't figured out her excuse before she arrived because she didn't expect to see anyone, so she told the truth. "Well, I broke up with my boyfriend and decided to come home for a bit. To help with the inn." The words lingered in the air and floated away from the table. She undecidedly stopped talking and awkwardly took a bite of food to signal Sheila that she had nothing more to say.

"Oh, I am so sorry. You're so young and beautiful. Any man would be lucky to have you." Sheila smiled sweetly, and Carly nodded blankly. She took a sip of water and turned to Sandra, hoping Sheila would read her cues correctly and talk to someone else.

"Excuse me," Carly whispered to Sheila and abruptly moved toward the house.

She heard Sheila whisper a little too loudly, "What did I say?" Carly ignored her and walked briskly, forcefully opening the sliding door.

Tears built up behind her eyes as she escaped to the bathroom. She couldn't fight them anymore. Today was not how she expected and just seeing Jackie, who was marrying Chris, who possibly knew something about her past, was too much for her brain and heart to handle.

She hid out in the bathroom longer than she should have but felt utterly broken inside. All she wanted to do was go to sleep, be alone, and figure out her next move. She had to tell Sandra because Sandra was possibly the only one who could understand her emotions. It seemed like Carly was adopted, and no one told her. Adopted or given up or abandoned. It was all semantics.

Carly pictured her mother, standing in the kitchen, wearing a blue sundress and white apron. In her memory, Ruth stood at the stove, flipping pancakes. Peter sat at the table and arranged the coffee accessories on a tray to carry into the dining room.

"Mom?" Carly had asked. "Do you think I will be as tall as you?" Ruth stood at almost 6 feet while thirteen-year-old Carly hovered around 5'2''.

"I got my height from my grandfather. Perhaps you will take after your father's side. His mother was fairly short."

Carly pulled her thin ash blonde hair into a ponytail, contrasted with Ruth's thick chestnut head. Ruth ducked into the pantry, searching for more syrup.

"Yes, my mother was on the shorter side," Peter confirmed as he organized the sugar packets and exited the kitchen.

Carly reflected on her parents' vague responses when she asked about genetics and family. She never fit in with her parents, and she wondered if it was because there wasn't an innate connection between them. Or perhaps they kept a secret from her, which prevented them from being honest.

The strained relationship started in her teenage years. Carly felt bitter and resentful for being stuck on the island and stuck with the inn. When she was in grade school, her friends ignored the age gap between their parents and Carly's parents, and although Carly noticed it, it didn't bother her. In high school, her classmates referred to Peter and Ruth as "Grandma and Grandpa." Carly at first laughed with them but eventually stopped laughing. Resentment for getting pregnant so late in life continued to build. Now, Carly wondered if Ruth was pregnant.

Carly never felt like her life was her own. She spent most of her life trying to please her parents and gain their acceptance. Confusion clouded her thoughts. She had no idea how she ended up with Ruth and Peter. Was it intentional or accidental? There were so many questions swirling in her head.

She made her way to the liquor cabinet and downed two shots of vodka to calm the chaos churning inside her before going back outside to pretend she was okay. She wiped her eyes and sat at the patio table, fully aware of how long she was gone.

Carly smiled at the group and stumbled into her seat. Jackie gushed about the photographers today. Sandra smiled across the table, and Joanie sat quietly, listening to the rant between Jackie and Sheila.

Sandra squeezed Carly's hand under the table as if to say, "Are you okay?" In response, Carly picked up her burger, drops of ketchup splattered her plate and took a bite. It was cold. She pushed her plate toward the center of the table and focused on her soda. The sounds and noises lulled in and out of Carly's brain like the gentle lap of Sebago Lake.

Carly turned toward Sandra, "I feel exhausted all of a sudden. After dinner, do you want to relax and watch a movie?" She indirectly alerted everyone that she was going to check out of the family festivities early.

Sandra and Carly sat for a few minutes, waiting for everyone to finish eating, and then helped clear the table.

"Joanie, are you sure it's okay if we stay in the carriage house?" Carly asked.

Joanie waved her off with a grin on her face. "Totally fine! You guys can head out. I have this," she motioned toward the kitchen. Relieved, Carly and Sandra walked across the lawn to the private cottage away from the chaos.

The two friends sat on the couch in the carriage house, each holding a glass of wine. "Are you okay?" Sandra gently asked.

"I'm okay most days. Other days, something sets me off, and I don't even know it affects me until I'm already in tears. I'm fine. I still can't believe I left him and am back home."

Sandra nodded.

"Sandra? I have to tell you something."

Sandra looked at her quizzically. "What's up?"

"You know that DNA test we took? I looked at my family link, and it said that Chris—Jackie's Chris—is my first cousin. I can't wrap my head around how that's possible. My parents aren't listed. Siblings aren't listed, but it says Chris is my first cousin. Chris was my neighbor growing up. My parents were friends with his parents. It doesn't make any sense." Carly started crying at the overwhelming lack of control she felt stirring inside her.

"Huh," Sandra replied. "That's weird."

"Yeah, and that's why I needed to leave Sebago so quickly. And that's why I left John." Carly paused in thought. "Well, not the only reason, but one of the reasons. I couldn't stay, knowing that this emptiness about who I am was growing within me again. I have so many questions. I need to figure them out! It would be unfair for me to stay with John if I was so distracted by my own issues."

"What are you going to do?" Sandra asked, circling the embroidery on the decorative pillow with her forefinger.

"I don't know. I need to find out about my past."

"Are you going to tell Chris?" Sandra asked.

Carly stared at the television straight ahead, debating what she should do. "I don't want to, but I feel like I have to. Jackie is going to kill me if I distract him from their wedding."

"Oh well!" Sandra cried incredulously. "Too bad. She's a grown-up. She'll get over it. You can't carry this with you for the next year. You have to tell him."

Carly nodded, unable to respond. The gnawing sensation deep within her belly was starting to swirl, and she needed it to stop.

"What are you going to do?" Carly changed the subject. "About Bianca?" Carly felt like a terrible friend for ignoring the avalanche snowballing out of control in Sandra's life. Or maybe it wasn't, Carly wasn't sure, because she hadn't asked Sandra about it since that night in Sebago.

"It's so crazy!" Sandra started, relieved to have a friend who wanted to listen. "I researched her all over the internet. I tried to find out as much information as I could about my past. I can't believe she's in California, the farthest possible state away. How did that happen? I messaged her through Ancestry but so far, no response. If she isn't a big genealogical person, she isn't going to get the message. So then I sent her a message online through her many social media accounts, hoping she responds. So far, nothing. I don't know what I am going to do if she doesn't get back to me! I cannot believe I have a sister!" Sandra's face and vocal pattern became animated with excitement.

"Really? Wow, you are so brave," Carly said sincerely. "What did you say?"

"I told her I was her sister, according to the DNA test, and I had a twin brother who died. I told her I had always been curious about my real family. And that I would love to connect but understood if she didn't respond because it was too painful or difficult for her." Sandra shrugged. "I haven't heard back yet."

"She has to write back to you! Is there any way you can find her email? Maybe you should google her husband, see if he has a business or something with a phone number or email address. There has to be a way!"

Sandra whipped out her phone, searching through the web. "His name is Walter. His last name is Mueller, so maybe that is her last name too? I know they're in California. One of her social media accounts has the place listed for her pictures, and most of them are in Vallejo.Here. Let me look it up." Her fingers flew as she thumbed the info into her phone. "Okay, Vallejo is in the San Francisco Bay Area. Great, now I have an area. Let me google Walter Mueller." Sandra scrolled through the results without saying a word.

"Well?" Carly asked.

"Maybe his parents were baseball fans. The majority of the results are for the major league player from the 1920s. Oh my gosh," her eyes snapped up from her phone. "What if that was his grandfather, and he is a multi-millionaire?"

Carly giggled. "I don't think so."

Sandra continued scrolling. "Where is San Jose?" she asked.

Carly shrugged. "I have no idea!"

"Oh! Carly! It's also in the San Francisco Bay area. I think I found him! He is the superintendent! Here. Look at his picture!" Sandra flashed her phone at Carly. "Look carefully. I'm going to pull up one of his pictures on Bianca's social media."

A few moments later, Carly stared at the same person whose picture appeared on the school website. "Yep, that's him! Shit! Good detective skills! What are you going to do?"

Sandra took a deep breath, smoothed back her hair, and said, "Nothing. I am going to wait. At least a week. If I don't hear anything from Bianca, I will reach out to him."

Carly smiled. "Girl, you are braver than I gave you credit for."

"Here's the thing," Sandra said, seriousness crossing her face. "I'm going to give it one week. I can't do this without you. You have one week to figure out your past, and if you come up with nothing, you have to promise me you will tell Chris. You have to because if you don't, you will be wondering for the rest of your life."

Carly averted her eyes to the coffee table and chipped away at the dried red wine that speckled the tabletop with her fingernail. "Fine."

Chapter 13

T he next day, Carly woke early and made her way to the kitchen to help Joanie with breakfast. The girls chatted about the previous few months while flipping pancakes and brewing coffee. The overall organization and confidence Joanie expressed throughout the breakfast-making experience impressed Carly.

"Joanie, you were made for this kitchen."

Joanie chuckled. "That's only because you haven't seen me in action in almost a year. Trust me, in the beginning, I was clueless. I couldn't cook, I was afraid to be around strangers, and I wasn't sure if I had made the biggest mistake of my life. Again." As she spoke, she poured the blueberry muffin batter into the tin and sprinkled cinnamon streusel on top.

The scent of pastries, bacon, and coffee filled Carly's nostrils and brought back memories of home. "I want to thank you for doing such an amazing job. We have been busy, we've gotten great reviews, and clearly, whatever you and Matt are doing is working."

Joanie nodded and paced the kitchen. Her arms overflowed with breakfast plates.

"I was surprised to see you yesterday. How are you feeling?" Joanie eyed Carly curiously.

Carly looked at her fingers, chipped pink paint that formed strange designs on her nails. "Yeah, sorry about that. I should have called."

Joanie reached over and gave her friend a tight hug. Carly melted into her and quietly sobbed.

She wiped her eyes with the back of her hand as she pulled away. "Thanks," she mumbled.

Joanie stood up straight and smoothed out her apron. "So, what are you going to do now?"

Carly tensed, not quite sure if this was the time or place to discuss her plans. "Well," she started, "I'm moving back here."

Joanie's blue eyes turned into saucers, and she quickly tried to hide her surprise by busying herself at the stove. "Oh," was all she said.

"I have to, Joanie," Carly defended. "There is nowhere else I can go. And I still own the inn. This place is still mine, legally. We can do it together. You're welcome to move back into the carriage house. Or I can stay there," Carly quickly added. "You don't have to leave. Honestly, I have other things on my mind that I have to take care of, so I can't fully commit to the inn right now. I still need you." Carly noticed Joanie's shoulders relax slightly.

Joanie smiled meekly and made her way into the dining area with sugar and honey for the tea.

They set up breakfast in silence. The two women passed each other, entering and exiting the kitchen, and silently transformed the dining room into a fun, summer oasis. Sea-blue tablecloths laid over the round tables, and vases sat in the center, slightly filled with sand, shells, and sea glass.

"Wow! This place looks great." Carly began to understand how the inn was doing so well without her.

Ten minutes before breakfast officially started, Sheila and Jackie made their way into the dining room. Joanie could hear them coming as they descended the stairs, each heel hitting the wooden step with a click. Joanie stood at the entrance to the dining room with a giant grin plastered across her face. "Good morning! Welcome to breakfast at Willowside Inn! Please take a seat wherever you would like!"

Sheila brusquely kissed Joanie on the cheek. "This looks wonderful. So professional. I see you have been taking decorator tips from your sister." Sheila side-eyed the table set-up and grinned at Jackie. Joanie stood, frozen, with an icy smile, unsure what to say.

"Thank you," was all Joanie could muster, and she hurried back into the kitchen to compose herself and finish bringing out the food.

"You okay?" Carly asked, seeing her friend shaken.

"My mother and sister are leaving tomorrow morning. Let's just say it can't happen quick enough," Joanie responded angrily. She grabbed the glass pitcher filled with freshly-squeezed orange juice, took a deep breath, and exited the kitchen.

Carly followed to assist with the final setup and then sat with Jackie and Sheila to touch base about the wedding.

"Hi, Jackie!" Carly said, enthusiasm coating her words. "How have you been?" She pulled out the third chair at the table and sat down before they could deny her a seat.

"I've been great!" Jackie responded. "The wedding is coming together, and Mom and I are just thrilled with all the progress we have made!"

"So, what type of things have you decided on so far?" Carly knew she should already know, but she hadn't been reliable with keeping in touch over the past few weeks.

"Well, I have my dress! It's stunning, beautiful, and not overly extravagant. It's perfect for a beach wedding. We have our venue," she splayed her arms out, motioning to the area around them. "We have our food, and we now have a photographer. The only thing I need is music and cake, but we will save that for another weekend." Sheila nodded in agreement.

"Great!" Carly responded. "Anything you need, let me know!" She turned to Sheila. "And when are you returning to New England again?"

Sheila took a sip of coffee. "I am going home with Jackie tonight and flying to Florida tomorrow. I don't know when I will be back. Maybe Thanksgiving or maybe Christmas. I will fly up if Jackie needs me again for planning purposes." She placed her hand on Jackie's and squeezed gently.

Joanie hurried around the dining room, which had filled up with guests. She poured coffee and asked about their plans while ignoring her family.

"That's so nice," Carly said blankly.

"Oh yes, this wedding is going to be one for the books! My daughter is going to look so beautiful in her dress."

"Mom!" Jackie hissed. "Don't show her a picture! It's a secret!" She was half-laughing, half-serious, and Carly could see a connection between the two women she had never experienced with her mother.

Carly never got married, and she wondered how Ruth would have responded. Ruth probably would have told Carly that any plans beyond the inn were unnecessary and wasteful. Carly imagined herself marrying someone from the island. It would likely be a person she knew or her parents knew.

A sour feeling swelled in her belly as she imagined marrying an unknown relative and her 'family' not telling her the truth. Carly wondered if she ever mistakenly kissed a relative and swiftly excused herself from the table to find Joanie.

"I'm going to find Sandra. See if she is up. I'll catch up with you later." Carly left the house through the back entrance and traversed the green grass to the carriage house, eager to depart all talk of weddings and happiness.

She found Sandra sitting on the couch, still dressed in pajamas, holding a tall coffee mug. "Hey!" she said, taking a sip. "How did you sleep?"

Carly nodded and smiled. "Pretty good. You?"

"So good!" Sandra exclaimed. "It felt great to sleep with the window open and hear the birds singing instead of trucks honking on the street."

They still had a car full of bags and boxes to bring in and unpack. Carly was unsure where they would go. She hadn't been able to sit down with Joanie alone to talk about her move back home. Joanie could remain in the apartment, but living in the carriage house felt like a step-down.

"I guess I'll be moving in here," Carly said, looking at the old, dusty furniture that reminded her of her parents. *Fake parents.* "Do you want to help me unpack the car and re-arrange some furniture?"

The girls emptied the car and dropped the boxes in the kitchen. They faced the bed against the window and moved the couch to the outside wall. Just those tiny changes helped Carly feel a little more in control of her surroundings and put her at ease.

"I think I'm going to head back today," Sandra said. Carly pouted her lips and said, "I'm going to miss you! When am I going to see you again?"

Sandra embraced Carly and kissed her on the cheek. "I don't know, but I have to get back to work before I can plan more time off. We'll be in touch. We're both on this DNA journey, Car, so we should lean on each other. I'm going to need you! Especially with Bianca. And you need me, with Chris."

Carly nodded, worried that her secret would crush her under the weight of fear and misunderstanding. "Promise. I promise we will talk every week, and we will walk this journey together. Call me when you get home."

The two women drove to the ferry in silence. Carly felt like her life in Portland had been a dream. She attempted to live a fairy tale story, but it wasn't meant to be. She reflected on her friendship with Sandra and how comfortable Carly felt around her. Sandra knew so many secrets within such a short period. They needed each other, regardless of the mess they both muddled through.

That was it—the final goodbye to her life in Portland. And just like a gale wind, the island swept her back and held her, unable to let her go, as she watched the ferry leave the dock.

Chapter 14

The following day, Carly and Joanie found themselves alone in the kitchen, cleaning up the last of the breakfast dishes. The inn was full, but new reservations for the rest of the season were slowing down. There were only a few more crazy weeks, and then Carly could focus on herself.

"How was the rest of your visit with your mom and sister?" Carly asked.

Joanie smiled. "Just great," she said sarcastically. "After breakfast, they spent the day attached to my hip. My mom begged to meet Matt, which I didn't want to do, but I did. After his shift, he came over briefly, fully dressed in uniform. My mother had a field day. It was so embarrassing. She spent the next three hours telling me how great it would be to have an officer in the house. An officer. Like it's 1950, and we are starring in a Marilyn Monroe movie."

"What did Matt think?"

"I think he was overwhelmed. He didn't know he would be walking into the Boardroom and would have to field eight hundred questions about his life, goals, and dreams. I felt terrible. I tried my hardest to shoo him out the door before my mother pounced on him. He's coming over in about an hour."

"Oh, good! I haven't seen him yet, and I miss him."

Joanie continued to scrub the last of the pans and placed them in the drying rack. She turned to Carly, "I was so happy when they left last night! They showed up unexpectedly, took my bed, and all my time. I finally got a good night's sleep because I didn't have to worry about waking them early in the morning or making sure they were having a good time." The two girls headed to the laundry room to start the next chore. "Do you want to hang out today? I would love to catch up."

Carly nodded and smiled warmly at her friend, "I would love to. I have no plans."

A few hours later, Carly, Matt, and Joanie were lounging on the couch in the apartment. It looked different than how Carly left it, and her heart broke a little for the erasure of her home. Carly had noticed that the carriage house was filled with Ruth's furniture but didn't realize that it came from her old apartment.

Someone removed the curio cabinet, Carly's grandmother's serving table, which held her linens, and the old chrome and red leather dinette set. In its place was a generic wooden table to eat at, a metal baking rack overflowing with linens, and an extra dresser. Joanie even swapped the rooms, so the bedroom was in the larger living area, and the living room was where Carly used to sleep.

Carly observed the changes. Joanie said, "It's easier for Matt if I am closer to the bathroom and farther from the kitchen."

Carly nodded in understanding. "It looks great!" Carly exclaimed, brushing off her sadness. She flopped on the couch and ran her hands against the brown plaid fabric and wooden arms that she hated as a child but grew to love as an adult.

"So, what brings you home?" Matt asked. "Unannounced?"

Carly rolled her eyes at her cousin. "Unannounced? This is my home!" She was laughing, but the hurt and anger bled through her words.

"Is everything okay?" he asked more seriously. Matt and Carly were cousins and had been raised on the island but didn't get to know each other until last year when Joanie moved in. Joanie stayed with Carly while on a newspaper assignment. She interviewed Matt for one of her pieces.

"John and I broke up. It wasn't working out." Carly looked down, embarrassed that she was so naïve, thinking that their relationship would work this time.

"I'm sorry," Matt said, unsure if he should proceed with questions.

"Yeah, it's fine. I don't want to talk about it." Carly waved her hands around her face to force the idea that it was no big deal. "I'm home for the foreseeable future. I can stay in the carriage house. I still need Joanie because I'm not quite ready to throw my life back into this place." She took a sip of soda to put a final period on her response.

Carly's eye gaze fixated on the television remote on the coffee table. Beige bags traveled from her lower lashes to her cheekbones. Fine lines wrapped around her lips, and the sparkle in her eyes dulled. Water filled her eyes and sat there like a glaze threatening to drip off the edges of a donut. She felt sad and tired.

Joanie rearranged the magazines on the coffee table, clearly uncomfortable with the silence and finite conversation. Joanie's blue eyes were bright, and she flashed a lightning-quick look to Matt, hoping Carly didn't notice. Joanie's lashes were long and dark, framing her mysterious eyes. Her plump lips shined from the lip gloss that she started to wear regularly. Her skin soaked up the sun and glowed healthily. She looked vulnerable but happy, despite her inability to handle conflict.

Carly broke the silence. "So tell me about you!" Her voice was cheery and enthusiastic. She spoke to them the way she would answer the phone when someone made a reservation. "How have you guys been? You look great!"

"We're doing great!" Joanie responded, glancing at Matt. She didn't want to give any other information, knowing that Carly was not doing great.

"Yeah, we have had a fun year together. Lots of fun." Matt's voice trailed off, unsure what to say. The awkwardness hovered in the air. "Hey, I have to go into town and grab some stuff for my renters. The sink is clogged again, and I told them I would fix it today. Does anyone want to go for a walk?"

Joanie smiled. "I would love to, but I have to go grocery shopping for breakfast tomorrow. Carly, why don't you go? You haven't been over to Matt's place yet, have you?"

Carly shook her head.

"Oh, I've done so much since you left! Painted the whole place and redid the landscaping. You'll love it."

Carly didn't want to go but could sense that she was a bummer pulling everyone else down. She nodded, thinking fresh air would help reset her mood. "Sure. Sounds fun."

They climbed into Matt's beat-up pick-up truck and rode the three miles to the other side of the island. It was too far for tourists to walk, so the double-lined road led to single-lane and gravel driveways. Random farm animals dotted the houses on craggy hills to accentuate the landscape.

Matt's family owned a farm for generations, and when they died in a car crash, Matt took over. He turned the barn into his own living space and rented out the house for money. It was a smart move since he was only one person and had no intention of being a farmer. Matt did what he could with the land and upkeep of the house but knew his parents would be disappointed if they were still alive. The land was undoubtedly not profitable for Matt, and he often questioned why he didn't break up the deed and sell it.

They pulled into the gravel driveway, and Carly saw the new farmer's porch Matt built off the front entrance of the old barn structure. The stained wooden planks glistened against the ivory door.

"Wow. The porch looks great!" Carly said.

"Thanks. I built it in the fall after you left. Joanie told me that her favorite childhood memory was sitting on her grandparent's porch, swinging back and forth with lemonade in one hand and a magazine in the other. I just had that concrete step, which looked awful, so she and I sat down one day, planned it out, and built it together."

"That sounds serious, Matt!" Carly responded, her chest warm with envy. "Have you ever built a porch for someone before?"

He laughed. "No, just Joanie. Carly, I'm old! I'm past my prime for dating. I want to settle down, and I enjoy her company. I love hearing her laugh and learning about what makes her sad, mad, and happy. I love to see her smile."

"I don't know Matt, that sounds serious to me," Carly said, walking through the front door. The inside of his place looked precisely as she remembered but better furnished. "Have you and Joanie gone shopping? Last time I was here, you were using a Rubbermaid tote to hold your TV."

"Yeah, she's slowly been working her way into my house. It's okay. I don't mind. I like having someone who needs me. Do you want a drink?" he asked, holding open the newly cleaned fridge door.

"Water, please."

They settled into the living room, and Carly noticed a picture of Joanie and Matt on his side table. The sun set behind the beach with majestic purple and pink hues streaking through the sky in the photo. Joanie and Matt were mid-laugh, and Carly wondered what happened right before the photo was taken.

"I love that picture," she said, nodding toward the silver frame.

"Thanks. We took that on our one-year anniversary."

"Congrats for making it one year," Carly said, raising her glass.

Matt smiled back. "So," he said, "what happened with John?"

Carly didn't want to talk about it out loud. She thought about it for months, recognizing the fault lines within their relationship that unexpectedly crumbled under the weight of life. "I decided that what he had to offer me wasn't what I wanted. I don't know what I want, but it wasn't that. I was alone all the time, he never made me feel special, and it was like we were roommates. There was nothing romantic about us. I was just someone to help pay the rent. It was a terrible decision to bring a boyfriend back from the dead and think that it would end with a fairy tale ending."

Matt's blue eyes looked into her crumpled face. "I'm sorry," he said quietly.

"It's fine. Thank you." She took a drink of her water and gulped loudly. Her heart was beating ferociously against her chest. "Can I ask you something?"

Matt nodded. "What's up?"

"This is going to sound crazy, but do you know anything about Chris Swanson's family?"

Matt shrugged. "I know his parents moved, but I don't know where. They sold their house. I think they sold it for a lot of money. He had a younger brother, Ronnie, and an older sister, Charlene. I graduated with Charlene. I think Ronnie lives in New York and Charlene lives somewhere in Rhode Island. Why?"

Carly waited impatiently. She knew all of this already.

"Okay, I have another question. Have you ever done DNA TODAY? You know, to figure out where your ancestors are from?"

Matt shook his head, "Nah, I don't care about that stuff."

Carly placed her fingers in her lap and twisted them against each other. She wiped her sweaty palms on her thighs.

"Can I tell you something? You can't tell a soul. Especially not Joanie."

A hollowness filled with hunger appeared in Carly's eyes. Matt reluctantly agreed.

She reached into her purse and pulled out her phone, fumbling with the app, trying to remember where the family contacts were. "Here," she said, shoving her phone to Matt. "Check out my relatives."

He skimmed the screen and slowly scrolled down. Chris and Charlene were both listed as first cousins. He continued to scroll up and down the page, looking for anyone from their family. Carly saw him rub his forearms, which had tiny goose pimples poking through his skin. "Chris and Charlene? I don't get it. We aren't related to them."

"That's what I thought! Thank you. I knew I wasn't crazy." Carly stood up from the couch and paced back and forth across the room. "It doesn't make any sense. How can I be related to them? And how is it that I don't have any of our relatives listed? Not one. Could it be that Ruth and Peter weren't my parents?" Carly started calling them by their first name out loud after she got the DNA results.

"Do you want to talk to Chris? Maybe he knows something." Carly shuddered at the thought that Chris knew a secret about her identity and never told her. But why would he? They weren't acquaintances. Could she drop her family drama onto his growing wedding drama?

"I can't talk to Chris right now. There is too much bedlam with the wedding. I can't be a distraction from Jackie's fairy tale unfolding. But I want to learn the truth. Will you help me?" Carly stopped, frozen in time, and shifted her body to face Matt. "Please," she pleaded.

Matt ran his long, slender fingers through his dark hair and rubbed the back of his neck. "I don't know, Carly. I can't help you and keep this from Joanie. She's going to pick up on it. We spend too much time together."

"You can't tell her!" Carly exclaimed. "I can't have this get back to Chris right now. She is too close to him." Carly shook her head assertively, her eyes filled with distress and fear.

Matt sighed loudly. "Fine," he committed reluctantly. "Fine. I will help you, but I can't make any promises. I work, I manage the inn, and I have a girlfriend that I love. I can help you, but you have to understand that I might not help you as much as you need."

"Thank you!" Carly exclaimed. "Where should we start?" Her mind was reeling as a spark of excitement ran through her chest. Fear and anxiety coursed through her veins as she imagined finding her mother or father and finally feeling like she belonged somewhere. What if they were dead? Or alive? What if she had a sibling? The questions and opportunities to feel whole again filled her with longing.

Matt and Carly pulled out her phone and scrolled through the DNA TODAY app. Too many puzzle pieces didn't fit together. They identified Chris and Charlene but couldn't recognize anyone else that sounded familiar.

Carly called the Historical Society and made an appointment with Mrs. Jackson, the woman who worked there for decades. Maybe she knew something and could shine some light into Carly's past.

On the way back to the inn, Carly stared out the window in silence while random memories dotted her psyche. They passed by a farm where Carly went to a party one summer and had her first kiss. She spent that entire summer at her best friend Dani's house. They told all the vacationing boys they were sisters. As they passed Sachem Pond, she recalled skinny dipping and getting caught by the police. Carly sighed. Those memories felt like a lifetime ago.

Carly felt like a shell of a person, her mind distracted and her aspirations empty. She hated feeling that way but knew that it would remain until she had closure about her past.

Carly, Matt, and Joanie sat in the large farmhouse kitchen, making plans for the remainder of the summer and into the fall. There were only two more weekends before Labor Day when the islanders would come out of their hobbit holes and survey the damage the tourists left in their wake. Carly's favorite month was September because the chaos of summer ended.

"So, what are we going to do?" Joanie asked. "About us?" She looked at Carly and motioned toward the inn.

"Well, I don't know! Live here together, I guess. You can keep working on marketing, taking care of guests, and doing what you do. I can live in the carriage house and help out as needed. I have other things that I have to take care of while figuring out what is going on with John and me. But nothing will change. I am fine doing my thing in the carriage house."

Joanie nodded. "Jackie is driving me crazy. Will you keep helping us with wedding planning?"

Carly waved her hands noncommittally. "Of course."

They ate salad and barbeque chicken together, with Matt cooking the meal. He and Carly exchanged side-eye glances throughout dinner. Joanie chatted amicably, not questioning Carly's tense body language or brusque responses to her questions and stories. Carly knew she could trust Matt but wondered how long he could keep this secret from Joanie.

Chapter 15

"Hi, Mrs. Jackson," Carly said, holding out her hand to the petite older woman with short, curly hair. Carly had never met this woman before, which surprised her since she had grown up on the island. Before meeting her, Carly read up about Mrs. Jackson on the website. She carried a wealth of knowledge about the island.

Mrs. Jackson's bony, frail fingers embraced Carly's hand. Carly gently squeezed, unsure how much pressure Mrs. Jackson's fingers could take before snapping in half. She wore red lipstick, which matched her nails. Mrs. Jackson smiled and revealed a tiny red smear across her front tooth. The fine lines around her mouth were prominent, despite the years of anti-aging serum Carly assumed she used.

"My name is Carly Davis," Carly continued, ignoring the lipstick.

"Ah, Peter and Ruth Davis. Yes, I remember them from years ago. They were one of the first people I met when my husband and I moved here in 1973."

Mrs. Jackson looked about ninety, which placed her about a decade older than Carly's parents. Carly noticed that her left ring finger was naked and wondered if her husband passed away.

Surprise and annoyance crossed Carly's face. She didn't think she had ever met Mrs. Jackson, yet her parents seemed to have made an impression on her.

"Did you know them well?" Carly asked.

"I knew them on and off for many years. I remember the first time your mom paraded you around and how excited your parents were. They always wanted a child, especially a little girl. They felt so blessed that God gave you to them. You practically fell in their lap."

A chill traveled up Carly's spine to her shoulders, and she shook the feeling away. She smiled encouragingly for Mrs. Jackson to continue.

"So, what brings you here, to the Historical Society?" Mrs. Jackson looked around the small room filled with books, periodicals, and antique furnishings.

"Well," Carly cleared her throat, "I am so pleased that you remember my parents. As you probably know, my mother recently died and left me the inn. Since her passing, I have—-" Carly paused, unable to put her thoughts into words. She what? Found out they weren't her parents? That someone stole her? Or could it have been a weird agreement between neighbors? Carly cleared her throat again. "I have done some research on our heritage, and I have some questions." She wasn't quite ready to confess to this stranger that she knew Ruth and Peter were not her parents.

Mrs. Jackson nodded, gripping the edge of the counter tightly to steady herself. "I see," she turned and walked around the room to look at binders of documents on the antique bookshelf. "What exactly do you want to know?"

Carly hesitated again. "Do you know anything about the Swanson family? They were our neighbors."

"Ah, yes," Mrs. Jackson said, playing with the pages of the original phone book for Block Island residents. "Doug and Rhonda. Doug's family had been here for multiple generations. When Doug and Rhonda sold the house and moved south, the Block Island line stopped. Chris, Charlene, and Ronnie wanted nothing to do with the island, so they left after high school and never returned. They were nice people." Mrs. Jackson had a faraway look in her eyes.

"What about their siblings? Was it Doug and Rhonda's family that lived on the island for generations or just Doug's?"

"Just Doug. Rhonda hailed from Ohio, I think. I'm not sure how they got together. One summer, in 1975 or 1976, Rhonda's sister lived with them. I believe that was her only sister. I remember the year because she was young, barely graduated high school, and worked with my son. He was slightly older than her. Doug had three siblings, but they all got married and moved off the island in the late '70s, early '80s."

Carly was born in 1977, so any of the four could be her parent, and she wasn't sure where to go next. "Your son. Did he know Rhonda's sister well?"

Mrs. Jackson eyed Carly from above the rim of her rectangular wire glasses, which were sitting below the bridge of her nose.

"No, I don't believe so. I don't even remember her name."

"What about Doug's siblings? Do you remember their names?" Carly knew she could ask Chris but didn't know how to transition naturally into that topic. Perhaps when they started planning the table assignments for the wedding, she could ask about his family.

"Yes. Doug was the oldest and the first to marry. He was given the house out of birthright order. After all the kids went to college, Doug's parents left the island, and Doug moved into the family house with his new bride. Doug learned how to run the farm, which produced most of the vegetables for the locals, and Rhonda was a clerk at the old grocery store. His younger sister, Mary, and two younger brothers, Stanley and Mitchell, were either working or in college when Doug returned, with Rhonda on his arm."

Carly nodded, trying to absorb all the names and their relationships to each other.

"Do you remember when I was born?" Carly asked.

Mrs. Jackson's shoulders stiffened, and she quickly turned to face the back wall, rearranging the clock and telephone sitting on the shelf.

"I do." Mrs. Jackson said, meeting Carly's eyes. "Your parents were in love with you."

"Is there anything you can tell me about my early years? My parents are both gone, and they never really shared stories with me about my early life."

Mrs. Jackson grimaced and glanced at her watch. "You know, Carly, I just realized I need to go. I have to meet my husband for dinner." She scurried around the building, shutting off lights and tidying up the shelves.

"Okay. Thank you for your time," Carly replied, incredulously. She noted again that Mrs. Jackson wasn't wearing a wedding band.

"Anytime. Please come by whenever you would like. Thank you." She practically pushed Carly out the front door and locked it behind her. "Have a great night." She turned opposite Carly and climbed into her car before driving away. As she sped by, she looked down, despite the wave and smile Carly gave.

Something didn't feel right. Carly left thinking about the four strangers she was briefly introduced to and wondered how and if they contributed to her history.

Chapter 16

Matt and Joanie crouched down in the flower beds outside his home. The weeds overpowered the garden he previously planted along the house's perimeter. The sun directly shined down on them. Now and then, they felt a reprieve from a passing cloud. Joanie told Matt that she would help with the upkeep of his home. So far, they repainted the front door, removed the trash, and pruned the rose bushes.

"Do you want to grab dinner after we finish?" Joanie asked, assuming it would be closer to dinner than lunch when she could finally shower.

"Dinner and a movie?" Matt asked, his muscular arms flexed and relaxed with every pull.

Joanie grunted as she yanked on a firm root. "Sure," she exhaled. "Your place or mine?" She didn't make eye contact because she was determined to finish the weeding.

"Yours. Just in case the guests need us."

Yes, the guests. It was the final week of summer, and Joanie silently cheered. The finish line was finally near. Her sister's wedding demands and her mother's nagging placed unnecessary stress on the entire summer, and Joanie could not wait for it to be over.

She nodded and attempted a grin at Matt as if to say, "You got it, boss." She pulled one last section and then lay on the grass, faced the sky, and breathed heavily. The warm grass prickled her exposed arms and legs, and she melted into the ground.

Matt lay next to her, placed his hand in hers, and squeezed.

"Thank you," he said to the sky. He turned his head, and their noses practically touched. "Thank you for this. For being here. For being with me. For everything." He gently leaned in, and his tender lips brushed against hers. Jolts of electricity coursed throughout her body. She grabbed the sleeve of her long-sleeved shirt and wiped the dripping sweat off her forehead before leaning in for a deeper kiss.

They stayed like that, for a while, hidden by the oak trees which overpowered the house. They stole kisses one by one, with no words spoken, and neither needed more. Joanie felt a longing build within her.

Matt pulled away, still holding her hand, and smiled. "I love you," he whispered for the first time in their relationship.

A giant stop light lit up in front of Joanie's eyes. She wanted to return the phrase, but her lips and tongue wouldn't cooperate. She stared into his eyes, her inner voice screaming, "I love you too!" but no sound exited her mouth. Her tongue felt like sandpaper, and she struggled to swallow. Her heart rate quickened, and her face got hot. Her entire body felt paralyzed and unresponsive.

The fear traveled from her mouth to her eyes, and Matt pulled away, recognizing his mistake.

He pulled himself up from the ground and changed the subject. "I'm going to take a shower," his voice seeped with melancholy.

"Matt!" Joanie cried. "Wait. I want to talk to you." Matt walked toward the house at break-neck speed. She doubled her gait to keep up with his long strides. She grabbed his arm, and he spun around rapidly.

"What do you want to talk about?" his steely voice and lack of eye contact pierced Joanie's heart.

"I-I-I'm sorry," she said, looking away. "I wasn't ready for that."

"I didn't realize that was something you had to prepare for," Matt spat out.

"No," Joanie cried. "It's not that! I wanted to say it back, I did, but my body froze. I wanted to, I did, but I couldn't!" Joanie didn't know how to explain what she felt at that moment.

Matt looked at her blankly. "I'll call you later." He walked into his home and closed the door in her face.

Joanie stood there, mouth wide open, shocked that her relationship teetered so precariously. She internally berated herself. Hot, angry tears coated her eyeballs and slowly rolled out, one drop at a time. She was mad at him for reacting the way he did, but she was angrier at herself for being a coward.

Joanie stood there, unsure where to go. She could stay outside his door, demanding he speak with her, but what if he didn't? Would she sleep there? She didn't have a car, and walking back to the inn would take close to two hours. She could call Carly, but then she would have to talk about their fight, and Joanie wasn't ready for that yet. If she started now, she would be home before the mosquitos came out to feast on her tasty blood. Joanie couldn't stay and think anymore. Her feet would hate her, but at least she would be home.

Those strappy sandals were cute at the store but not intended for exercise. A blister formed on the back of her heel an hour after she left, and Joanie felt the sting with every step. It was too late to turn back. Her mouth was parched, and her sopped hairline felt sticky against her fingers. All she wanted was to shower, get in her pajamas, and lay in bed.

On the way home, she thought about Matt and how things turned so sour. She had to tell him, but she was afraid that he would find her defective or broken and would toss her away just like Troy did. Her relationship with Troy was perfect until she said, "I love you." He was the first man who ever held her heart, and after she admitted her love, he crushed it in his hands while she watched. She was only seventeen and had never repeated those three words since.

Joanie didn't realize Troy still had a hold over her until all the feelings of paralysis came back with those three words. At that moment, with Matt, she saw Troy hovering over her. When she said "I love you" to Troy, he ripped open her pants like a rabid dog and pulled until she was exposed. For the longest time, she blamed herself, because she went to the party with him. She drank alcohol by choice. She wore a crop top that accentuated her flat belly. At that time in her life, she liked the attention. She knew she was taking a risk, and she did it anyway. She was with her boyfriend, who had always made her feel safe. Her parents loved him. Didn't they know what was best?

Joanie buried that part of her decades ago. Memories of Troy ran rampant within her like a pack of wolves frantically searching for prey. She didn't know how to get him back in the dark corners of her mind. She stood in the shower, crying for her pain and her need to protect herself.

Joanie knew she had to tell Matt but couldn't until she got her emotions in check. She did love him, but he could never fully understand her or how she operated until he knew her story. Joanie curled up in bed with a bowl of ice cream and a movie. She wanted to take tomorrow off but knew she couldn't. It wasn't even an option. Nothing felt right, and she cried herself to sleep in desperation for things to go back to the way they were before those three words traveled through the universe.

Chapter 17

Y our parents were so happy when you practically fell into their lap. Carly couldn't get that image out of her head. She imagined her parents, sitting on the wooden swing together, rocking blissfully, when a baby fell out of the sky and into their laps. It didn't make any sense.

Carly walked down the dirty basement stairs, and a musty scent overpowered her senses. The floor was damp and cool. Cobwebs hung from the wooden posts. Carly ducked, avoiding the spiders, and approached the stack of soggy cardboard boxes.

She poured over the picture albums nestled in brown boxes and plastic totes. Photos of her, Ruth and Peter, at her second birthday party. Pictures of her and Ruth on the first day of kindergarten. Pictures of her and Peter, fishing in the Atlantic for her 10th birthday. Carly pulled out album after album and never seemed to find the images of her birth. There weren't any photos of a wrinkled, pink baby swaddled and encased in a handknit beanie. No photos of the proud mom and dad, holding their one and only child. Carly continued to search until all boxes were exhausted. Her first birthday was the earliest family moment she could find.

Ruth and Peter never directly answered her questions. Eventually, she stopped asking because it never seemed that important to get the finite details. Ruth told her she was born at the inn because she wouldn't make it in time to a hospital. Supposedly, Peter spoke to the physician, who walked him through the labor and delivery process. Chris's parents assisted Peter. Ruth and Peter told her she wouldn't have made it safely without the help of Chris's father.

Carly listened to her parents tell her this beautiful story about how their family evolved. In the story, her father brought her into this world, being the hero, and her mother remained calm and confident. Carly never questioned the details, but now, as an adult, she started to wonder if it was true because there was no picture evidence.

She made a mental note to find her birth certificate as soon as possible.

Carly pushed the boxes toward the basement wall, unsure where to look. Her parents got her a passport when she was a child, and that was always the most accessible document to retrieve when applying for a new job. She couldn't remember the last time she held her birth certificate in her hands.

Carly moved up the stairs methodically, her shoes clicking rhythmically. Even though it was after breakfast, Joanie hunched over the kitchen table, staring out the window. She didn't turn when Carly opened the door or entered the kitchen.

"Ahem," Carly cleared her throat as naturally as possible. She winced at the sheer volume of her throat clearing.

Joanie turned to face her. Her puffy eyes, dried, cracked lips, and wet cheeks revealed heavy, frequent crying. She wore gray sweatpants and an oversized Block Island t-shirt. Carly hoped she didn't wear that to breakfast.

Carly rushed to her side, sat in the rugged, wooden chair, and held Joanie's gaze for an uncomfortably long time. "Are you okay? What's wrong?"

Joanie attempted to smile, but it was more like a grimace as she continued to fight back the tears. She knew that if she started talking, she would cry again and eventually run out of tears. In response to Carly's questions, she shrugged her shoulders and turned her body away from her.

"Did something happen?" Carly asked.

Joanie nodded, a sob escaping from her lips, her chest heaving.

"Is it your family?"

Joanie shook her head no, wiping away the wetness above her cheekbones.

"Is it Matt?"

Joanie nodded her head yes, unable to formulate the words.

Carly could see how distressed she was, so she hugged her, hoping to quell her sadness. "Do you want to talk about it?"

Joanie shrugged, rolled her eyes, and wiped above her cheekbones. "He told me he loved me."

Carly sat there, frozen, wondering how she was supposed to respond. Her gut told her to cheer and clap and praise the beauty of their relationship but knew that that reaction would be ill-received. "Wow," was all she said, hoping Joanie would continue.

"And I couldn't say it back, so he told me to leave. I walked home last night. I didn't call him. Then at midnight, he called me drunk and angry. He told me that being with me was the worst decision he'd ever made. Told me that I was a bitch and a tease." Joanie looked at Carly, pleading with her eyes, "That's not true, right?"

Carly stroked Joanie's head and hugged her against her shoulder. "No, Joanie. Not at all. He's angry. By you not saying those words back, he probably felt stupid. What he said isn't true. It was probably just the alcohol talking."

"I don't know what to do," Joanie said. "I'm so hurt by what he said. I do love him. I do, but those three words are triggering for me."

"Why?" Carly asked, hoping she wasn't overstepping.

"I was dating this boy, Troy when I was in high school. He told me he loved me. I told him back, and then he raped me. Ever since then, I have never told someone I loved them. It's not that I don't, but bad things happen. I never had a serious enough boyfriend since Troy until Matt to even say those words." Joanie stumbled through her thoughts. She rambled on. "When he said it yesterday, my entire body froze. I was suddenly transported back to that party in the woods. Beer was everywhere. Loud music playing. And Troy. I was afraid, and my whole body froze. The same thing happened yesterday."

Carly pulled Joanie in tighter and held her friend until her shoulders stopped heaving up and down, and her breathing was quiet.

"I'm so sorry," Carly whispered into her ear. "I'm so sorry."

The girls stayed together, in the kitchen and then the apartment, until night fell.

The conversation eventually moved to the wedding. Carly pulled out two beers from the fridge and tossed one to Joanie. "I can't stand my mother," Joanie said, ejecting the bottle cap with a "Welcome to Block Island" beer opener.

"Yeah, your mother is one of a kind," Carly said diplomatically.

"One of a kind?" Joanie scoffed. "How about pretentious and righteous and entitled? How's that for some adjectives?" She took a swig of her beer.

Carly smiled. "Did she make it home okay?"

Joanie shrugged. "I don't know. She never called to check in. I don't know how she ended up like that. She used to be fun and carefree, and spontaneous! Now, she is having an adventurous day if she wears sneakers to church. I don't know how my dad puts up with her." She paused and then continued. "Yes, I do. He golfs. He does what he wants, she does what she wants, and they live happily ever after."

"How is Jackie?" Carly asked. "Was she happy with the weekend here?"

Joanie snickered under her breath. "Oh yeah, it was great. She shows up unannounced, demanding that I drop everything to attend to her wedding appointments, and then leaves once she gets what she wants. I cannot wait for this wedding to be over. I like Chris, I do, but I don't know if he knows what he is getting himself into."

Carly tried to smile, but the mention of Chris swirled her belly like a whirlpool. Carly realized she was in control of her situation, and the stress she was causing was purposeful. She couldn't seem to stop the rapid acceleration of her emotions.

Carly put her beer down. Her ancestry, birth certificate, the baby photos, and Mrs. Jackson were too much to process. She needed a day with Sandra, walking and talking until all of their problems disappeared. It felt like it had been an eternity since she last saw Sandra, but in reality, it was only a few days. There was so much to tell her since she left.

"I know it was a surprise for me to show up unexpectedly, but I want you to know, nothing will change. I am dealing with my own stuff right now, so I need you to help with the inn unless, of course, you don't want to. But I want you here. I like having you here." Carly stopped mid-thought.

"Do you want to talk about John?" Joanie asked.

Carly shook her head. John was the last thing on her mind. "It just didn't work out. I haven't spoken to him since I got here. I'm sure Sandra has filled him in. I have no interest in talking to him right now." More like no available brain space to think about him, she thought. She only had room for one catastrophe in her life, not two. "I'm going to head home," she said, giving Joanie one last hug. "I'll see you in the morning."

Chapter 18

J oanie glanced out the kitchen window and saw a dark shadowy figure across the grassy field. He took long strides toward the house, unaware that someone was watching. It had been four days since that dreadful phone call in the middle of the night.

Joanie ignored his calls and texts and eventually turned her phone off. Every time her phone dinged, she longingly searched to see who it was, debating back and forth whether to answer it or ignore it. She needed more time.

Matt's face looked especially dismal. Worry penetrated the creases in his forehead, around his lips, and his eyes. Joanie looked away, searched for a dishrag to dry the dishes, and ignored her clammy hands and shallow breathing. She wasn't ready for this.

Any confrontation had always been difficult for Joanie. She spent her entire life trying to be accepted by her family, so she never learned how to handle conflict. Joanie acquiesced to the demands of others because it was easier. She never dealt with Troy, never spoke of that night to anyone. Troy pulled away from her, blamed it on leaving for college in a different part of the country, and Joanie let him go. She felt conflicted because she did love him. What he did to her was her first time, so perhaps that was how love worked.

When she was eight and Jackie was five, Jackie threw a rock that broke the shed window in their backyard. She didn't do it purposefully, but Joanie knew that she was older and partly responsible. Jackie was her only playmate, and she needed her around, so Joanie took the blame and the punishment. That was the start of Joanie's need to please others. It eventually snowballed to her parents wanting her to join the Swim Team, even though Joanie hated her body and would do anything to hide it. She even applied to the same college as Troy, thinking that he would want her if they could be together every day.

And now, Matt was approaching the door to the kitchen, and Joanie had nowhere to hide. She knew she was not at fault for her reaction but didn't know how to share that with Matt. Joanie heard the turn of the doorknob and froze, ignoring the sound of shoes scraping against the doormat.

Joanie turned a hard left and closed the bathroom door behind her. She ran the water to give herself a few moments to regain her composure. Her inner voice ran amuck, with a series of greetings flowing over and under each other, making it hard for her to concentrate.

"Joanie?" Matt called through the door. "Are you okay?"

Panic set in. She had been in there too long. She looked at the bathroom window, gauging if she could fit through unscathed. Fearful that she would get stuck, she saw no other option. The door swooped open, and Joanie stood face to face with Matt.

"What do you want?" she asked, rubbing above her cheekbones, hoping the redness didn't give her emotions away.

Matt's eyebrows furrowed, and he pursed his lips. "I wanted to talk. Can you talk?" He spoke quietly and slowly. His hands pushed into his jean pockets, and he rocked on his heels.

"Fine," Joanie responded. "I'd like to talk outside. Let's go for a walk." Joanie didn't want to look into his eyes.

They quickly moved outside to the road. Joanie led the way with quick, long strides. Her heart raced, and her body tingled.

"Joanie, slow down," Matt said, skipping behind her to keep up.

Joanie stopped and waited. She looked into his eyes and smiled. "So, what did you want to talk about?" She continued walking but slowed her pace, now walking beside him instead of in front.

Matt skipped to keep up. "I'm sorry," he exclaimed, grabbing her arm. She swiveled around more violently and erratic than she hoped. She didn't want to show him how much he hurt her.

"It's no problem," she responded, breaking from his hold and continuing down the curvy street.

"But it is!" Matt called to her back. "I don't know what I said, but I know I can be a mean bastard when I'm drunk."

Joanie felt her heart shatter at her feet. He had no idea what he said, how he said it, or how he made her feel, yet he threw out half-hearted apologies without understanding the implication of his words or actions.

"No problem," she said again through gritted teeth. She abruptly turned around to head back to the inn. "I have stuff I have to do," she said, breezing past him, ignoring his pleading eyes and stiff shoulders.

She walked around to the front entrance and noticed Matt slowly following behind. Joanie saw Carly struggling with grocery bags and waved, rushing past. She didn't want to talk. Joanie heard Matt call to Carly as she stumbled into the house.

***

Carly looked up and grinned. "Hey, Matt!" She rested the brown paper bag on the ground and waved back.

"Do you need some help?" he approached her with a quick step. She nodded in thanks.

They made their way into the carriage house, and Matt dropped a bag onto the cluttered counter. He looked around and recognized old furniture from the main house with a mix of new designs contradicting the general tone of the house. He saw his grandmother's retro chrome table next to the black and white chevron dishtowels hanging from the small two-burner stove.

"Have you seen Joanie today?" he asked innocently, hoping that the topic felt natural.

"Yeah," Carly said, opening and closing the refrigerator. "You?"

Matt shrugged his shoulders. "Kind of."

Carly didn't look at him. She continued putting the groceries in the refrigerator. "How was she?" Carly asked, opening the cabinets.

"She didn't seem great." They tiptoed around the topic. Carly refused to give too much information about their conversation.

Carly turned and looked at him, waiting for him to continue. He looked tired. His ruffled hair, untucked clothes, and bristly beard reminded Carly of a homeless person she'd seen in Portland. He looked like he had a rough night the night before.

"Did something happen?" Carly asked, distracting herself with an old cookbook she found on one of the shelves. She had no intention of making a recipe from it but needed to prevent making eye contact.

Matt shrugged again. "It's a long story," he mumbled.

Carly couldn't share what she knew, even though the words were ready to tumble out of her mouth. "I'm here if you want to talk," she responded.

Matt sighed deeply and rubbed his eyes, elbows resting on the counter. He pulled out a chair, and Carly followed. "I told her I loved her. She didn't answer. I got pissed and made her leave. I pulled out some drinks. That's all I remember. I don't know if I did something stupid, but I think I did. I do have some outgoing phone calls in the middle of the night to her, but I don't remember what I said." Matt continued rubbing his forehead. Carly bit her lip, preventing herself from sharing information that wasn't hers to share.

"Have you tried talking to her?" Carly asked.

Matt nodded. "Yeah, I did. She didn't want to talk." He motioned out the front window. "I was there a few minutes ago."

"Cookie?" she asked, offering a chocolate cream cookie. She tried desperately to remain silent. He took the cookie and ate it in two bites.

"What do I do?" he asked with chocolate-streaked teeth.

Carly shrugged. "Keep trying."

Matt sadly and slowly nodded. "Yeah. Thanks. I have to run. Thanks for the cookie." He grabbed his keys and headed out the door.

Carly thought about Mrs. Jackson and the weird way she closed up the building when pressed for more information. Carly didn't know if she would find anything of importance, but there were boxes in the basement she had never gone through before. Carly noticed the boxes tucked away behind the stairs when she was looking at the baby photos. Maybe her birth certificate was buried in one of those boxes.

Downstairs, Carly found scrapbooks and shoeboxes filled with memorabilia from Ruth and Peter's early life. She found old photographs, newspaper articles, and movie ticket stubs that were yellowed with age. She found novels and magazines from the fifties and sixties that must have held a place in

Peter's heart, but Carly was unsure why. Although these items from Ruth and Peter's past were interesting, they didn't provide any clues about her birth.

Carly pulled out the bottom box. It resembled a wobbly diamond from the loss of integrity from the damp basement. As she pulled, the bottom of the box separated, the humidity too great.

"Ugh," Carly mumbled, looking around the room for another box to transfer the items. She found a plastic tote nearly empty near the holiday decorations and pulled it over.

Carly found a dilapidated box from her childhood that she never knew existed. She found a baby blanket, barely big enough to cover her adult torso. The yarn felt soft and warm against her forearm. Carly wondered who gave this blanket to her, thoughts moving toward her birth family.

She found another adult-sized shoe box filled with baby books and baby clothes. Carly held up each object, trying desperately to pull up a memory, but nothing emerged. At the very bottom of the shoe box was a folded-up newsletter from the Block Island quarterly. At the very bottom of the second page was an article about her parents and the inn.

Carly glanced at the top of the page. Her father's choppy block lettering scrawled **Summer 1976**, the blue ink smeared with age. Someone saved the article approximately one year before she was born. Carly scanned the paper, searching for clues. Her heart pounded, her hands shook, and her eyes scanned furiously from word to word. BUSINESS SPOTLIGHT, the article said. Right underneath was a photograph of Ruth and Peter, one young man, and two young women.

Ruth looked beautiful, with her long, straight, black hair hanging to her shoulder blades. She wore bell-bottom jeans and a flower headband in her hair. Carly analyzed her mother and noticed a relaxed airiness to her posture and a lightness in her smile. Presented before her was a carefree woman that Carly never knew, and she wondered what made her turn so cold.

Peter stood next to Ruth, round glasses covering his bushy eyebrows and thick mustache hiding his upper lip. He had one arm around Ruth's shoulder and one arm around one of the young girls. Carly looked more closely at the woman, wondering who she was. The woman leaned into Peter, her shoulder wedged into his armpit. Ruth stood on the other side, her body turned away from Peter, creating a space between them.

The woman next to Peter was beautiful and young. A floral maxi dress wrapped around her thin frame and a wooden beaded necklace accentuated her collar bones. Her straight blond hair feathered out at the sides. Her eyes, outlined with black mascara, stared back at Carly. The woman grinned broadly, her head tilted toward Peter, mid-laugh.

The other woman and man in the photo looked vaguely familiar. They appeared young, like the woman leaning into Peter, and stood on the other side of Ruth. All five of them stood behind a sign that said, "The Willowside Inn." The house towered behind them.

Carly looked at the photo again, unsure who the three people were. She read the article, looking for clues, but there was no mention by name who they were. The article mentioned Ruth and Peter owning the inn and praised the business. The three people beside them were a mystery to Carly. Her breathing slowed and became shallow. Her lungs felt deflated, and the room felt hot against her skin. Carly rubbed her hands on her pants, hoping to preserve the old document, and stood up quickly.

She folded up the paper and placed it back in the box, next to her baby blanket. Something didn't feel quite right. She needed to know who they were. Those three people could be the answer she needed. Thinking again, Carly placed the folded-up newspaper in her pocket, saving it for her next visit to see Mrs. Jackson.

Chapter 19

L abor Day was the last major weekend of the summer. Joanie had a packed house full of parents, grandparents, and children for a family reunion on the beach. The place was alive, full of cheerful chatter, thudding movements of doors slamming and children running down the hall, and the bell to the main inn entrance dinged consecutively as the families embarked on their family outings.

Today was Sunday, and Joanie already survived two of their three breakfasts. The kids loved pancakes and requested all flavors. She pulled together a platter of blueberry, cinnamon, chocolate chip, and buttermilk. By the time breakfast was over, someone had left one lonely pancake on the platter. Joanie picked it up and took a bite.

The dining room and kitchen were a disaster, but the feeling of freedom and finishing the last big weekend boosted her spirits. She got to work. The weather was cloudy and cool, a sure sign that fall was emerging. Joanie pushed up her sleeves, wiped her hands on her apron, and loaded the dishwasher.

She felt her phone buzz in her apron pocket against her leg. Her wet hands prevented her from answering. She ignored the vibration until it stopped. Glancing at her phone, she saw a missed call and a text from Jackie. The text read: **We need to go shopping. Operation party favors. Wednesday?**

Joanie groaned at another demand placed upon her about the damn wedding. She didn't want to go wedding shopping. She wanted to enjoy her final Wednesday alone, savoring the introduction of quiet. Joanie texted back:**Sorry. Busy that day. Maybe next week?**

It had been a few days since she saw Matt, and she wondered when or if he would reach out to her. She hid her melancholy mood with forceful effort. She hoped that her misery didn't splash over into her conversations with Carly or the guests.

Even when she needed him, she refused to call him, like when the faucet in the washroom wouldn't stop dripping. Instead, she pulled out her pliers and a do-it-yourself video, chanting to herself that she didn't need a man.

Joanie wondered if seeing Jackie was what she needed. Jackie only cared about herself and never asked about Joanie. Jackie probably didn't even remember Matt's name. If Joanie carefully responded to Jackie's conversation, she could go the whole day without giving an ounce of information about her current life.

She had a long list of things that needed to get done but couldn't seem to get motivated. Instead, she strode outside and checked the vegetable garden that Matt planted. A bundle of cucumbers, tomatoes, and squash greeted her. The colorful array brightened her mood as she filled her bag with dinner for the next few days.

"Hey, Joanie!" Carly called from the entrance to the carriage house. Joanie smiled and waved.

It felt slightly uncomfortable having Carly back on the property. Joanie enjoyed running the inn solo, even though it wasn't hers to run. Having Carly nearby made Joanie feel anxious, like always being watched or judged, and never quite capable.

Carly didn't share a lot of experiences about her life in Portland. Joanie barely knew John and maybe could pick him out in a lineup. When Carly's mother passed away, so much had happened. John came back, Carly practically gave the inn away, and then she left. Carly was in love with John, and Joanie wondered how she and Matt had survived when Carly and John didn't.

Carly pulled the straps of her duffle bag over her shoulder. The bright orange canvas bag peeked out a pillow from the zipper. "I'm heading out to Portland for the next few days. Will you be okay?" Joanie assumed she was asking about running the inn.

"Yep!" Joanie exclaimed, a grin on her face. "Yeah, we'll be great. What are you doing up in Portland?"

"I'm going to spend a few days with Sandra. Do you remember her?"

Joanie nodded, still picking the tomatoes off the vine. "Have a great time! When are you coming home?" Joanie asked casually.

Carly winced, realizing that home was here. "Wednesday. Just a few days to get away and relax before the fall weather sets in."

"Okay, have fun!" Joanie called out sweetly.

Carly readjusted her backpack, threw it on her other shoulder, and walked down to the ferry.

She stood on the ferry deck, listening to the waves lap against the boat as it traveled to Rhode Island. Memories of Ruth flooded her mind. All the trips back and forth to do Ruth's laundry and visit her in the nursing home took up time in Carly's life.

When Peter died, Carly was more unprepared and more devastated than when Ruth passed. Ruth guilted Carly to return home and help with the inn, and Carly was angry. Carly felt guilty because she was the only one who could competently help. She felt backed into a corner and did what Ruth expected, putting her life in Portland on hold.

Eventually, Ruth's dementia became too much for her to juggle the guests and the finances. Silly, simple mistakes became bigger, embarrassing mistakes. With the birth of the internet, their reputation was flailing, especially when Ruth forgot to secure a booking and had to turn a family of four away on her doorstep because they didn't have an available room. Not only did they lose the guest, but they lost many new guests who researched reviews before booking.

Ruth ended up in a long-term care facility for the next decade of her life. Carly was thrown back into the hospitality business, even though she ran away from the island at her first opportunity.

Carly looked out at the ocean and wondered what her mother thought of her now. She knew all her secrets and inner thoughts. Carly felt the disappointment in her failed relationship push her down, below the water's edge.

Peter and Carly had a special connection. They spent Saturday mornings walking into town and getting a chocolate-covered donut from the local donut shop. He read to her every night before bed, and a love for reading evolved throughout her childhood. She always felt enough around her dad and never felt that same level of acceptance from her mother.

Maybe her dad was her dad. The thought flew into Carly's mind like a hawk swooping down to catch prey. Perhaps her father had an affair with the neighbor's sister, and a child was born. That would explain Ruth's coldness toward Carly and her lack of acceptance over the years. Carly's heart quickened, and her fingers went cold.

She needed Matt to take the DNA test. If they were still related, that was what happened. Peter had an affair. It felt crazy to Carly, and she shook her head at the absurdity of her imagination.

Carly quickly sat down. Her stomach rose and fell with the ocean waves and repeatedly crashed into her heart. She wanted to feel relief at the potential explanation, but all she felt was fear and sadness.

She thought about her parents and how they interacted when she was a child and an adult. Her mother and father worked together, but they had separate responsibilities. Her mother cooked and cleaned while her father spent his time outside, beautifying the yard. She couldn't recall her parents holding hands or sneaking kisses. That lack of intimacy felt ordinary. She couldn't remember any tension either, and that apathy felt normal too.

Carly's mind raced like a speed track on opening night. If Peter was her father, who was her mother? Carly thought about Mrs. Jackson and her comments about Chris's aunts. Mrs. Jackson said that Rhonda's sister was only around for one summer, and she worked with Mrs. Jackson's son. Mrs. Jackson was the same age as Ruth and Peter. That meant that if Peter fathered Carly with Rhonda's sister, there was a significant age gap between the two.

Carly pulled out the old newspaper article from her bag and carefully looked at the body language between Ruth, Peter, and the unknown adults. She couldn't be sure, but there appeared to be a closeness between Peter and the woman in the maxi dress. Peter was at least twenty years her senior, and Carly shuddered. She couldn't imagine her father cheating on her mother for a younger woman. Nausea rose, and Carly wondered if it was due to thoughts about her dad or the turbulence of the boat.

Carly continued to sit and stare ahead at the distant coast. She was suddenly exhausted. Carly considered the potential affair between her father and another woman and wondered how she fit into their relationship.

As people muddled around her and grabbed their bags to depart, Carly stared straight ahead. She couldn't think anymore. She was numb from her discovery. Sadness for Ruth filled her heart, and compassion toward a possible birth mother grew. Carly hid her face under her hat and allowed the tears to roll down her cheeks slowly. No one noticed because they were all wrapped up in getting off the boat.

Carly strolled down the ramp. She was the last to depart and dreaded the next few days. Not only would she share her thoughts with Sandra, but she also agreed to dinner with John. She rubbed the back of her neck, bit her lip, and continuously readjusted her hair.

As she moved along the plank, her heart sank further. Instead of Sandra, she saw John. He was smiling widely, bouncing from foot to foot, waiting for her.

Chapter 20

"John, what are you doing here?" Carly demanded.

"I'm here to pick you up!" he replied, enthusiasm lingering on his words.

Carly looked around, her lips pursed. "Where's Sandra?" she asked suspiciously. Did he think she was going to sit in a car with him for three hours? The weight of her overnight bag dug into her bare shoulder, but she refused to show any weakness.

"Something came up. She's planning on having you stay with her, but she couldn't do the six-hour drive today. She called me last night in a panic, asking if I could come and get you."

"Since when are you Sandra's friend? You don't even know her." Carly's tone held more accusation than she intended. Her eyebrows squished together, and she touched the base of her neck. She wondered if John knew her feelings toward him since she shared them with Sandra. The connection between John and Sandra felt like a betrayal.

"We're not. She had my number from when you left me, and you went to the lake. She said she didn't want to cancel on you," he said defensively. His crossed arms illuminated his height and the previous power he had over her.

"Great. So now I have to ride with you?" John's face dropped at Carly's rudeness.

"Or you can cancel and go back to the island." He kicked his toe on the gravel drive.

Carly considered her options. Should she sit in a car with John for three hours to see the only person she could talk to about her parents or take the next ferry home, unsure when she would reconnect with Sandra again? Carly didn't understand how John and Sandra became friends, despite what John said, but the three-hour ride would give her ample time to not only ask about that but explain to him why she left. Did she owe it to him? Probably. Did she want to talk to him? Absolutely not.

Carly sighed and looked off into the horizon. Eventually, her eyes met John's, and she saw the pleading request in his raised eyebrows and slightly forward posture. "Fine!" Carly said vehemently. "Fine. I will go with you." She threw her bag over her other shoulder, giving in to the weight of her situation.

They walked silently to the car, and Carly climbed into the passenger's seat. The ride back to Maine was quiet until they got to Boston. John tried to make small talk, but Carly was uninterested in hearing about his life. She didn't want to ask about the apartment or initiate the topic of their relationship. Carly spent the first half of their trip looking out the passenger window, thinking about everything that went wrong in their relationship.

"Do you want to grab some food?" John asked the front windshield, not taking his eyes off the road.

Carly responded to the passenger window. "Sure."

They pulled off the highway a few miles before the New Hampshire border.

"Do you want to do the drive-thru, or do you want to go inside?" John asked.

Carly had to use the bathroom but didn't want to provide an opportunity to talk to John directly. "Let's do the drive-thru. I want to see Sandra," Carly said. She could hold it for another hour or two, she decided.

By going through the drive-thru, there was no need to look each other in the eye.

John took the final bite of his burger, followed by a sip of soda. "What happened to us?" he asked, glancing at Carly from the corner of his eye.

It was the first time they had spoken since he asked if she was hungry twenty minutes earlier.

"Nothing," Carly responded.

"What do you mean, nothing? It had to be something. Was it because I didn't go with you to the lake?" John asked.

"It was nothing!" Carly's voice rose in pitch, and she internally cursed herself for getting emotional. She started again, making sure to use a steady tone. "It was nothing. Nothing had changed in the ten years we were apart. I mean, I changed, and you changed, but we didn't change together. Our life was the same. I felt like we should have been different by now. I don't know, maybe together more. I was lonely. Just as lonely as I was without you. I decided that the life we still had was not what I wanted. It was nothing. Really."

John swallowed loudly. "But you knew! You knew when you moved in that we would only be together six months of the year. You knew that, and you still chose to come home with me." He didn't look at her but continued to cruise up the highway.

"I did. And I thought it would be enough, but it wasn't." Carly said, changing the radio station.

John didn't respond.

"I am sorry for just leaving. I had to get back to the island. I missed it, and as much as I hate to admit it, it is my home." She didn't want to talk about this anymore. Stuck in a car with John was too much pressure.

John nodded meekly. "I'm sorry I wasn't enough for you," he said quietly. The engine revved as he accelerated.

When they got to Sandra's, the sun shined brightly in the sky. Shadows fell on the road from the clusters of buildings dotting the city. Carly desperately needed a bathroom. She texted Sandra during the ride to make sure she would be home when they arrived.

"Here you are," John said, glancing at the triple-decker building.

"Thanks for the ride," Carly said politely.

"Yeah, I'm glad we talked." Carly ignored the hint of sarcasm dripping from his words.

"Good luck. With everything." She didn't know if she should hug him, kiss him on the cheek, or wave. Everything felt contrived and fake. Instead, she smiled at him and exited the car before she hesitated and made the situation more awkward.

As soon as the door closed, John's vehicle peeled away from the curb before Carly could adjust her overnight bag on her other shoulder. She breathed a sigh of relief for making it to Sandra's in one piece. She was going to kill Sandra when she saw her.

Carly walked up the concrete steps and climbed the stairs to Sandra's apartment. She knocked on the door three times and waited. Carly looked around the stairwell and thought about their talks and walks around the city. She missed having her friend nearby.

The door swung open with gusto. "Hi!" Sandra cried with a smile across her face, her arms outstretched for a hug. Carly threw her arms around her friend, and they danced in excitement.

"I am going to kill you!" Carly cried in jest. "You stuck me in a car with John for three hours! That was so cruel of you!" She grinned widely, excited to see her friend.

"Sorry! I had a last-minute appointment today, and I couldn't miss it! I didn't want to cancel on you. I bumped into John at the grocery store a few days ago and told him you were coming up. He was asking about you. He seemed excited. Yesterday, when I found out I had an appointment this morning, I called him to see. He offered to pick you up. I'm so sorry! I should have told you, but I thought if you knew, you would've canceled on me." Sandra spoke rapidly.

"I almost did! I almost turned around and took the ferry home! You have no idea how pissed I was when I saw him standing there."

"I'm sorry!" Sandra laughed. "Did you at least get to talk to him? Get some things off your chest?"

Carly nodded. "Kind of. We didn't have much to say. We both looked out the window and avoided eye contact. I told him why I left. He seemed surprised. He thought everything was fine."

Sandra pulled out two beers from the fridge. "Here. You sound like you might need this."

Sandra and Carly sat down at the table to talk. There was so much to share. Thoughts about Mrs. Jackson, the wedding, John, and her dad tumbled around her head like a dryer carrying a sneaker. Carly needed help figuring out what happened with her parents and needed Sandra's support. She had two days in Portland to formulate a plan.

Chapter 21

Carly and Sandra woke up early the following day to walk the city, just like old times. The temperature was mid-sixties, with a slight cool breeze coming off the ocean. Carly packed her sneakers, knowing that they would spend time outdoors.

"How's the family search coming along?" Carly asked Sandra as they hustled past the row of restaurants and art galleries.Carly was curious the night before but couldn't seem to bring up such a heavy subject when the mood was so light.

"Good! She never responded to my messages, so I keep researching her, trying to piece together her life. I knew her husband would get my emails because of his job. I felt weird contacting him, but I had no other options. He hasn't written back yet."

"Is it driving you crazy that she hasn't responded yet?"

Sandra nodded. "Yeah, but I was trying to put myself in her shoes. If she didn't know about me, this could feel like a total shock, especially if our birth mother raised her."

"Or, what if you have the same father but different mothers?" Carly asked, thinking about her own situation.

"Could be, you're right. I have no idea. I was thinking of hiring a private investigator, but I doubt I have enough money for that. Ever since Tim died, a part of me died with him, you know? It was devastating to lose a sibling, and now suddenly, I have another one. I know it doesn't replace Tim or the hole he left in my heart, but maybe it will ignite something in me that died a long time ago. Maybe she will provide some closure as to why my parents gave us up for adoption. All I can do is hope, you know?" They stopped next to a tree overlooking the harbor and sat on the grassy hill. "Granola bar?" Sandra asked, holding out a snack.

Carly shook her head.

"I hope one of them responds. Even if Bianca doesn't know anything, you know? It will at least help me fill in the gaps of my life."

The two women sat silently, staring at the waves rocking the boats docked in the harbor. Carly missed Sandra these past few weeks. Joanie was nice enough, but they weren't friends. They were work acquaintances.

"How about you?" Sandra asked. "Any progress with Chris?"

Carly gave Sandra her theory that her father knocked up Chris's aunt and somehow got the baby.

"Wait," Sandra turned to face Carly. "You think your dad had an affair with his aunt, got a young girl pregnant, ended up with the baby, and your mom still stayed married to him? That doesn't make any sense, does it? Wouldn't you have heard something? Don't families stay on the island for generations? Wouldn't someone remember if your mom had a baby but was never pregnant?"

Carly hadn't thought about that, but Sandra was right. Someone somewhere would have said something weird about her past.

"You're right. It's probably my overactive imagination. Maybe my mom got pregnant by another man and played it off as my father's child." Carly thought about it. "It still doesn't make sense because my mom was in her mid-forties when I was born. It feels unlikely to me."

"I think you need to talk to Chris. He has to know something or have weird memories or vibes from his family. So what if he's getting married? Life happens; life goes on. It's going to drive you nuts if you don't."

"Matt knows. I had to tell him. He's the only family I have nearby, and according to the DNA test, we may not even be family. He told me he would help me figure it out." Carly took a sip of water. "It's a mystery."

By the time the girls got home, their foreheads were dripping with sweat. The temperature rose rapidly, and the humidity increased moment by moment. Carly showered and changed into more comfortable clothes. Her saturated hair rested below her shoulders, and her nose felt burned. She bounced on her toes, humming to the radio, happy to be spending time in Maine on her own. At that moment, she felt free.

"Guess what?" Sandra called through the bathroom door. Carly was standing in the steamy bathroom with a towel wrapped around her body.

"What?" Carly hollered back through the door.

"I got an email! From Bianca!" Sandra shouted back. Carly heard the excitement in her friend's voice and knew that the email was positive. Carly quickly dried off her body and threw on clean clothes. She swung open the door and embraced her friend in a bear hug.

"No way! What did she say?"

Sandra's eyes lit up with hope, and she spoke a mile a minute. "She told me that she knew about me and always wondered if she would meet me! She said that our mom, Judith, had my brother and me when she was seventeen. Her parents threw her out of the house when they found out she was pregnant, and my father denied us as his. My mom ended up moving in with her aunt and uncle on a farm in the Midwest and gave birth to us. She gave us up for adoption and then returned home to California. Three years later, she married and gave birth to Bianca and my brother. I have a brother! His name is Randy, and he's ten years younger than me. Bianca is five years younger than me. Can you believe it?" Sandra cried, tears dotting her cheeks. "I found my family," she whispered. "I can't even believe it. I wish Tim were here. He always wondered."

Carly threw her arms around Sandra again and squeezed her tight. Her friend half-laughed and half-cried into her shoulder.

"You know, when we were kids, we had to do this family tree assignment. I hated it. My mom told us repeatedly that we were French Canadian because that was her history, but I knew that I had no French. I mean, look at me. Look at my skin tone. There is no way I was French, but I did the project, researching her past. I had to present it to my classmates, and I could hear them snickering when I went into my white-European heritage. They all knew I was full of shit, yet the teacher and my parents encouraged me to do it, and my teacher gave me an A. It was such a joke. I shouldn't blame my

126

mom, though, but I did for a long time. She supposedly didn't know about my past, but if I was going to make up my history, at least give me a believable country, like Brazil, or Honduras or something."

"Did Bianca tell you about your heritage?" Carly asked.

"No, not yet, but the DNA test said I was mostly from the Mediterranean area. I don't look French or Canadian. I can't wait to talk to Bianca! We are going to talk this weekend. I am so nervous!" Sandra exclaimed.

"It will be great! Don't worry. She is probably just as excited as you are!" Carly reassured her friend. She felt a tinge of jealousy cross her mind, and she quickly swept it out. Like Sandra, she would love to have good news, but Sandra took the hard step and reached out to a family member. Carly was too afraid of rejection right now. Maybe in a week, she would feel more assertive and could start the conversation.

"Let's celebrate! To your new family! Let me take you out to dinner. We can have all the desserts and all the drinks. It will be fantastic!" Carly suggested.

The two women relaxed for the rest of the afternoon and then dressed up for a night on the town. Short skirts, high heels, and sparkly tops decorated the girls as they made their way to dinner. A bottle of champagne, chocolate-covered strawberries, and laughter filled their night. It was indeed a night to celebrate.

Chapter 22

Joanie glanced at her vibrating phone, with Matt's name displayed across the screen. Her phone pinged with messages and missed calls all day long. If Joanie was honest with herself, she missed having him around.

Joanie picked up the phone to answer, but it stopped ringing. She was too late. Instead, she texted Matt: Do you want to talk?

He responded immediately and said he would be over in ten minutes.

Joanie looked down at her oversized nightshirt and cotton shorts. With no one staying at the inn, she felt an obligation to sleep in and relax. Her body kicked into high gear without her realizing the sudden change in her movements. She sashayed to the bathroom, taking long strides, and jumped in the shower to freshen up.

She heard a quick rap at the door as she pulled on her shirt. Joanie glanced at herself in the mirror and dragged a brush through her wet hair, hoping it looked halfway decent. She ran lipstick across her lips and mascara quickly along her lashes. She dashed to the door, took a deep breath in, smiled widely, and turned the doorknob.

"Come in," she said with a breathy tone, trying to appear nonchalant. She couldn't read his body language yet, so she stepped to the side to allow him to enter. No physical contact until she knew the intention of his visit.

She led him into the kitchen, and they sat at the table.

"Would you like a drink?" she asked politely.

"Nah," Matt responded. His big, round eyes, overgrown stubble, and his hair pointing in all directions sent a quiver through Joanie's body. He looked as sexy as she remembered, and her heart responded instantly. His eyes darted around the room, his posture slumped, and his voice quivered.

They sat in silence for a few moments, not quite looking at each other in the eye, but looking all around each other's eyes. Their eye gaze moved from eyebrows to the tip of the nose, to the lips and cheekbones. Everywhere but the place that would spill the secrets of the soul.

Joanie cleared her throat. "Sorry I haven't answered your calls or texts. I needed some time."

"Joanie," Matt started. "I'm sorry. It was immature of me to act the way I did. When I said I loved you, I meant it. You hurt me when you didn't feel the same."

A pit in Joanie's stomach started to grow, with flashbacks of Matt rejecting her and Troy using her. She knew she had to tell Matt, but she felt like it was too early. She trusted him but didn't know if she trusted him with her most shameful secret. She didn't know if she was ready to share the weakest, most naïve version of herself.

"I've had a lot of time to think," Joanie started, avoiding the topic of love. "I miss you. I miss seeing your face, I miss laughing with you, and I miss touching you and being with you. I love you, Matt, but you have to understand that I was caught off guard when you said that.I was raped at a party after I told my boyfriend I loved him." Her voice quivered, and Joanie directed her anger of that night at herself.

Stop being weak! Her inner voice screamed, willing the tears to stay back.

Matt looked at her with concern in his eyes and didn't say a word. He leaned in closer to her and held her hands in his, looking at her with anticipation.

"I never told anyone about that night. Well, no one except Carly, since I had to tell her about why you weren't hanging around like usual." Joanie threw Matt a weak smile. She made it sound like his presence at the inn, the place where he technically worked, was an annoyance, even though she loved having him around. She cringed, hoping he didn't take her comment the wrong way.

Matt's voice filled with tenderness. "I had no idea. I'm sorry." He gently kissed her on the cheek.

Joanie waved her hands. She didn't want to talk about it with anyone, let alone Matt. "It was a long time ago. I've been careful to guard my heart over the past few decades." Joanie said sadly. "I know I love you, but I felt paralyzed."

Matt interrupted her. "I would never hurt you."

Joanie nodded. "I know that in my heart, but my head keeps telling me to be careful. Because Troy, my boyfriend of two years, hadn't hurt me until that night. I blamed myself. I blamed the alcohol. I thought I deserved it for leading him on in some way."

"It wasn't your fault," Matt said, his voice cracking.

"I did love him, but I was in high school. I don't know if I knew what love was, and I wasn't ready to have sex in a dark field with my classmates on the other side of the bushes."

Joanie swallowed the lump in her throat, reliving the fear of that night. Her body, frozen, was pinned to the ground. His hand clamped over her mouth, his free hand ravenous, pulling at her clothes like a flock of crows eating roadkill. The pain shot through her like a rocket shoots into space, flames extending down to Earth. Lights flashed behind her closed eyelids as he rocked above her, grunting like a disgusting pig. She wanted to cry and scream, but her body couldn't move. The heat inside her grew like an inferno. Troy finished within seconds, and he stood over her as she crumpled into the fetal position. He pulled her skirt down to cover her thighs in case anyone saw her through the bushes. He left her there alone with her silent sobs and a pile of vomit next to her.

Joanie stood up and hugged Matt tightly, tear after tear rolling down onto his shoulder. Her sobs were quiet, but the heaving of her shoulders illuminated her distress. Matt stroked her hair until she pulled away from him. Her mascara ran down her face in two black, muted lines.

"You are so beautiful," Matt whispered, running his thumbs across her cheekbones.

"I'm sorry," she said.

"Thank you for telling me. I wish I knew earlier. I hope you know that I am different than him. I promise to protect you and love you and take care of you." Matt spoke slowly and deliberately. Joanie nodded, sniffling.

"I need to get a tissue," she said, wiping her nose and heading into the bathroom.

In the vanity mirror, she looked at herself and saw the puffy, red eyes, swollen face, and smeared makeup. She washed her face with a warm washcloth, hoping to remove all the pain she relived in the kitchen.

She looked in the mirror again and saw Matt standing in the doorway, watching her.

His tall physique leaned against the door frame. He walked behind her, kneeled, and wrapped his arms around her back. His long arms crossed at her belly button. He kissed her lower back one time and then stood up.

He leaned into her splotchy face and kissed her under the eyes and on the corner of her mouth. He traveled to the tip of her nose and finally on her slightly chapped lips from crying.

A charge of electricity traveled back and forth between the two as his kisses deepened and intensified. Joanie hopped up on the bathroom sink and wrapped her legs around his waist, pulling him closer.

Matt pulled away and looked into her eyes. "I love you," he said.

Joanie had no reason to hide behind her past anymore. "I love you too."

Matt picked her up, her legs still wrapped around him like a spider, and carried her to her bed. He gently laid her down and traced the perimeter of her body with his index finger. Joanie shivered at the light touch, her pleasure receptors firing like the Fourth of July fireworks. She closed her eyes, and the world around her disappeared.

There was no inn, no wedding, no overbearing mother, no rape, no fear. Just Joanie and Matt, alone with no distractions. She let go of her past, pain, and anxiety and jumped off the cliff with Matt. Her body responded to his fingers and lips, and moans and cries escaped from her frantic mouth. She focused on his touch and allowed herself to let go.

He gently undressed her and looked at her naked body. "You are so beautiful. Can I make love to you?" he asked.

She nodded, biting her lip in anticipation at the pleasure that was coming. Matt slowly stripped out of his clothes and gently lay on her, pressing his warm body onto hers.

Joanie arched her back, responding to his movements until she couldn't take anymore. She desperately wanted to tell him to stop because it was too much, but she needed to follow through and let herself disappear into him. Electricity ran up her torso, and her head exploded, lights flashing behind her eyes. Matt's body stiffened with her, and then he collapsed against her, his chest pressed against her breasts.

She had never allowed herself to feel so free with a man. She relaxed underneath him, and Matt rolled onto his side, next to her. Naked and together, they stayed, exploring each other's bodies and building the love and trust between them.

Suddenly, Joanie heard Jackie calling through the closed front door. "Joanie!" she called, knocking rhythmically. Joanie froze, still topless in her bed, lying next to Matt. Her entire body tensed.

"What the," she groaned. "Why is Jackie here?" she whispered to Matt, seething. Every time Joanie had a moment, Jackie barged in like a tornado, ripping up all the good in her life. Joanie threw on her pants and tank top, and Matt tip-toed to the bathroom, clothes bundled in his arms. He kissed her nose and raised his eyebrows questioningly.

Joanie looked in the mirror and threw her tangled hair in a ponytail, hoping Jackie couldn't smell the scent of love or lust in the room.

She flung open the door widely. "Jackie!" she exclaimed. "Is everything okay?"

Chris stood behind her, clearly uncomfortable showing up unannounced. He didn't say a word and eyed Joanie, waiting to see how the rest of the conversation unfolded.

"I've been calling you all morning!" Jackie exclaimed. "Where is your phone?"

Joanie shrugged.

"I even called the inn, but there was no answer."

Joanie shrugged again. "Usually, I don't answer the phone unless I am physically in the inn. I

hate feeling tied to my job, even when I'm technically not working. I check emails and voicemails twice a day."

Jackie stood, incredulous. "Joanie, you run an inn.You are working twenty-four hours a day. And what happened to your hair? Did you serve the guests looking like that?" Jackie gawked.

Joanie shrugged again, motioning for her family to enter her small apartment. She hurried into the kitchen and lit a candle scented like clean cotton. Joanie glanced at herself in the mirror and smiled. Her puffy eyes, red chin, and mangled hair reminded her that life was messy but beautiful.

"What are you doing here?" Joanie asked again. She removed the sugary sweet intonation pattern in her words. "Is everyone okay? I told you I was busy today."

Chris sat on the edge of the couch, looking from his fiancé to his future sister-in-law. Joanie didn't know where Matt was or if he was going to make his presence known. She glanced at the bathroom door, wondering if it would be rude to assume he wasn't coming out or rude to think he was.

"Yeah, fine! I got a call yesterday from our photographer. She canceled on us! Can you even believe that? Totally out of the blue. I even put down a deposit! The wedding is seven months away! Can she even do that? I've been emailing all night with the other photographers. We have to find one. I thought we could go into the photography studios today and check them out."

"What? I can't!" Joanie exclaimed, shocked at the forwardness of her sister.

"Come on!" Jackie protested. "Chris had today off and everything! I even made him take tomorrow off. We're going to spend the night."

Joanie glared daggers at her sister. "You can't just come here demanding I follow you around or demanding a place to sleep without even asking!"

Chris touched Jackie on the arm. "Jackie, I told you this was a bad idea," he whispered.

"Chris. We're getting married. We need a photographer. We don't have time to waste, sitting around, hoping something falls into our laps." She turned back to Jackie. "Is Carly here? She knows everyone."

Joanie shook her head. "She went up to Maine for a few days. She should be back tomorrow."

Jackie turned to Chris. "Can you take Friday off too? We can wait for her."

Chris meekly grinned, rolling his eyes and shrugging his shoulders. "Fine, yeah. I can call out Friday. Let's make it a vacation," he said sarcastically.

Jackie squeezed his arm in agreement. "I promise it will be great!"

"Jackie, you don't even know if Carly can help you. And Chris lived here! Doesn't he know people on the island? Why do you need to wait for Carly?"

"Chris left the island almost twenty years ago. His family is gone. His house is gone. There is no one left for him to get in touch with." Chris rubbed the toe of his shoe against the shaggy carpet, and pink traveled throughout his face. His shoulders slumped forward, creating a turtle shell around his standing body.

"Wait. Let me get this straight. You show up, demanding I come with you to search for another photographer. And you need a place to stay. For two nights. While I am working? You are unbelievable!" Joanie threw up her hands in exasperation.

"Come on!" Jackie whined. "You have an extra house on your property."

"Someone lives there! Carly lives there! You can't just take her place!" The absurdity of this conversation sat on Joanie's last nerve. She couldn't believe Chris followed Jackie, like a puppy, and had no objections to her demands. Based on Chris's body language, Joanie knew that he was uncomfortable with this confrontation but not strong enough to say no.

"Jackie," Chris interrupted, touching Jackie's forearm. "We can go home and come back. We don't have to stay overnight."

Jackie turned to him, raising her voice in authority. "Yes, we do! I am not leaving here until we have another photographer lined up!" Chris sat down, sulking in the oversized couch cushion.

Joanie glanced at her bathroom door, wondering if Matt was eavesdropping. It would be nearly impossible for him not to hear the conversation.

"I have to go back to the inn. We currently have three empty bedrooms. You are welcome to take one for the two nights. If I get a last-minute reservation and I need the room, you're out. The room, sheets, and bathroom are all clean. You are welcome to come down early to help me with breakfast. I have things to do." Joanie stood from the couch and opened the door.

Jackie remained on the couch, her arms crossed.Chris stood, welcoming the request to leave.

"Seriously," Joanie said. "I have stuff to do. The inn is open. You have room three. Go, go!" She shooed them with her hand toward the door.

Jackie reluctantly got up from the couch and threw her Prada purse over her shoulder. She stopped in front of Joanie and wrapped her arms around her. "Thank you, thank you, thank you!" She grabbed Chris's hand and pressed her body against his as they walked to the main entrance.

Joanie had never stood up to Jackie before, and Jackie seemed unconcerned and underwhelmed. Chris's unease with the conversation fueled Joanie's mouth. She walked into the bathroom and announced that she was showering. Jackie was not going to make her feel incomplete because her hair was unkempt.

"Damn, Joanie. Your sister is brutal!" Matt said, giving her a passionate kiss on the lips.

Chapter 23

The forty-eight hours with Sandra was worth sitting in a car with John. During such a pivotal time in her life, seeing her friend made the uncertainty she was about to face bearable. Carly and Sandra searched the internet for information about the Willowside Inn and Block Island news from 1976. They were unable to find any information about a child. Carly decided that her best sources to help her rearrange the puzzle pieces were Mrs. Jackson and Chris. Seeing Sandra so excited after connecting with Bianca gave Carly a renewed sense of hope.

Warmth spread throughout Carly's body, and a lightness permeated her chest. When she left for Portland, she was anxious and alone, with the DNA secret pressing against her lungs and making it difficult to breathe. She struggled to think coherently because her mind was racing with what-ifs. But now, the what-ifs turned into and-thens because she knew there was hope at the end of her journey. It might not end well, but it would end with closure.

Carly stepped off the boat and immediately noticed the quietness of the town. Today was Thursday, and the number of bicycles zipping in between cars decreased. Fewer walkers filled the sidewalks, and most people wore jeans and a sweatshirt instead of the bathing suits and shorts commonly worn in the warmer months.

Carly hoisted her overnight bag onto her shoulder and headed up the hill. It was after dinner, and dusk settled in the sky. The blueness of the sky adjusted to a light gray. The orange sun muted the blue behind the low-lying clouds. Carly wanted to get back to the carriage house to sit on her couch, kick off her shoes, and eat. Her brain was tired of thinking.

Carly opened the screen door and found a note taped to the front door requesting a visit to the inn. Carly ripped the paper off the door, crumpled it in her hand, and turned on all the lights. Her apartment looked the same as she remembered. The clutter-free counters, empty sink, and neat bed calmed her mind.

She quickly texted Sandra telling her she got home safely, and thanked her for her hospitality. She scrolled through her text messages and noticed an unread message from Jackie: **Hi Carly! I am on the Island until Friday. I would love to see you before I leave.**

Ah, that explains the note, Carly thought.

Jackie was sometimes hard to handle, and she wondered how Chris tolerated her high demands and constant needs. Carly was unaware that Jackie would be visiting this week and wondered where she was staying.

Carly crawled into her bed with a bowl of soup and a grilled cheese sandwich and turned on the television. She watched a movie without actually watching it because her mind was elsewhere. *Who were her parents, and how did she end up with Ruth and Peter? Were there signs she missed throughout her childhood? Should she talk to Chris?* There were too many questions, and none of them had reasonable answers. Eventually, she couldn't take it anymore and turned her light off. She had to shut her brain off.

The following day, Carly woke up feeling refreshed. Sleeping in her bed was a million times more comfortable than sleeping on the hard, lumpy futon in Sandra's living room. Since the futon was in the apartment's main room, Carly fell asleep late and woke up early. Sandra's living room window faced the sunrise, so Carly woke with the yellow and orange hues each morning. They had stayed up most of the night talking about family questions, which somehow comforted Carly to know she wasn't alone.

She strode over to the kitchen entrance of the inn and found Joanie running around, cooking breakfast for two guests staying at the inn. Jackie sat at the table drinking coffee. "Good morning!" Carly called out with a wave.

"Carly! You're back! I'm so happy to see you!" Joanie exclaimed. "Jackie came down for a visit." She waved toward her sister, who was watching

Joanie prepare for the morning.

"Hey! Did you get my text?" Jackie asked.

Carly nodded.

"I met with a new photographer yesterday. I am hoping to run by his plan with you before we go."

"Sure thing," Carly said. "I don't have much going on today. I thought you already had a photographer."

"I did!" Jackie started. "She canceled on me a few days ago and didn't even give me a reason! Can you believe that? It's so unprofessional."

"Hey!" a deep voice said from the doorway.

Carly pulled back at the sight of Chris. Her heart stopped, and her breath caught in her throat. She reminded herself to play it cool. "Hey!" she muttered with a wave.

"How was Portland?" Chris asked, sitting next to her.

"Oh, you know. It was Portland. I saw John for a bit and spent a few days with Sandra."

"Who's Sandra?" Chris asked.

"Oh, just a friend from up there," Carly responded nonchalantly. "It's good to see you, Chris!" Carly studied his face. They had the same color hair and the same hair texture. Glossy and blonde. They both had blue eyes, and both wore a rose-hued tan from the summer sun.

Carly didn't know when she would see Chris again and needed to get him alone. She felt like the universe was throwing her an opportunity to seize control of her situation.

"How is John?" Chris asked.

"He's good. We spent about three hours together. We talked about ourselves and why it ended. I felt good talking with him and officially saying goodbye. So, Jackie, when are you leaving?" Carly knew that although she was talking to Chris, Jackie was the one who made all the decisions in the relationship.

"We are catching the five o'clock ferry. Today I was going to explore the island to see if I could find any other locations for wedding photos. Do you want to come?"

"Sure," Carly said. She was distracted by Chris and her deep desire to see him alone. She needed Matt's help. "Joanie, what is Matt up to today?" Carly turned to Joanie, who was busy flipping pancakes.

"Um…" she hesitated, tossing the bacon. "He's working until two and coming over around two-thirty. I need him to fix the leaky faucet in one of the guest rooms."

Carly instantly concocted a plan to get Chris over to the carriage house with Matt.

"Great! You know, I need him to stop by the carriage house too. Last night, I noticed that the exhaust fan in my bathroom stopped working. It's probably easy enough, but I don't know if there is a switch somewhere or if it's electrical. Can he pop over when he is done over here?" Her plan sounded authentic enough.

Joanie nodded, "Sure, I will let him know when I talk to him." She carried out the rest of the food to the dining room to serve her guests.

Carly made small talk with Jackie, listening to her go on and on about the table decorations, flower arrangements, and the invitation list.

"Chris," Carly interrupted, "how many people are you inviting from your side of the family?"

"We made the guest list, and he has twenty-five family members and ten friends," Jackie answered for him.

Carly nodded. "Are you inviting your aunts and uncles and cousins or just your siblings?" Carly didn't realize she was fishing for information, but she held her breath until he responded.

"My immediate family and my parent's siblings. I wasn't all that close to them, but I told my parents they could invite ten people, and they opted for their family over their friends."

Carly nodded again. "Oh, I didn't realize you had aunts and uncles. Do you have cousins too? I don't recall them ever visiting."

"Yeah, my mom and dad both have siblings. Some already passed away, but the majority are living. I didn't know my cousins, so they aren't invited to the wedding, but my aunts and uncles are. I told my parents that our numbers were limited. They understood."

Carly's heart skipped a beat at the thought of meeting one of her parents. It could be a man, or it could be a woman, she wasn't sure yet. Suddenly, she needed to insert herself into the wedding plans and learn pieces of her past through Chris.

"Oh, that's great that they weren't offended by leaving anyone out of the invite list. I imagine it was stressful figuring out who was coming and who wasn't."

Jackie looked at her diamond, and prisms of light flashed across the wall. "Yeah, it was tough, but we wanted to keep it small—less than a hundred people, including the bridal party. Oh, Joanie, the bachelorette party will be in Boston in March. I hope you can make it."

"Uh-huh," Joanie mumbled as she exited the kitchen.

"How many people are in your wedding party?" Carly asked.

"Just three. Joanie and my best friend from college are my bridesmaids, and my best friend from high school is my maid of honor."

"That's going to be perfect," Carly said. "Who do you have, Chris?"

"That's the reason I only have three," Jackie answered. "I would have had more, but Chris couldn't think of anyone worthy to ask, so we compromised on three. He picked his brother to be his best man, his sister, and his roommate from college will be groomsmen."

"Wait a minute. Is Charlene going to be wearing a tux?" Carly interrupted.

"Yeah," Chris responded. "I don't know if you knew this, but my sister is gay. I gave her the option of being a bridesmaid or a groomsman, and she opted for the groomsman. I think she feels more comfortable with Ronnie and me than she would if I made her wear a dress and hang with girls she doesn't know."

"I think she'll look beautiful."

"Yeah, she is going to wear a feminine tux. She's going to look stunning."

"I can't wait to see everyone," Carly said sincerely. "It's been way too long."

They sat at the kitchen table, eating leftover pancakes and muffins that Joanie baked from scratch. Carly's mood brightened. She realized that talking to Chris put her at ease. Her heightened sense of anxiety dropped as she asked Jackie about the new photographer. The wedding distraction and all the debacles attached to the wedding plans prevented Carly from dwelling on her problems.

After Carly finished her coffee, she, Jackie, and Joanie headed out to the beach to find the perfect place for pictures. Carly took them to Dinghy Beach, which faces the sunset and has a gorgeous view of the bay, the cliffs, and the boardwalk. It was far enough away from the hustle and bustle of town and had that rugged, natural feel. No matter which way they turned, they faced nature.

Dinghy Beach was far from the inn, but it would be a beautiful backdrop. The photographer could stop at every beach if Jackie insisted. If she felt spontaneous, she could decide on her wedding day and tell the limo driver to take her somewhere beautiful for photos.

They returned to the inn a few hours later, and Carly returned to her home. She texted Matt quickly: **Call me. Operation Family.** She was worried that Joanie would see the text and ask questions, so she made it as vague as possible.

A little after two, her phone rang. "Hey, what's up?" Matt asked.

"Did you know Chris is here?"

"Yeah, he came a few days ago."

"I didn't know that! I need to talk to him alone. I told Joanie that I need you to come over and fix something in my bathroom. I need to see Chris. Can you convince him to come over with you? And make sure no one else comes. I need to talk to him alone."

"I'll do my best," Matt said. "I'll see you in an hour."

"Thanks, Matt! I am going to tell him what I found out. And, did you do your DNA test yet? I wonder if we are related."

"Yeah, I did. I just got my results. I didn't open the email or look at it yet, but I think they are there."

Carly's heart stopped for the second time that day.

Chapter 24

That afternoon, Carly paced around her small home from room to room, thinking of ways to tell Chris: *Hey Cuz....I got my DNA results, and the weirdest thing popped up!...... How have you been? Did you ever think it was strange that we were always together as kids but never really hung out?....Hey Neighbor, I believe we're cousins. Do you want a beer?*

Everything felt odd as it rolled around her head and out her mouth into the silence of her home.

Carly heard a knock on the door and her heart stopped, yet again. Her body froze, her left arm extended to reach the doorknob, but her legs remained firmly planted to the ground like an oak tree. "Come in!" she called, her pitch too high and staccato.

Matt entered. "Hey, Car, Joanie told me you have a fan that's not working?" He looked her in the eye, his face giving away nothing.

"Yes, in the bathroom."

Chris was right behind him. "Hey, man, do you need any help?"

Matt shook his head. "You know I thought I would, but her bathroom is too small for both of us. Why don't you wait here, and I'll be right out?"

Carly quickly followed Matt toward the bathroom. "See?" She called loud enough for Chris to hear. "It's not turning on." She leaned back and threw a glance toward the living room. Chris was looking at his phone, distracted by something. She leaned forward close to Matt, "Thank you! Give me, like, ten minutes."

She pulled away from Matt and rapidly approached Chris on the couch. "Hey! Do you want a drink while you're waiting?"

Chris held up his water canister and shook his head. "I'm good," he said, still scrolling through his phone.

Carly stared at him, sensing the time ticking down.

"Hey," she said again, touching his arm to gain his attention. "I need to talk to you about something." Her voice was soft and tender. She took a deep breath, forced down her shoulders, which pressed against her ears, and rolled her neck from shoulder to shoulder. She felt like she was ready to dive into a pool for a swim meet.

"Are you okay?" he asked.

Carly took a deep breath. "Yeah, I'm okay. Listen, I had my DNA done, and the weirdest thing came back. You and I are first cousins." She stopped to gauge his emotion. He squinted at her and furrowed his eyebrows.

"Wait, what?"

"I'm serious. It says it right here." She thrust her phone out at him with the contact list on display. On the first page was the name Christopher Swanson.

He took her phone and looked at the screen, still confused about how this happened and how he didn't know about it. "That doesn't make any sense," he whispered.

"I know!" Carly was relieved that he couldn't find the logic either. The question about her parents drove her insane and kept her up night after night. "It doesn't make any sense. I have no idea how we are related. Is it through my mom? My dad? Your mom? Your dad? Am I related to Matt? It's so crazy."

Chris looked at her quizzically again.

"Wait!" Carly cried. "Give me my phone." She scrolled through the page until she got to second cousins. A notification indicated that she had a new contact. "Oh my God." She jumped up from the couch. "Matt! We're still related!" she hollered into the bathroom.

Matt stuck his head out the door, and smiled.

"Matt, can you check quickly? I need to know if you are related to Chris too."

Matt pulled out his his phone, fumbling with the app. After a few moments, that felt more like a lifetime, he responded, "No mention of Chris anywhere."

He returned to the bathroom and closed the door.

Carly turned back to Chris. "If I'm still related to Matt, that means that my dad is my dad. He's not related to you, so that must mean that one of your aunts is my mother! Right? Does that make any sense?" Chris slowly nodded in agreement.

"I guess so," he replied, still working out the inner connections of their family tree.

"Chris, who are your aunts? Like, your first aunts. Your mom and dad's sisters," Carly clarified.

"I have two aunts. My dad had one sister, Mary, and my mom had one sister, Delilah."

"Is there any way my dad had an affair with one of them?" Carly practically sat on Chris's lap. They looked at the phone between them like a shared movie screen.

"I don't know. I have no idea," Chris responded. "Delilah and my mom had a falling out. Delilah was younger than my mom by about ten years. Mary, I don't even remember her visiting. I don't remember Delilah ever visiting either. I don't think so, Carly. It sounds far-fetched."

Sweat pooled in Carly's palms and her toe tapped the floor. Her frustration grew. "But don't you get it? DNA doesn't lie! We are related! I need to figure out how."

Matt came out of the bathroom carrying his toolbox. "All set, Carly! It should be working just fine."

"Huh?" Carly turned to him. "Oh, right. Thanks."

Matt sat in the chair across from them, looking back and forth.

"I'm sorry to spring this on you. I know you have enough on your plate with the wedding and everything, but I need to figure this out for myself. If you remember anything or hear anything, please let me know!"

Chris continued to sit there, dumbfounded on the couch. "Sure."

Joanie and Jackie burst into the room, their chatter on flower arrangements overpowering the increasing tension. Chris put on his biggest smile and kissed Jackie on the lips. "Hi. When should we catch the ferry?"

Jackie glanced at her watch. "We need to leave in ten minutes."

"I'll double-check the room and pack our bags," Chris offered. As quickly as Jackie entered, Chris left.

"Is he okay?" Jackie asked. "He looked kind of pale."

"Yeah, he's fine," Matt said. "He has a lot on his mind."

Carly sat quietly on the couch, letting everyone else chatter about nothing. Two potential mothers. Her father had an affair. How did she end up in the care of Ruth and Peter? How did she never hear a rumor or a story about her past? She imagined that her arrival, her falling into the lap of Ruth, as Mrs. Jackson said, was a memorable event. Mrs. Jackson's lack of eye contact and quick desire to leave the room indicated that she knew something.

How was it that Carly never sensed the scandal? She was going to find out. She was going to find her mother.

Chapter 25

Carly didn't know what to do with all the new information and plausible explanations that jumbled in her brain like a washing machine on high. She sat with it for a few weeks, wondering if she should reach out to Chris for more information, Mrs. Jackson to get the gossip, or play dumb and contact another cousin on her DNA match list.

Carly wondered if Chris shared his news with Jackie or if he was sitting with it frozen from moving forward like her. His parents had to know something, but Chris said they never commented that Carly was different.

September turned to October with cooler temps chilling the year-round residents, and brighter colors littered the landscape. As expected, the inn was slow this time of year. Carly retreated to the carriage house, night after night, spending her evening going down one rabbit hole to the next about secret adoptions. She needed to find her birth certificate and see what it said. She wished Ruth and Peter were still alive.

Sandra spent three days with Carly, the two of them hunkered down in the carriage house, searching for their identities. "I need to find my birth certificate," Carly said.

"How do you not have a birth certificate?" Sandra asked. "How did you get a job in Maine?"

Carly shrugged. "I have a passport."

"You've had a passport your entire life? You need a birth certificate to enroll in school," Sandra argued.

"My parents handled all the paperwork for school, even for college. When I graduated high school, my dad took me to Europe for a week. Ruth stayed at the inn with the guests. Ever since then, I've always had my passport for legal documentation."

"How did you get a license?" Sandra questioned.

"I had to go to the mainland to take my test. My parents handled all the paperwork while I was with the driving teacher. I never questioned it. I got back from the test, and they gave me a license." Not having a birth certificate never concerned her until now.

"It's an easy fix. We can call the town and get a copy. They should have a copy, even from forty years ago."

Carly pulled out her phone and searched for Town Hall. She dialed the number and spoke to Mrs. Richardson, the school secretary from her childhood. "Hi, Mrs. Richardson. This is Carly Davis. I was hoping I could get a copy of my birth certificate?" She gave Mrs. Richardson all the details to verify her identity.

"Carly, we don't have anything on file. You weren't born here."

Carly swallowed a mouthful of air and coughed into the phone. She threw a wide-eyed glance at Sandra, waving her arms to gain her attention. "What do you mean? I was born at the inn."

Carly could hear keys tapping through the phone. "No, dear, you weren't. I would contact Providence. They might have more information for you."

Carly swallowed, but her mouth was parched, and a foul taste consumed her taste buds. She hung up the phone. "She said I wasn't born here," Carly repeated.

"What?" Sandra exclaimed. "I knew it sounded fishy!"

Carly immediately found the phone number for Providence City Hall and spoke with a pleasant woman. "Hi, I am looking for a birth certificate," she croaked.

After giving all the necessary information, the woman provided another piece to the jigsaw puzzle. "Carly, I don't have a birth certificate for you. I do have an adoption certificate, which names Ruth and Peter Davis as your parents. Is that correct? I can send you a copy to your address."

Carly's tried to respond, but the room spun, and her vision went black. When she came to, Sandra was sitting next to her, rubbing a wet washcloth over her face.

"Are you okay? You scared me," Sandra said.

Carly nodded. There was no phone nearby, and Carly wondered if she imagined the conversation. "What happened?"

"You fainted."

Carly sat up, but the room spun clockwise. She placed her hand on her forehead and closed her eyes. "But what happened? Why did I faint?"

"It looks like you were officially adopted. They are sending you a hard copy and suggested you call with any questions."

Carly nodded again. She had proof that she was adopted and that her fake parents lied to her for her entire life. Carly seethed with fury at all she sacrificed for Ruth and Peter.

That night, Sandra cooked Carly dinner. The kitchen smelled like cumin and melted cheese. Carly's mouth watered, while looking at the taco toppings.

"What would you do?" Carly asked, swigging a beer and eating tacos. "I mean, what would you do." It came out as a statement instead of a question. "I feel like I can't pester Chris. If he wanted to be a part of this, he would have by now." The taco shells were stuffed a mile high with every topping available in her fridge. Sour cream oozed out one end as she bit into the shell.

"I already told you! Go back and see that old lady who knew you when you fell into your parents' lap."

Carly rolled her eyes.

"Come on, Car, that's a weird thing for her to say. She knows something!"

"Ugh!" Carly exclaimed, taking another drink. "Will you come with me?" she asked Sandra. "Please! I would do it for you! I'm afraid I am going to chicken out if I have to go alone."

Sandra filled another taco shell. "Why would you chicken out? You already talked to her. She was nice, right?"

"She was, but she practically kicked me out when I asked about my birth. She knows something about my family and me. I don't know what exactly."

Sandra shrugged her shoulders.

They had been talking about this all day. They traveled down every possible scenario, and Carly filled a notebook with what-ifs and broken dreams.

"What about Matt? So, he's still your cousin, which is awesome, but has he been any help?"

"Matt's parents are dead, so he doesn't have anyone to ask either. I was thinking of talking to Charlene or Ronnie, but they probably don't remember me. It was weird enough talking to Chris. I can't imagine out of the blue contacting them and telling them we're cousins." Carly took a bite of taco, the crunching sound bouncing around the otherwise silent room. "Matt's been busy working on his house. I have this weird feeling that he and Joanie are moving in together."

Sandra looked at Carly.

"It's just a feeling!"

"Oh, that's exciting. Does that mean you would take over the inn again?" Sandra asked.

"Take over? I still own it, thank-you-very-much. But yes. It's been great having a little extra time to devote to my family search. I don't know. It's just a hunch. I haven't heard one way or the other, but they are always together now! They're attached at the hip!"

"I will go with you tomorrow to see the old lady who knows it all. We'll figure it out. Don't worry."

Carly squealed in delight and wrapped her arms around her friend. Nervousness and excitement competed within her. "Thank you!"

The following day Carly and Sandra climbed on a tandem bicycle and rode to the Historical Society. Having so few tourists meant open roads, speed, and wind blowing gently through their hair. Carly took delight in hearing Sandra scream in glee as they went over gravel and up and down frost heaves that developed in the road. By the time they got there, their legs were numb, their hair was a wind-swept mess, and laughter echoed over the gently rolling hills.

"We made it! I was hanging on for my life!" Sandra cried. "I'm too old for this!" she said jokingly.

They smoothed down their hair and walked into the main lobby. A middle-aged man stood behind the counter and smiled upon greeting them. He looked familiar, but Carly wasn't sure why.

"Hello," he said, reaching out his hand to introduce himself. "My name is David Jackson."

Both girls shook his hand.

"Are you by any chance related to Mrs. Jackson?" Carly asked.

"Yes, that is my mother," he said. "She is away this week."

Carly stared at the man, dumbfounded. She pulled out the newspaper article from her messenger bag and contemplated exposing her secret.

"You're her son?" Carly asked again.

David nodded.

"I don't know if you can help me, but I am researching my family. My father is Peter Davis, and he and my mother owned the Willowside Inn."

Carly saw a flash of recognition cross David's face as he readjusted his glasses.

"Are you from Block Island?" Carly asked.

Sandra stood beside her, looking back and forth.

David nodded. "Yes, I grew up here. I left in 1980."

Carly judged his age to be about twenty years older than Carly.

"Great! I came across this newspaper article in my parent's basement. Do you by any chance know who these people are?" Carly unfolded the paper to show David.

He chuckled to himself. "Yes. That is Doug and Rhonda Swanson and one of their relatives. I can't remember her name, but she stayed here for a while, working at your parent's inn."

Carly heard him, but she didn't allow herself to process the information. She needed to learn details, so she continued firing questions.

"You knew my parents! And your mother knew my parents also. Do you remember when I was born?"

David shook his head. "No," he replied.

"Do you remember me at all?"

"I remember you when you were a toddler, but my memories are few. My parents frequently attended cookouts at your parent's inn. Sometimes I went with them."

"Are you sure?" Carly asked.

David shrugged. "I don't remember anything else."

"This woman here," Carly said, pointing to the woman next to her father. "You don't know her?"

"She was only here a short time. I think she was living with Doug and Rhonda, helping with the kids. I'm sorry I couldn't be more help."

Carly snatched back the paper and folded it neatly in her palm.

"I have one more question," Carly said. "Your mom said that I fell into my mother's lap. Do you know what that means?"

David looked at her quietly shuffling papers on the counter. "I don't know what that means, but I recall hearing stories about a baby showing up in a basket somewhere. I didn't pay attention. Block Island gossip wasn't my thing. Sorry."

Sandra nodded toward David and turned to Carly. "Come on. We should go." Carly stood up, grabbed the newspaper article from David's hands, and numbly walked to the door.

They walked their bikes back to the carriage house in silence. Carly's mind raced, and her chest tightened. Her spine stiffened as anger took hold. Her entire life was a lie.

When they got back to the carriage house, Sandra pulled out a blue notebook from her backpack. "Okay, what do we know?" she asked.

"David is lying. He knows more than he is letting on."

"You don't know that for sure," Sandra said.

"Yes, I do! Mrs. Jackson remembered a relative because she worked with and was friends with her son. Here was her son, and he pretended like he didn't even know her!"

Sandra rocked back and forth on her feet, "Okay, I am writing that down as a questionable fact. Maybe we will find out more."

Carly settled into Peter's old cozy blue armchair that had thinning fabric on the arms and butt. Carly rubbed the arms of the chair, feeling the fabric push below her short fingernails. The friction almost felt painful and pleasurable simultaneously.

"Well. Let's start at the top. Ruth and Peter raised me. Matt and I are still second cousins. Chris and I are first cousins. Matt and Chris are not related, which means Chris and I are related on my dad's side. Chris has two aunts, which means two potential mothers. My father has to be my father because if he weren't, Chris and Matt would be related, right?"

Sandra furiously jotted down clues and drew lines connecting everyone.

"So that brings us to the situation," Carly continued. "Let's pretend that my dad got one of Chris's aunts pregnant. I have no idea what the situation is, but maybe it was a one-night stand or a summer fling. He doesn't know, I am born, and someone...maybe Chris's parents or grandparents dropped me off on the doorstep because...." She stopped, reviewing the notes. "I don't know." Carly stopped again, her imagination running wild. "What if my dad never knew that I was his child? What if both my parents had no idea where I came from? Or, what if they did? Maybe that's why my relationship with my mother was so rocky. Maybe that's why my mom never seemed happy."

Carly knew she wasn't making any sense, but it felt good to let all her thoughts out like an overfilled balloon flying around. Her words were going in every which way, and once she started talking, she couldn't stop until her lungs emptied.

"That's quite the theory," Sandra responded.

Chapter 26

"Mom, you can certainly stay here," Joanie said into the phone, rolling her eyes. "Yes, Jackie and Chris too. And Dad. Yes," Joanie stumbled around the kitchen, checking the cabinets to see what she needed for Thanksgiving. Food was triple the price on the island, so she planned to take Matt's car on the ferry to buy groceries on the mainland.

"Great," Sheila said. "We will be there on Wednesday and leave on Friday. I think that is plenty of time."

Joanie agreed. Two days wasn't a long time, but it felt like an eternity when you were stuck with Sheila.

Joanie spoke with Carly about closing down the inn on Thanksgiving. It could be a busy time due to families visiting for the holiday weekend, but it could also be slower because few people lived on Block Island year-round. Still, she knew her parents were coming and didn't know if she could handle random guests and Sheila simultaneously.

Thanksgiving was in three days, and Joanie had a million little things to do before all hell broke loose. She confided in Matt, fretting about the stress of the weekend, any time he would listen. She knew that she was an annoyance, but she couldn't stop.

It had gotten to where Matt kissed her every time Joanie brought up Sheila or Jackie's name to cause a distraction. It worked most of the time.

Matt stayed at her house more and more often, and the bathroom counter was a mish-mash of men's and women's toiletries all tossed together. Her already cramped closet was busting with memories of Matt. His oversized sweatshirts hugged the coat rack, and his work boots splayed against the wall in the corner of their bedroom. Joanie considered it their bedroom when Matt's items suddenly appeared on his side of the bed. The bed was no longer just for lovemaking but also for sleep.

They stayed up late at night, dreaming about living together and building a life together. Matt modified his home to fit her tastes, requesting she move in once Carly's midlife crisis was over.

Joanie stood in front of the refrigerator with the door wide open. "Sure, Mom, you can do some of the cooking. Just send me a list of what I need to buy, and you can make it Thursday morning."

Joanie sat at the table, overwhelmed that the next few days would be a disaster. Her mother called herself the Queen of the Holidays because she knew how to host. Sheila lay appropriate silverware on the table, whipped up table centerpieces, and paired appetizers with wine. Joanie never cared about any of that, and she almost wondered if she should let Sheila take over and do it all. It would make Sheila feel good about herself and make Joanie's next few days much less stressful.

Wednesday morning, Joanie made her last breakfast of the week and got to work, cleaning bedrooms and bathrooms after the guests left. She had three hours to get it all done before chaos erupted like Mount Vesuvius.

"Hey, Joanie!" Carly called through the empty hallway.

"In here!" Joanie said, tangled in a blue comforter. She straightened the floral design against the king-sized bed.

"Do you want me to be here when Jackie shows up?"

"Yes! Please! Matt will be here too. I have so much to do. I need you to distract them or at least keep them out of my hair. My parents are coming in on the last ferry, so I have a little time. Jackie is on her way now."

Carly spent the day helping Joanie get the rooms situated. As they walked down the staircase in the old Victorian home, the front door swung open, and Jackie waltzed in. She held an oversized suitcase in one hand, a large satchel in the other, and sunglasses perched on her flaming red hair.

"Hey, girls!" Jackie called into the foyer.

Carly and Joanie greeted her, lugging down the cleaning bucket and laundry basket.

"Happy Thanksgiving!" Jackie called out again. Her bubbliness was nauseating.

"Hey," Chris said, approaching from a distance behind her. Grocery bags stuffed with food hid his large frame.

They dropped their bags at the base of the stairs and made their way into the kitchen. Chatter about the weekend and the wedding filled the room.

"Carly, did you ever contact those horse farms asking about a white horse we could borrow?" Jackie asked.

Joanie stifled a chuckle.

"I did, actually," Carly lied. "I couldn't find any available."

"Bummer! I wonder if I can have one shipped in from a farm in Rhode Island."

Joanie made bug-eyes to Carly. "Yeah, maybe."

"What time are mom and dad coming?" Jackie asked.

"Probably in a few hours. Matt's coming over. I was thinking of doing something easy for dinner, like make-it-yourself subs. We're going to eat non-stop tomorrow. I don't want to cook tonight."

"Sure, whatever," Jackie responded.

Chris was silent today, Joanie noticed. He was often quiet, but today he didn't even make eye contact, which was unusual.

"So, Chris," Joanie started. "How's life?" It was a loaded question, and she knew it.

"Eh, you know. Busy."

Carly occupied herself in the kitchen, pouring drinks and plating a veggie platter. She had been quieter than usual too. The vibe in the kitchen felt uncomfortable to Joanie, but Jackie didn't seem to notice.

Jackie flipped through a wedding magazine. "Look at these pictures! It's stunning in the winter snow," she said.

"Sure, but it's cold, and you're risking getting married alone because of snow storms. I would never get married in the winter," Joanie said. "It's too questionable."

"Yeah, true, but look how gorgeous these women are. Their cheeks are rosy, and the snow is brilliant white. It's beautiful."

Joanie shrugged. "Sure, but I would still never do it. Winter is so depressing."

Jackie dropped the magazine and placed it upside down on the table. "I love winter," she defended.

Joanie shrugged again, ignoring her sister's steely eyes, and looked at her phone, willing Matt to call so she could escape from her sister.

***

That evening, the entire family squeezed around the large kitchen table. Poker chips precariously sat in a pile, and each person obtained a portion of tokens in various colors. Joanie hadn't seen her father since Christmas, and he looked good. Golfing and Florida sun seemed to be what he needed to survive living with Sheila.

"Full house," Chris said, splaying his cards face-up on the table.

"Damn! I had two pairs," Matt said. They were the only two left in the round. Chris reached around and scooped all the chips to the edge of the table.

Poker was a card game Joanie and Jackie grew up around. Their parents hosted a poker event every other Saturday night in the basement of their home with all their couple friends. Joanie and Jackie sat on the stairs, eavesdropping, wondering when they would be invited to play.

When they hit eleven and fourteen, they joined their first Poker tournament with their mom and dad. Sheila was a tricky player who knew how to bluff. She taught the girls when to fold and when to persist. Although it wasn't Joanie's favorite game, it was one of her beloved family memories. It was the only time she received praise because Jackie never finished a game. She would start, but then she would get bored and leave the table. First, she was distracted by her dolls, then her friends, and then her boyfriends. Poker was the only time Joanie felt superior to Jackie and worthy in her parent's eyes.

Now, laughter, chit-chat, and noise reverberated off the kitchen walls as the poker chips flew from pile to pile. The empty beer cans filled the sink. Sheila and Jackie refused a drink because they only drank wine, and Joanie was all out. She bought her dad's favorite beer instead. Everyone but Jackie and Sheila clinked cans.

Later that night, Joanie found herself in the kitchen with Matt.

"That was fun," Matt said, hugging Joanie from behind, his arms wrapped over her shoulders.

"It was!" Joanie concurred. "We always loved to play Poker when I was a kid. My parents are great players. I always wondered if I would ever get to be as good as they are. It's the only time I feel confident around them. Usually, they make me feel like I am this big," Joanie held up her thumb and forefinger with an inch of space between to demonstrate her inferiority.

"You are amazing. And beautiful. And kind. And loving." Matt said.

"Thanks," Joanie turned to him and kissed him gently on the lips.

She stretched her back and yawned, expanding her mouth like a frog catching flies.

"Tired?" Matt asked tenderly.

"Yes! I have such a busy day tomorrow. I probably should get some sleep."

Matt and Joanie headed to her apartment with the intention of sleep, but the desire to become one was too strong to ignore. She may not have slept the entire night through, but she was satisfied.

Chapter 27

The tinging of metal on glass filled the room. The family and friends sat around a large table in the formal dining room. The buffet trays of food spread between them, and their glasses were full. Empty plates begged for food, and the savory smell of rosemary and sage watered their mouths.

Dinner preparations went off without a hitch. Sheila cooked Thanksgiving dinner for so many years. It was now a well-oiled machine. Jackie husked the corn and made the corn pudding, Carly made the stuffing, Matt peeled the potatoes, and Joanie prepped the sweet potato casserole. Chris dressed the turkey, Sheila made the pumpkin pie, and Joanie's father sat watching football in front of the television. Everyone except Joanie's father played a part in the preparation of the meal.

All eyes turned to Jackie, who tapped her glass vigorously. She stood up, wearing a black dress with an empire waist and a floral cardigan over it. "Hi," she began. Everyone smiled nervously, wondering if they could start dumping food on their plates.

Joanie glanced around the table, wondering if Jackie was giving grace. She held out her hands and grabbed onto Matt's hand. Everyone followed suit until the ring of people created a human chain.

"No, no," Jackie said. "Chris and I have an announcement." Chris's blue eyes became as big as saucers. He stared at her with eyes wide, lips pursed, and skin pale. He appeared guilty but surprised. He quickly stood up and leaned into her ear. She ignored him.

"What is it, dear?" Sheila asked. "The food is getting cold."

"Mom! This is important!" Jackie whined. "Chris and I just found out that we are expecting!"

A huge smile spread across her face. Chris's face turned red. Sheila dropped her fork, and the ting echoed throughout the room. No one said a word.

"Congratulations, man!" Matt said, breaking the silence.

"What do you mean?" Sheila asked, forcing a smile on her lips and badly portraying excitement.

"A baby, Mom!" Jackie sat down in her chair and pulled it in close to the table. "You're going to be a grandmother!" she beamed.

"Ah, a baby. That is," Sheila paused, "wonderful! When?"

"Well, we found out a few weeks ago. We are having a baby in July."

"Congratulations!" their father said, raising his beer.

Everyone else around the table followed suit, wondering what exactly this meant for the wedding. Would Jackie get married if she was showing?

"So, the wedding is happening sooner than we expected. We are going to get married in January."

Sheila choked on her sparkling water and looked around the room. "January? But that is two months away. We have so much to do." Sheila squeezed her eyes shut and clenched and unclenched her fists resting on the table.

"We haven't figured it out yet."

"But January. You may still have morning sickness."

"No, if we get married at the end of January, I will be fifteen weeks pregnant. I should be fine."

"Wonderful," Sheila repeated, but based on her sarcasm, it was not wonderful.

Joanie, Carly, and Matt watched the conversation unfold like spectators at a tennis tournament. The tension in the room continued to build, yet the winner was not yet declared. Chris appeared excited, but Joanie could tell he was terrified. Tiny beads of sweat formed around his brow, even though it was cool enough to wear a sweater.

Jackie's face turned to stone. Sheila denied Jackie the significant congratulatory response she expected. Sheila made sure that Jackie understood just how inconveniencing her actions made the entire event.

Joanie rarely felt sympathy for her sister, but they were grown adults, and Sheila didn't need to shame Jackie. There was no reason Sheila couldn't pretend to be happy or hide her disdain. The only person who showed genuine excitement was Joanie's dad. He was oblivious to Sheila's bitterness and held up his beer bottle cheerfully exclaiming, "Congrats! I'm going to be a granddad!"

To Joanie's surprise, what started as a great visit had just taken a momentous turn. A wedding, and a baby. Poor Chris was in over his head, and it was apparent that he was about to have a mental breakdown. He smiled blankly and pushed food around his plate to occupy his attention.

They ate in silence. Joanie inwardly panicked about having a January wedding instead of an April wedding because everything was affected. They couldn't have the wedding outside because of the weather, wedding photos on the beach would be gray and drab, and there was no indoor place to accommodate one hundred people.

Occasionally, Jackie threw out an idea, but Sheila quickly squashed it. Sheila didn't want to hear the details. Sheila was always more concerned about her friends' thoughts than understanding the motives and intentions behind her children's actions. Joanie threw glances at her sister, communicating that she wanted to talk to her alone, in private, and gave her a nervous smile to ease her concern.

Immediately after dinner, Carly excused herself from the party, feigning exhaustion. Everyone probably knew it was a lie, but the circus within the four walls of the inn was overpowering any sort of resentment toward Carly for leaving early. Joanie wished she could go with her.

Matt and Joanie stayed until after they cleaned the kitchen. Sheila downed two more glasses of wine before disappearing into her room. Joanie's father and Jackie sat in the kitchen, talking about her pregnancy and the weather under the bright overhead lights. Chris was silent, next to Jackie.

"Hey, I think I am going to go home. Take a shower and relax. I think you all need to stay here and talk. Call me when everyone goes to bed. I will come back over." Matt gave Joanie a quick kiss on the lips, and Joanie silently begged him to stay. "I love you," he said.

Joanie grinned and wrapped her arms around his neck. "I. Love. You. Too," she said, breaking up each word with a staccato.

Matt snuck his head into the kitchen. "Later!" he said with a wave. "I'll see you tomorrow."

After Joanie heard the door close behind him, she walked back into the kitchen. Without Sheila there, the negative vibe cleared out of the room, and laughter reverberated off the walls.

"Congratulations!" she said to Jackie and Chris. "I can't believe I am going to be an aunt!" Joanie never thought she would desire the title "Auntie," but her insides felt warm and fuzzy. She imagined taking her niece or nephew shopping or out for ice cream. Joanie was happy for Jackie. It seemed like everything she wanted was coming to fruition all at once. "When did you find out?"

"Three weeks ago," Chris said, staring at the center of the table, playing with the saturated wrapper on his beer bottle.

"I'd been nauseous and sick for days and thought I had some sort of virus. It turns out I was pregnant. I couldn't even believe it. I'm thirty-seven, Joanie. How the hell did I get pregnant?" Jackie flipped her hair over her shoulder.

"Thirty-seven isn't that old. People have babies all the time at thirty-seven," Joanie responded.

"Yeah, well, I thought I was too old to have a kid. I guess not." She sounded glum.

"So you're due in July. You can still get married in April. I've learned through the years that first babies don't show for a while. No one will even know."

"Joanie, I will be seven months. There is no way I won't be a whale. People have babies at seven months. We have to get married sooner."

"But January is so soon. And so cold. And the weather is so unpredictable. You may not have anyone come. The ferries barely run in the winter." Joanie thought a January wedding was a terrible idea.

"It's all a mess. We already sent out the save the dates, so we need to contact our guest list immediately."

"What if you come down to Florida?" Joanie's dad spoke up, interrupting the doom and gloom of all the changes. "Get married at the golf club. January is a slow time of year. Make it a destination wedding. If people want to come, they'll come."

Joanie snickered, "Mom would kill you!"

"Yeah, Dad. Good idea, but Mom would be livid. She doesn't even care that we are having a baby. She only cares about showing off to her friends how amazing she is, and this pregnancy blip does not make her strong Catholic beliefs look good." Jackie had strong feelings about Sheila, and Joanie was surprised. Jackie and Sheila always seemed close, like two peas in a pod.

"Oh, forget your mother!" he exclaimed. "She'll get over it. She was surprised, that's all. She would love to have you get married in Florida. You'll still have the wedding you want. Outside, warm weather, not looking pregnant, which is what you want," he looked at Jackie, "and your mother will be excited to be able to help you plan."

Jackie sneered. "Yeah, right, Dad. But if you want to talk to her, go for it. I'm done talking to her about the wedding until she gets over her bad attitude. I don't want that stress. It's not even her wedding."

They continued to chat about the wedding, their options, and the pregnancy. After a few more drinks and slices of apple pie, Joanie excused herself for the night. It sounded like Jackie, Chris, and their dad were feeling better and more optimistic. Sheila never returned from her room, and Joanie saw the sadness in her father's eyes. Joanie rarely witnessed her father openly disagree with Sheila, and Joanie was happy it was because of Jackie. Both girls were trying to prove their worth to Sheila, and it was nice to witness their father's immediate acceptance of their choices.

Today was the first time Joanie didn't have to get up at dawn to serve others in the past eight months. She felt reassurance in her connection with Matt and was grateful for the simplicity of their relationship. From the beginning, Joanie urged him to go slow and be patient with her. She knew that it would be a long night but felt relieved that she could sleep until noon if she wanted. Joanie texted Matt. She had a man to make love to all night long.

Chapter 28

The following day, Carly panicked. A wedding in January was only two months away. She had two months to figure out who her mother was because there was a chance that she would be in attendance. Now that the celebration was in the winter, there was a good chance no one would come, but Carly held onto hope that maybe, just maybe, her mother would be there.

Carly called Sandra to troubleshoot her options. "Jackie's pregnant. The wedding is now in January. All I know is that I might have been dropped off on my parent's porch when I was a baby. My father is my father, but my mother could either be Delilah or Mary," she quickly summarized. "What do I do?"

Sandra sat quietly on the other end. "David told you everything he knew. Supposedly. Chris knows you are related but has pulled away from you ever since. Are his parents still alive?" Sandra asked. "They might be who to contact next."

"Yeah, they are. I don't know where. Chris doesn't talk about them. His two siblings are still alive, and they're both in the wedding."

"Are any of your parent's friends or families still alive? Maybe they would know something."

Carly shook her head, but Sandra couldn't see. "My parents would be in their 80's if they were still alive. My mom's siblings are mostly dead. One is in a nursing home with dementia. My dad lost contact with his family, so I wouldn't even know where to look."

"Did you say your dad? Carly, you have all the DNA stuff at your fingertips. Maybe you can pull an aunt or uncle from there and contact them." Carly nodded.

"I could look," she said quietly, not quite sure how comfortable she felt contacting a stranger. "Speaking of contacting family, have you talked to Bianca yet?" Carly changed the subject, trying her hardest not to overpower the conversation.

"Yes! We video chatted yesterday for Thanksgiving. Her kids are beautiful! We've been talking every week, just catching up. It's been great."

Carly felt a ping of jealousy but pushed it down.

They chatted about Bianca and her family and Thanksgiving and Christmas plans. Carly went through the conversation on autopilot, all the while wondering how she was going to find her birth mother.

She needed to talk to Chris before he left. It was the only chance she had.

Carly abruptly hung up with Sandra, grabbed her coat, and dashed out the door, taking long strides to get to the inn as quickly as possible. The entire family moved about the kitchen, chatting about their plans for the day.

Chris sat at the table with an oversized mug of coffee sitting in front of him. He half-smiled when he saw her, and Carly returned an enthusiastic wave. "Morning, everyone!" she called out. Her chipper tone and sudden appearance caused the group to turn and acknowledge her.

"Morning, Carly," Joanie's dad said. Everyone else continued with their conversations. Joanie wasn't there yet. Neither was Matt. A quick plan loosely formed in Carly's head, and the words were out of her mouth before she could think.

"Chris, can you help me in the carriage house? My closet door came off the runner, and I can't get it back on. You're tall. Would you mind helping me?"

"Sure," he said. He immediately stood up from the table and kissed Jackie. "Be right back."

"Bye," Jackie quickly responded, turning her attention back to the coffee pot, which was slowly dripping. She fumbled around the kitchen, looking for sugar and clean mugs.

Chris exited with Carly, and they made their way to the carriage house.

"What closet door do you need help with?" he asked.

"I don't. Here, take a seat," she said, pulling out a kitchen chair.

Chris sat. "What's up?" he asked blankly.

"We need to talk. About us. About our family."

Chris waited for her to continue. When she didn't, he responded, "Carly, I can't help you. I don't have the mental capacity to go on this wild ride with you."

"Please," she begged. "Please." She looked down at her hands, wondering if she should share the secret held within Pandora's Box that she was grasping tightly. It stewed, rolled around, and tainted all the memories of her father. "My dad had an affair with one of your aunts. I don't know which one. My parents adopted me when I was about a year old. I don't know how they got me, but apparently, there was a rumor going around about a baby and a doorstep. I don't even know if my dad knew that I was his biological child. I don't know if my mom knew he had an affair. I have so many questions, Chris, and it's eating me alive. I need to find out who my mother is and what happened." Carly began to cry, slowly first, and then more rapidly. The truth behind the spoken words triggered an avalanche of anger, sadness, and bitterness toward her situation, and she wondered if life would have been easier if she never knew. "Please," she whispered.

"Carly, I'm getting married. I'm having a baby. My life right now is shit. I don't know if I can afford to support a child. I love Jackie, but she has been crazy ever since we got engaged. If I take on anything else, I am going to lose my shit. My head does not have any more room for drama."

"You don't have to do anything!" Carly pleaded. "Just give me a lead. Give me the name of someone who might know something! Are your grandparents still alive? They must know something! Can you give me any information about your two aunts or someone who knows them well? I am going crazy thinking about all the possibilities. I am going to lose my mind! I need help!"

Chris sighed, grunted, and sat back in the seat, his tense shoulders crooked against the straight back of the chair. Carly waited, dying inside. He was her last hope.

"Fine. Let me hook you up with my cousin, Teegan. She's the daughter of my Aunt Mary. I can also connect you with my cousin Rick, who is the son of my Aunt Delilah. You say it's either Mary or Delilah, right? There you go. I'll send you their email addresses, and you can go to town."

Carly clapped her hands frantically and threw her arms around Chris. "Thank you!" She felt a resurgence of hope push through her fear. "Now, I have to figure it out before January. Thanks, Chris! I have two months to find my mom." She sat back down and looked at Chris's weary face. "Seriously. Thank you."

He nodded. "Anything else you need?"

Carly pulled out the folded newspaper. It had been folded and refolded so many times, a faint crease cut through the woman in the maxi dress, cutting her body in two. "Do you know who these people are?"'

Chris looked at the article and bit his lip. "Those are my parents."

"Yes! Did you know they worked so closely with my parents? I never knew they worked at the inn!"

Chris shrugged, looking at his watch. "Jackie's going to wonder where I am," he interjected.

"I know." Irritation tainted Carly's words. "Did you know they worked with my parents?" Carly asked again.

Chris shook his head. "I had no idea. My parents were friendly with your parents but never talked about them beyond being neighbors."

Dread filled Carly. Chris commented on his parents but not on the woman leaning into Peter. Maybe she wasn't anyone of importance. "What about her?" Carly pointed to the woman in the maxi dress.

"I have no idea, Carly. She doesn't look familiar."

Carly's hope shattered at her feet. It seemed like every person she spoke with led her straight to a dead end. "Thanks," she mumbled, still wondering how Doug and Rhonda were important enough to be included in an article about the Willowside Inn.

"I have to go," Chris said. He rocked on his feet. "Jackie's probably wondering where I am."

"Thanks again," Carly said as she watched the most recent clue to her past walk away, leaving more questions in its wake.

***

The following week, Carly got up enough nerve to reach out to Teegan and Rick. Chris set up an email thread between the two family triangles and explained the situation before introducing Carly. Carly was terrified that she would be rejected and eventually abandoned.

Her biggest fear was that Teegan or Rick would find out they were siblings and shut down. She had no idea what feelings they had about the situation or if they would accept her, become angry at their mother, or be disenfranchised by the entire ordeal. She had no idea what kind of mothers Mary and Delilah were or what type of trauma or experiences Teegan and Rick had as children.

The initial email from Chris was generic: **Hi. This is your cousin Chris. From Block Island. I have a friend who found out she and I were first cousins, and now she is trying to figure out if your mother is her mother. I don't have any information for her, so I thought I would get her connected with you. –Chris.**

Rick had not responded yet to the email, even though Chris verified he had spoken to him on the phone. Carly wondered if Rick was in shock or if he expected this sort of thing from his life. Teegan responded that night. She included Chris and Carly in her reply: **Hi Carly! Yes, Chris filled us in on your problem, and I get it. I would be freaking out too. If you want, you can call me, text me, email me, or message me via social media anytime. I will try to help you. –Teegan.**

Carly sat with her email for a few days before finding Teegan on every social media platform. She stalked her profile pictures and public wall. She opened up the photos of Teegan and enlarged the image on her phone, searching for an immediate connection in the way her freckles dotted her nose or how her hair awkwardly waved at the end. Carly looked and looked, praying for an answer.

She texted Chris, asking for background info about Teegan. Where did she grow up? Was she an only child? Were her parents married, and did they stay married? Did he notice anything weird about them when they were kids? Weird, like hiding something? Sometimes Chris responded, and other times he ignored her, probably too wrapped up in baby and wedding chaos.

Carly called Sandra, desperate for guidance. "What do I do?" she asked.

"She sounds open. You have to call her. Don't do it over email. An email will drive you crazy. There's too much downtime in between responses. Set up a time to call her, write down your questions, and talk to her. See what she knows." Sandra said calmly.

Carly gulped down the giant peach pit in her throat. Taking that next step could cause an avalanche and make or break her identity.

"You're right," Carly replied. "You're right. The worst that can happen is she says no."

"You should ask her to take a DNA test. The more people that take it, the easier you'll figure out how you're all connected."

Carly swallowed again. Asking her to do that felt too forward, but Carly would be able to put another piece into the puzzle if she were willing.

"Good idea," Carly said, writing down DNA in her notebook.

As soon as she hung up from Sandra, she texted Teegan: **I would love to talk. Are you free tonight?**

Within five minutes, Carly's phone dinged. She held it upside down and quieted her breathing. She willed herself to turn it over, and her hands miraculously cooperated. Carly read: **Yes. 7:00?**

Carly's heart sped up and pumped against her sternum. She typed quickly and hit send before she could stop herself.

The weight crushing her lifted gingerly off her chest. Carly no longer felt trapped under the guise of mystery but felt rejuvenated for coming this far. Besides Sandra, no one else knew how deep she was into her family drama. She wished Chris were a little more helpful, but she understood why he was so distracted.

The sun started to set, and Carly's stomach grumbled. She hadn't decided what she wanted to eat for dinner. The air was brisk and chilly. Carly shivered in her oversized sweatshirt as she raced across the lawn to the main house.

"Joanie?" she called through the kitchen. "Joanie?" she called again.

She found Joanie waist-deep in the walk-in closet, digging through a box of Christmas lights. "I've never done this before," she said. "Should I call Matt?"

"Nah. We can do it!" Carly exclaimed. "It isn't that hard. We figured it out last year. We can figure it out again."

Joanie laughed. "Last year, you were so in love with John, you didn't care about the decorations. All you put up was the wreath on the door."

"That wreath was beautiful. Just what we needed!" Carly laughed.

Joanie grabbed all the tangled lights and started to uncoil them. "You seem to be in a happy mood," she commented.

"Tonight, I will be chatting with Teegan, my maybe-half-sister!" Carly said gleefully.

"No shit!" Joanie said. "How did that happen."

"Well, Chris connected us."

"Chris?" Joanie asked, plugging in a strand of lights.

"Yeah, Matt didn't tell you?" Carly told him to keep her secret, but she didn't expect him to keep it for so long.

Joanie's eyes darted around the room, and she bit her lip. She narrowed her eyebrows and tapped her fingers on the floor. "Tell me what?"

"That Chris and I are cousins. I found out a few months ago when I did a DNA test, and I asked Matt not to tell you because I didn't want it to get back to Chris."

Joanie's eyes narrowed as she continued to pull apart the tangled lights. "Oh, wow. I had no idea."

"I'm sorry," Carly said, searching for her eyes. "I didn't know what to do with that information, and I confided in Matt because I needed to know that we were cousins. I needed to figure out how Chris and I were related. I didn't tell anyone except Sandra."

After a moment, Joanie asked, "So are you and Matt still cousins?"

"Yes! That means Chris is my cousin on my dad's side. I still don't know how, but we are. I also found out that I am adopted, which I never knew before. It's a mess."

Joanie's shoulders drooped, and she lowered her head. She asked a few questions but didn't request the specifics or the timeline. She kept her eyes down, focused on accomplishing the decorating task, and spoke to Carly with a flat affect and monotone voice.

"It's weird that you two are cousins and never knew." Joanie struggled with the strand of lights, threw them on the floor, and quickly changed the subject. "I have no idea how I am going to get these separated!"

"Yeah, me too, but I have narrowed it down to two aunts that might be my mother. I am this close," Carly held up her thumb and forefinger an inch apart and an inch away from her eye. "I will find out the truth."

"Are you going to the wedding?" Joanie asked.

"Do you have any details?" That was the real reason she came over. She needed to know exactly how much time she had before missing her opportunity.

"January 24th. They're getting married on the golf course in Florida. She's inviting everyone, and if they come, they come. If they don't, they will send gifts. She wins either way."

"Any unicorns?"

Joanie guffawed. "Unicorns are the last thing on her mind. She's too preoccupied figuring out whether or not she can trust my mother making all these decisions."

"Is she going down there before?" Carly asked.

"Yes, she's going down with Chris a week before the wedding, and then they are honeymooning. All the decisions will be finalized or tweaked that week. I am so happy I won't be there."

"Wait," Carly interrupted. "You aren't going to the wedding?"

"We have to figure it out because of the inn. It can't go unattended, and we need the business if there is any," Joanie said.

Carly nodded, reached down, and pulled apart the lights balled on the floor. "Whatever time you need, I will stay here and run the inn. You shouldn't have to miss your sister's wedding because of a job."

"Ha!" Joanie laughed. "But what if I want to? Staying here is the perfect excuse for me not to go."

Carly nodded, but her head was already spinning. Carly needed to be at the wedding if her mother was in attendance. If Joanie didn't go, could she go? Would that be weird? She barely knew Jackie. Chris was her friend, but an estranged friend, at this point. Everything felt wrong, like a dead-end in every direction. Optimism fell away, and Carly felt tied to the couch with shackles. She was so close to finding and meeting her mother.

"We'll figure it out," Carly said flatly.

They spent the next few hours untangling, hanging, and rearranging furniture to the tunes of traditional Christmas carols. The windows glowed with candles, and the village sat on the mantle, lit up with white lights. They pulled up the artificial tree and placed it in the corner of the sitting room, ornaments intentionally placed on the branches. By the end of the night, Carly and Joanie transformed the interior into a Christmas wonderland. The scented candle aroma of trees and snow lightly permeated the furnishings in the house. It looked beautiful, and Carly knew Ruth and Peter would be proud.

Carly placed the last empty box in the walk-in closet and headed home. Decorating was a great distraction from Teegan and the wedding dilemma. She expected to dash home, excited for the phone call, but her fear of rejection slowed her down. She thought maybe if she moved too slowly, she would miss her opportunity. Sure, she would miss it, but it would have been her choice, not the result of someone else's choice. Carly didn't want to be responsible for the success or failure of the conversation.

A few minutes past seven, Carly picked up her phone and dialed Teegan's number. She was surprised to hear a high-pitched, bubbly voice on the other end of the line. Teegan sounded young. Like, twenty-something young. Carly pulled up her laptop to check out her pictures on social media. Teegan looked around early-thirty, but Carly was a terrible judge of age.

They talked for a while. Carly wanted to communicate like a person, but her fear kept her in a professional state. Carly asked about Teegan's job (a preschool teacher, which made sense as to why she sounded so young), her age (thirty-one, which placed her a whole decade younger than Carly), and where she lived (Cleveland, Ohio). After they conversed polite, social exchanges, Carly went in for the kill.

"So, tell me about your mom. What's her story?" Carly asked.

"She's nice. She's married to my dad. I have two brothers. We grew up in a nice home in the suburbs. What do you want to know?"

Carly thought for a moment. "How old was she in 1976?" Her age would be the dead giveaway if Teegan were her sister.

"Let's see. I was born in 1985, and my mom was twenty-four, so that would make her fifteen. Why?" Carly swallowed. This was not her sister. Mary was not her mother. Peter was in his forties when Carly was born. If he had sex with a fifteen-year-old, he would have been arrested on the spot. Carly crossed off Mary's name from her notepad.

One word stared back at her. Delilah.

Carly didn't want Teegan to feel used, so Carly stayed on the line. Her shoulders relaxed, and her feet rested on the ottoman. Carly asked Teegan about Chris and if they were close, and how often she visited Block Island. Teegan said that she had never been to Block Island, at least that she recalled.

Carly thought about Chris. Contacting her must have been so awkward. It sounded like they didn't even have a relationship.

After Carly hung up with Teegan, she texted Chris: **Can you talk?**

After a few minutes and no response from Chris, she called. He answered with a gruff voice and low volume. "What's up?" he asked. "I'm working."

"I just wanted to thank you for everything you have done for me. I know how uncomfortable it must've been to get me in contact with your family. Thank you. Really. From the bottom of my heart."

Chris paused. "What happened?" he asked.

"I just talked to Teegan, and Mary is NOT my mother. I am 100% certain. Unless Peter was a child molester, there is no way."

"Gee, you sound kind of happy to realize your dad wasn't into little kids," Chris laughed. "It's no problem. Really. I wish I could help more, but I just can't right now. I have so much shit on my plate. I'm losing my mind."

"If you need anything, please reach out. I mean, about the wedding. Or the baby. Or whatever," Carly stumbled. "Just reach out. Thanks again."

They hung up, and Carly sat there, giddy with excitement.

She knew Delilah was her mother. Relief deep in her gut rolled around. She spent the rest of the night searching for any information about Rick Parker. Social media pulled up nothing, and Carly wondered if he had another name. She hoped that Chris would have good news for her the next day.

Chapter 29

"**M**om," Joanie stated with authority. "Stop. Just stop. You're acting crazy. Stop stressing. It's not your wedding!"

Sheila went on and on about Jackie and Chris and the turmoil they caused her. "Can you believe I am pulling off a wedding with less than two months' notice? I have done everything, and she has done nothing to help."

Joanie couldn't believe Sheila blamed Jackie for feeling overworked. Sheila insisted on having a unicorn and sea glass candle holders for all the guests. She insisted that the wedding photos occur on the beach and the rehearsal dinner at the Country Club.

Jackie told Joanie she felt out of control. Her hormones spiked and plummeted like a roller coaster, she and Chris fought about the wedding every day, and Sheila stuck her nose in every decision.

"Mom, I don't know if this is what they want," Joanie said.

Jackie confided in Joanie that she felt torn between appeasing their mother, having the wedding of her dreams, keeping the baby safe, and considering her husband's requests. She told Joanie that she felt like every limb was being stretched in different directions, and eventually, she was going to rip into pieces.

"Joanie, I don't care. They are getting married, and it is going to be beautiful." Her icy voice echoed through the phone.

"Mom, it's a low-key wedding. There may only be a handful of guests. Invitations just went out. You can't expect people to drop everything to fly to Florida for a weekend. Just take a breath. I don't even know if I am going to make it."

Sheila sucked in an audible breath through her nose and held it for a few moments before violently expelling it from her abdomen as a deep sigh. Joanie imagined steam billowing out of Sheila's ears.

"You are going to that wedding! You are IN the wedding. You are her sister. You will be there," Sheila demanded. Sheila tsked disappointment the way she did when Joanie told her she was moving to Block Island.

"Mom, I WAS going to be there when it was here. You can't just pick up the wedding and fly it two thousand miles away and expect me to drop everything with no notice. I will know by Christmas if I can be there. Sorry. I have a job."

"A job? You barely have a job," Sheila said, her true feelings spilling out of her mouth. "Carly has a job. You are just the fill-in. You are doing a favor for a friend. That is hardly a job."

Joanie felt her face burn, simmering up from her neck to her forehead. "Thanks, Mom, for the support and confidence in my life choices. I have to go." Joanie forcefully hit the end button, wishing she held a landline so she could slam it down on the receiver. "UGH!!" she screamed at no one in particular.

She immediately picked up the phone and called Jackie.

"Hey!" Jackie chirped.

"Our mother is insane. She has lost it!" Joanie cried.

"Yeah, she's driving me crazy too," Jackie said. "Honestly, I don't even want to get married. I mean, I do, but not like this."

Joanie's fingers tensed around the phone, her breathing short and choppy. "I can't stand her. She is so self-absorbed. Jackie, I'm sorry. I love you, but I don't know if I can go to your wedding. I don't know if I can leave work for a week, and I don't know if I can be around Mom without ruining your day."

"I get it," Jackie said glumly.

"How are you feeling?" Joanie asked.

"Sick as a dog. The first trimester is almost over——thank God! I am so tired of waking up to the toilet bowl and then continuing with my day pretending like I don't have an alien growing inside me."

"I'm sorry," Joanie responded. "Don't worry about Mom. If you decide to back out or elope, or whatever, she'll get over it."

The two sisters hung up, and Joanie ventured outside to find Matt, busy shoveling the driveway. They had gotten their first real snow storm of the season, and although they didn't have any bookings, he didn't want a surprise guest to slip and fall on the driveway.

Joanie approached, the ice cracking below her boots. Matt turned. "Hey," he said, eyeing her while still shoveling.

"How's it going out here?" she asked.

"Great, almost done."

"I just talked to my mom and Jackie. I told them both I may not be going to the wedding. It's too stressful. My mother is out of control right now."

"Whatever you decide, I'm good," Matt responded. "If you go, I will take care of the inn. Maybe you and Carly can plan a girl's trip for that weekend, and if you decide to show up at the wedding, then great. If not, go to Disney, have some fun. Go to the happiest place in the world."

Joanie mulled it over, considering her options. *That could be fun to have a travel buddy and get away from the cold for a few days*, she thought. "My mother would kill me," she responded, with a grin on her face. "I think I might do it." She smiled brightly and picked up the other shovel. As her muscles contracted and relaxed with every scoop and toss, she felt her spirits rise. She was not going to let her mother control her life.

***

That evening, Carly came over to pick up her mail. "Knock-knock!!" she hollered into the kitchen. She sat at the table with her laptop and pulled up the online banking. They were still coasting on their summer profits, and Carly felt a wave of relief as she anticipated that they would survive another off-season.

She glanced down at her phone and saw email and text notifications illuminated on her home screen. Finally, she opened up her email and saw a message from rparker. She didn't know who that was and figured it was spam.

Her skin prickled when she read the subject line: **DNA results**. Her heart rate quickened, and she looked around nervously. She was afraid to read the email in the presence of others. Her legs felt weak and shaky, threatening to collapse like a detonated building.

She swallowed and opened the email. **Hi Carly. My name is Rick. I am Chris's cousin. I'm sorry it took so long for me to write back. I think you may be my sister. My mom used to talk about the child she gave up when she was in her early twenties. My grandparents took her in because she was jobless, pregnant, and single. After the baby was born, my mom started using drugs. Probably from the stress of being a new mom and feeling like a complete failure. My grandparents refused to support her unless she got clean. She ran away with the baby and came back three years later, clean and childless. No one knew where the baby went, and no one asked. My mother never gave us details. It was too painful. She married when she was thirty to my father, and they had my brother and me. Thank you for reaching out. I hope to talk to you soon. –Rick**

Carly reread the email, still not fully comprehending the severity of its message. Her mind was blank, empty, unconscious, and unable to think. Her hands chilled like the December snow. Her legs tensed, and her belly ached. Heat radiated from within, her heart beating furiously and skipping a beat. Carly wondered if she was dying, and she stood up without thinking. She paced the room from the refrigerator to the door, around the table, and back again.

She wanted to cry and wondered how she was holding it together. She had two brothers. She had a mother. Questions bumped in her brain and spilled out her ears. She stood against the edge of the kitchen table and slid down to the cool tile. She pulled her legs into her chest and squeezed, as tight as she could, digging her fingers into her legs, trying desperately to inflict pain, but her jeans were too thick. She released a single, desperate sob, emptying her lungs and her soul of everything that was keeping her alive. Her wail echoed throughout the kitchen. Hot tears rolled steadily down her cheeks.

Her entire life was a lie. Her mother was never her mother. Her father may have carried this secret to his deathbed, or he never knew. Both scenarios twisted Carly's heart. Carly cried for her father's betrayal, her mother's naivety, and her abandonment. She wished she knew earlier, but would it have been any different? Delilah wasn't ready or able to be a mother. Carly felt guilty for not feeling grateful to Ruth and Peter for taking care of her and keeping her alive.

Minutes later, or maybe it was hours, Joanie and Matt stumbled into the kitchen, laughing happily about something. Carly didn't acknowledge their boisterous laughs or rapid rate of speech. The kitchen door swung behind them. Carly sat frozen in time, watching her life go on without her.

Joanie stopped mid-sentence and saw her friend crumpled in a ball on the floor. Carly's face was white with red puffy eyes, hair disheveled, and heartbroken. Joanie ran over and wrapped her friend in a hug, unsure of the circumstances. "Carly!" she cried. "What happened?"

Carly looked at her friend and realized that her private display of vulnerability was suddenly public. She wiped her eyes aggressively. "I found my mom," she whispered.

Joanie pulled her tighter, and Carly sobbed into Joanie's shoulder. Joanie finger-brushed Carly's hair out of her eyes, wiped her tears, and whispered, "Are you okay?"

Carly laughed in disbelief. "Yeah, I'm okay—just processing. I have so many questions, and I can't think. I needed to get it all out." She giggled nervously and noticed Matt for the first time.

He slowly approached and gave her an awkward hug, his long arms pulling her close to him. "Rick?" he asked.

Carly nodded. "Yeah, he emailed me."

The three of them sat huddled in the corner. Joanie grabbed a blanket and draped it over their legs. Carly pressed herself in between Joanie and Matt, and the two of them held her up like scaffolding holding up a broken pillar. There was no noise. The three sat in silence until Carly felt strong enough to go home and be alone with her thoughts.

***

That night, Matt snuggled up against Joanie and wrapped his arms around her torso. "You're such a good friend," he whispered in her ear.

Joanie twisted, her body pressed flat against the bed, and she looked at Matt. "She's hurting. She needs someone."

"Yeah. I felt so uncomfortable there, watching her cry, not able to help her," Matt confessed. "I'm her cousin. I've known her my entire life. I should know how to comfort her."

"Matt, no offense, but you're a guy. Guys aren't overly emotional. She probably wouldn't be able to talk to you about it because you wouldn't know what to say. So I wouldn't worry about it," Joanie looked into his eyes. "Plus, you're her cousin, but you aren't overly close."

"Do you feel like you can talk to me?" he asked.

Joanie nodded. "Yeah. It's weird. When I am with you, I feel like I am home. I can just be me. I don't have to think about what everyone is thinking or if I sound stupid. You put me at ease. I can talk to you about anything." Joanie thought about their fight and her trust in sharing her past with him.

Matt held her close and paused, the words stuck on his lips. "I need to tell you something." He swallowed and stopped. "I omitted some information about myself because I was afraid to tell you. So much time passed that I felt weird bringing it up. But I think I have to because I love you, and I want to be honest with you."

Joanie froze, her body tensed, and her cold feet pressed against the footboard of her bed.

"I was married."

Joanie's face contorted into a mix of surprise, anger, and disbelief. "What?!" she exclaimed, hoping he was joking.

"I was married. Before," Matt said again. "I'm divorced now."

Joanie sat up in bed swiftly, pulling on her sweater. "What? When? This doesn't make any sense!" She couldn't believe Carly never told her after all this time. That Matt didn't tell her at some point within the past year. Feelings of betrayal and scenes of decorating for Christmas flashed in front of Joanie. Matt kept Carly's secret from Joanie, so why wouldn't Carly keep Matt's secret too?

"No one knew. No one. Not my parents, not Carly, no one. My girlfriend and I went to Vegas. One night after too many drinks and too much gambling, we ended up at a chapel. I don't even remember that night. I was twenty-three. I woke up the next morning with a piece of paper folded and stuffed in my pocket saying we were married. We were living together at the time, so we went with it. We thought we would try it out."

Joanie stared at him as he fumbled for the words to reassure her that it was indeed no big deal.

"After about six months, we broke up, filed for divorce, and that was it. Marriage over. Girlfriend, or wife, gone. I didn't tell anyone. I felt like an idiot for marrying her in the first place, a bigger idiot for not remembering the night, and the biggest idiot for paying thousands of dollars to a lawyer who wrote up the papers for a marriage that lasted six months."

"I can't believe you didn't tell me!" Joanie cried. "What was her name? Do you still talk to her?" She felt jealousy zip through her as she thought about the woman who was his wife before her. Joanie stumbled back, surprised at how she assumed she would eventually be his wife.

"I'm sorry I didn't tell you. Her name was Glory. We met at college. I haven't talked to her in over ten years since her mother died. I heard through the internet and sent her a card. I swear, Joanie, that's the last time I saw or heard from her."

Joanie felt her heart drop to her feet but didn't understand why. She would have expected to be surprised but not angry. She had a past too. Joanie wasn't sure if it was his lying that flamed anger within her or the sacred vow of marriage he so quickly threw away that scared her. Either way, she was angry and needed to get away from him.

Suspicion grew as she questioned the validity of his story. What else was he hiding? They had been dating over a year. Matt had numerous opportunities to tell her about his past marriage, and he chose to keep it to himself. Joanie's imagination ran wild as she created an unbelievable life he shared with Glory and wondered what really happened. True love, jealous ex-wives, and children galloped around the dark recesses of her mind and slowly burned a hole in her heart. She wanted to ask questions, but the fear and doubt in pursuing her life with him stomped on her trust within his answers.

"You need to go," she said, opening the door. "I need some space." Spittle shot from her mouth, but she didn't care.

Matt collected his car keys and wallet and turned to face her at the door.

179

"I'm sorry," he said. "It was nothing, and I should have told you."

Joanie nodded, unable to speak, and closed the door as he turned to leave.

She picked up a glass bowl and threw it at the door, screaming in angst. The shatter reverberated throughout her tiny apartment, and suddenly it was silent. She could only hear the hum of the electric heater as it warmed her up from the icy outside.

She felt like everything around her was disintegrating. She needed to talk to someone but didn't know who. She was alone.

Chapter 30

C arly texted Chris almost every hour until he finally called her to tell her to stop texting.

"I'm at work!" he hissed into the phone.

"Chris, I have to talk to you! This is important! Please! Can you give me three minutes?" she begged.

He sighed loudly, annoyance penetrating his voice. "You have three minutes. No more," he said coldly.

"Rick emailed me."

"I know. He cc'd me on the email. I read it," Chris responded. Carly felt somewhat betrayed that Rick shared this personal moment with Chris without her consent. She also felt ignored that Chris didn't think to call her after this life-shaking revelation.

"Oh," was all she said. A moment later, she tried again, chipper this time. "So what do I do? I know Delilah is my mother. Are you in touch with her?" she asked anxiously, playing with her necklace.

"I'm not. Delilah and my mother had a falling out when I was a kid. The last time I recall seeing her was for a funeral. I can't remember who. I was just a kid, but that was the last time I saw her. After that, my parents wanted nothing to do with her. They never said why."

Carly's mind processed all this information. "Don't you get it?" she cried. "My father slept with your aunt. She gave birth to me, realized she couldn't take care of me, probably went to your parents asking for help. They knew my parents wanted a kid. Maybe they knew my dad was the father, and they dropped the baby off on the porch. Your mom disapproved of what they were doing, so they had a falling out." Carly hadn't thought about it before, but it made complete sense as the words tumbled out of her mouth.

"I only have one more minute," Chris chimed in. "I don't know, Carly. It seems far-fetched."

"Only because you aren't looking at the clues!" she interrupted.

"Yeah, maybe. I have no idea where she is or if she's still alive."

"I'm emailing Rick back," Carly said. "Maybe he can help me."

"Okay, good luck. I have to run." The words came out like an eight-syllable word.

"Thanks for listening. Talk to you soon," Carly said sarcastically. She hung up the phone, amazed at her detective skills. She figured it out!

She pulled up the email and reread it. Carly responded and included Chris in the message because it would look weird if she deleted him. It took her forty-five minutes to formulate a paragraph asking for information about his mother, her age, and where she lived. Finally, Carly deleted it all and wrote **Can I call you? What's your number?**

She hit SEND before she could question her response and delete it for a final time.

Her leg shook, and her toe tapped against the hard floor. She wondered how long it would take for Rick to write back. She could either keep busy or obsessively pine for her phone to ding. She grabbed a shovel to clear her walkway from the previous snowstorm. The snow was hard and heavy, but it felt good on her muscles to push herself through the emotional strain pressed upon her. Twenty minutes later, she moved onto the main driveway and widened it with short, heavy heaps of snow. She needed to calm her body, and shoveling in the cold was just enough to numb her mind and muscles.

When she got back inside, she grabbed her phone and opened up her email. There it was. His number glowed like a winning lottery ticket. Carly hit the number before she could think. The phone rang in her ear like an oncoming freight train. She considered hanging up, but a deep, male voice answered before she could disengage the call.

"Hi Rick, this is Carly." The words tumbled and fell like a waterfall down a mountain. "I just saw your email."

"Hi, Carly. Nice to meet you." He sounded kind enough. His voice had the after effect of southern drawl, and Carly wondered where he grew up and where he lived now.

An awkward silence filled the space between them. Carly knew it was her turn to speak, but nothing was coming to her. There were so many questions but no clear-cut direction on where to start.

"Uhhh..." she said, feeling her neck redden under her turtleneck sweater and rising to her cheeks.

"How can I help you? It sounds like you're my sister," Rick began.

At the word sister, Carly felt a prickle of tears threaten to fall.

"Yes, I don't know who I am." She told him the story of the DNA results, Mrs. Jackson, Chris, and Mary. "What do you think?"

Without his DNA results next to hers, there was no way to know if she was speaking to her brother. Instead, she wanted to see his face and identify the traits they shared.

"It could be," he said. "My mom never talked about it. I only heard about the baby when she was fighting with my grandparents when I was a kid. They died a long time ago. The details are fuzzy."

His grandparents were Chris's grandparents, and possibly her grandparents too.

"What did they say?" Carly asked. She had to know.

"Just that it wasn't the baby's fault Mom couldn't get clean. They tried their hardest to help her, but that didn't mean they would raise the child for her. If she messed up one more time, she was out on the street. And they did. From what I gathered, that was the last they saw of the baby. They didn't have any rights to the baby, even though it sounded like my mom wasn't able to take care of it."

The baby. The child. She had a name, and it was Carly Davis. She knew Rick was trying to be polite, but her maybe-mother gave her away to strangers. She deserved to have a name.

"Do you know what my name was?"

"Nah, sorry. No one ever said your name."

Carly's heart dropped in sorrow. She wasn't wanted, and she wasn't worthy of being known as a person with a name. She tried to hang up, but her hand pressed the phone against her ear. She hoped for more resolution, but she only had more questions.

"Where do you live? Where did you grow up? Did you have a happy childhood?" Carly shot out the bullet questions in rapid succession.

"My parents and I lived in Ohio for most of my childhood. My mom and dad moved to Florida because it was cheaper. I followed. I live near Tampa, and my parents live about a half-hour away."

"Are you married?" Carly changed the subject.

"Nah, not yet."

"How old are you?" Carly asked.

"Thirty-six."

"Do you have any siblings?" She already knew the answer.

"Yeah, one brother. His name's Charlie." Carly thought it was odd that Chris never mentioned a brother.

"How old is he?"

"Thirty-two."

"Is he married?"

"Yeah, married with three kids."

Carly's heart dropped to her belly button. Two brothers and three nieces and nephews? Anger flared out Carly's nostrils at Delilah for denying her the family she always wanted.

"Where does he live?" she asked.

"New York."

"So, what do you think?" Carly asked after a moment of silence. "Could she be my mother?"

"Could be. As I said, I don't know. Everything seems to match up, but it feels unreal."

Carly nodded in agreement even though he couldn't see her. "Would you like to video chat with Charlie and me? I'd like to see you guys face to face." Carly asked.

"Yeah, I can ask him. I'll email you. When Chris contacted me, I thought he was full of shit, but now I wonder. I'd like to see you, see if we look similar."

Carly knew in her gut that Delilah was her mother. She had a general idea of why Delilah gave her away but still didn't understand the relationship between her and Peter and how Ruth and Peter secretly adopted her.

Carly said goodbye to her maybe-brother and sat with herself, unsure how to feel or if she even wanted to feel.

A few days later, Carly and Joanie found the perfect Christmas tree for the carriage house. The inn could look classy with its artificial tree, but the carriage house would smell like the holidays.

When Carly was a little girl, Peter and Ruth took her to the only Christmas tree farm on the island. It wasn't even a farm, but more like a farm stand. The trees were shipped over for the islanders who lived there year-round.

Every December, she and Peter picked out the perfect tree. It couldn't be too tall or too fat and required enough branches to hold the many ornaments and lights. Then, they drove home with the tree strapped to the roof, even though the farm was less than three miles away from the inn.

Peter stood up the tree, and Carly and Ruth decorated the branches with old, new, unique, and ordinary ornaments. When they finished, the tree glowed rainbow colors, and a radiant yellow angel adorned the top.

Once Peter died, and Carly moved back home, Ruth was unable to manage a real tree. Carly convinced Ruth that an artificial tree would be best, but of course, Ruth wouldn't have it. It was a battle between the two women, and in the end, Carly won.

Now, standing in the parking lot with their parkas zipped to their chin, Carly and Joanie selected an imperfectly perfect tree. It was short and stocky, with many branches to hang ornaments and memories. One side of the tree was bushier than the other, and one single branch stood tall on top of the tree. It would be perfect for a golden star, Carly thought.

"So," Joanie interrupted. "What are your plans for Christmas?"

Carly shrugged. "Sandra invited me over, but she also invited her new family. I think it would be too weird for me to be there. I want them to experience their new family with just them. I probably will stay home and enjoy the quiet. You're going to Florida, right? Do you need me to watch the inn for you?"

The attendant strapped the tree to Matt's truck, which Carly borrowed for the day.

"Yeah, I will be gone for two nights. Matt will be here too. Maybe you guys could have your own little family thing. I feel terrible leaving him on Christmas, but he can't take off work, and if I'm not going to the wedding, I have to see my family for Christmas."

Alarm bells rang loudly in Carly's ears. "Did you decide you aren't going?"

"I can't," Joanie replied. "If my mom thinks I'm going to drop everything for her, she's wrong. I can't, and I don't want to. She'll get over it." Joanie threw up her hands in exasperation, her volume increasing with every word.

"Is she that bad?" Carly asked although she had an inkling of an idea of what it was like to grow up as Joanie.

"Worse than that. The worst."

"You need to do you. How old are you? Forty? You're a grown woman. You don't need to prove yourself to anyone. I love you, just the way you are."

Joanie hmphed.

"Sorry to bring up the wedding," Carly cringed at the sore topic, "but what are the wedding plans now?"

"Wedding on the golf course and the beach at my parents. My mother is a psycho and wants to make all the decisions. Jackie is finally seeing her for her true colors, which is why I don't want to be there. The wedding is taking place in Clearwater."

"What part of Florida is Clearwater?" Carly asked.

"It's right near Tampa."

Carly's heart skipped a beat, knowing Rick lived in Tampa, and Delilah wasn't too far from there. "Jackie invited me to the original wedding," she said sweetly. "Does that mean she'll invite me to the wedding in Florida? I could benefit from a vacation."

"Yeah, if I'm here with Matt, you don't have to stay and watch over the inn. I got it."

Carly turned on the car and drove out of the parking lot.

Somehow, things started to turn around and fall into place. Carly was going to meet her family!

Chapter 31

C arly looked at the two men she believed were her brothers and was blown away by the round eyes, thin lips, and glossy hair. They even spoke with the same intonation pattern, which felt strange since they lived in entirely different parts of the country. If those men wore wigs, they would pass off as her sisters.

Carly knew she was the outsider, unfamiliar with both of them, and she had to play it cool. She didn't want them to text all night to each other complaining about how boring, or needy, or undeserving she was of their siblingship. Instead, she needed them to text about how excited they were to meet her and want to get to know her better.

They talked for about twenty minutes, and the questions flew off her tongue like confetti escaping from a pinata. She learned that Rick was single and a mechanic and Charlie's wife was named Talia. His three girls were named Josie, McKenna, and Scarlett. Rick loved baseball, and Charlie lived in the suburbs. Rick never went to college, and Charlie was valedictorian. The amount of factual information about these two men overwhelmed Carly, and she wondered if she had first date jitters or job interview anxiety.

Delilah was sixty years old, which meant she was twenty when Carly was born. Carly sighed with relief, knowing that her father wasn't into obscenely young girls, which was a thought that crossed her mind when learning about Mary. She wondered how Delilah and Peter met but didn't feel comfortable asking her maybe-brothers if they knew anything. That question would be for Delilah.

Delilah got clean when she met Larry, Charlie and Rick's father. She spoke about her sobriety their entire lives and often spoke of her regrets, making Carly feel a little less unwanted.

Larry was a decade older than Delilah, which may have been a consistent attraction for her, considering Peter was twenty years her senior. On the other hand, Delilah may have been looking for a father figure or someone who experienced more life than her. Whatever it was, Larry fell for her, and Delilah needed him. The result was thirty years of marriage before Larry died of a heart attack unexpectedly.

From what Carly gathered, Delilah was much closer to Rick. Carly wondered what the story was with her relationship with Charlie.

Carly's impression of Charlie was that he was more social than Rick. On the video chat, he wore a sweater vest, which reminded Carly of Peter. His short, blond hair and blue eyes gazed at her from the screen.

Rick had longer hair that stopped just below his ears. His face was stubbled and bristly, and he wore a t-shirt and baseball cap. They looked like complete opposites, similar to Joanie and Jackie. Carly wondered if the two men were close.

As the conversation ended, Carly felt pressured to ask about the wedding because she was running out of time. Her hands were wet, and she wiped them on her denim jeans before readjusting her hair. Finally, when there was silence and Carly believed she would miss her chance if she waited another moment, she blurted out her request.

"I am going to a wedding in January. In Florida. Right near you, Rick. It's actually for your cousin, Chris. I don't know if you or your mom got an invite or not, but I am inviting you. Would you like to come and meet me? And please, bring your mom too. I must meet her, and I don't know when I'll have another chance." Carly held her breath, waiting. She didn't know if Chris invited Delilah, but Carly assumed she could take Joanie's ticket.

No one responded, and Carly lowered her eyes to her hands, which crumpled a damp tissue.

"Sure. Are you sure you want me to bring my mom? She can be a handful. Am I supposed to tell her about you?"

"No, please don't. If you do, she won't come. Invite her to the wedding, tell her it is for Chris, her nephew, and it's less than an hour away. Tell her there will be free food and drinks. Tell her whatever you want, but please don't tell her about me."

Charlie chimed in, "Come on, man, it could be good for her."

"Sure," Rick said. "I'll see what I can do. Send me the info—-date, time, location, that kind of thing. If we can't make it, I'll let you know. Otherwise, expect to see us there."

Carly was ecstatic on the inside but cool as a cucumber on the outside. She didn't want her maybe-brothers to think she was strange or decide they didn't want to keep in touch with her.

They all waved to each other goodbye, and the call disconnected. Carly turned up her radio and danced to the music, alone in her kitchen, feeling alive for the first time in months.

Once the euphoria dissipated, she reached for her phone and called Sandra.

"You won't believe this!" Carly exclaimed. She felt like she was in the middle of a dream. The joyous feeling threatened to mutate into a nightmare. One more month, and she would know her answer.

The following week, Carly walked on cloud nine, filled with nervous energy and unparalleled excitement. She thought about the wedding and if it would be weird to show up without Joanie. In the not-too-distant past, Jackie considered Carly to be her wedding planner because she organized all the Block Island plans. Sheila took over that role, but Carly was still ready to play. She spent many hours emailing, researching, and calling places for Jackie. Carly deserved to be at the wedding. Not to mention Chris was her cousin.

She thought about what she was going to wear. First, she wanted to make a brilliant impression on her maybe-mother. Second, she wished to make Delilah regretful for giving up Carly. Finally, she wanted her brothers to meet her and want to see her again.

She had to wear something comfortable but professional because she needed to find out what happened between Delilah and Peter and how she ended up in their life. Carly scanned her closet and pulled out the black fitted knee-length dress she last wore to her mother's funeral. She put it back quickly and pulled her hand away like the fabric scalded her. She flipped through all the hangers and decided she needed to go shopping to find the perfect ensemble.

She thought about the risks of meeting her maybe-mother unannounced. Delilah would probably turn away, angry darts thrown from her eyes to her boys for scheming with Carly. Carly had been practicing what she would say: *Hi, Mom. Remember me?*; *Hi, my name is Carly Davis. Chris is my cousin. How do you know the bride and groom?*; *I hate you! (followed by pounding fists on her shoulders).*

No matter how she approached it—calm, angry, or innocent—-it never felt right. Nothing she practiced would feel right until the words were spilling out of her mouth like an overflowing bathtub.

The only person she could talk to was Sandra because Sandra understood the emotions and the fears attached to this sudden reunification. Carly texted and called Sandra multiple times a day, which bothered Carly because she had never been this needy. She searched for reassurance that she wasn't making a colossal mistake.

Carly researched airfare and hotels and secured both with a pit of fear rolling around her belly. It was happening. Carly was going to meet her family.

Chapter 32

C arly and Matt looked at each other across the table and ate from overflowing plates of Chinese food. Finally, it was Christmas, and the two of them were alone. Christmas music played faintly over the radio, and a fresh dusting of snow coated the outside world.

"Cheers," Carly said, raising a glass. "To family. Merry Christmas."

Matt raised his glass and nodded. "Merry Christmas."

They ate their food in silence. Carly wondered what Rick was doing and if he was with Delilah.

"So, what's up with you and Joanie?" Carly asked abruptly. It had been three weeks since their fight. Joanie came to Carly, upset about the marriage, and Carly could give her no words of advice because she was also in the dark. She told Joanie to give Matt the benefit of the doubt.

"It's been weird. She's been weird. She feels like I was withholding information from her, which I was, but it was only because I knew she would act like this." Matt took a big bite of eggroll, and soy sauce seeped down the sides.

"I had no idea you were married," Carly said. "If I had known, I would have told her."

"No one knew," Matt said simply. "I haven't talked to Glory in years. It was a mistake, and we both agreed it was a mistake. There are no hard feelings between us. It's truly in the past. I wish Joanie realized that because I like her. I love her."

Carly nodded, wondering why Matt didn't tell her from the beginning. She tried to put herself in his shoes. A single man, living on an island with people who knew his entire history and family history, unable to meet someone new. Then, he falls in love with a woman who knows nothing about him. It probably felt too risky to tell her.

Carly understood but still felt sympathetic towards Joanie. "Have you talked to her?"

"Eh," he took a sip of beer. "Not really. Just the cordial conversation about the inn. She told me she isn't going to Jackie's wedding, which means I'm not going either—-which is fine!" he defended. "Now we have nothing to talk about."

"I'm sure she'll come around. I know she loves you."

"What about you? How are you feeling? About everything," Matt asked.

"I'm still processing and still have so many questions. I can't figure out how I ended up with my parents with no one knowing, and I can't figure out if my dad knew that he was my father." Carly poured herself another glass of water, her chalky mouth preventing her from swallowing.

"What are you going to say to your mother?" Matt asked.

"I don't know. Whatever comes out of my mouth. I can't think about it too much. I have to see her and see her reaction to me first. I'm terrified she doesn't want to meet me." Carly looked down and picked at her fingernails. Suddenly, she looked up silently with urgency in her eyes.

"What," Matt inquired.

"You can help me! You work for the police and have access to everything! I searched online for info but came up blank. Can you search the database for information about a baby in a basket around 1977?" Carly's eyes glistened with hope.

Matt looked at her. Carly could see the uncertainty in his eyes. "I don't know, Carly. 1977 is a long time. That would take forever."

Carly didn't want to push him. He had already done so much, keeping her secret from Joanie and pretending to fix things in her house so she could talk to Chris.

She nodded. "I get it. If I come back empty-handed from the wedding, will you help me?"

Matt took a deep breath and audibly sighed. "Fine."

Carly clapped her hands quickly, her jubilant face exposing her excitement. "Thank you!"

"Are you going to ask Chris's parents about Delilah?"

"Probably," Carly continued to smile, a plan forming. "I'm going to get as much information as I can. I'm nervous, though. This could screw everything up. I could lose it all." She took a bite of rice and smiled, herbs stuck between her teeth.

"Life's too short. You're what, forty years old? Screw it. Just go up to them and tell them you know. Then, introduce yourself to Delilah. Tell her you're Peter's daughter. See what she does."

Carly nodded. He was right. She wasn't a child anymore. She was a grown adult who didn't need a mom, but she did need transparency about her past. The only person who could give that to her was Delilah. She would be brave, carry confidence, and expect the worst because anything better than the worst would only add disappointment to an already disappointing situation.

Carly and Matt sat in silence, each lost in their own dilemma. Carly's anger toward her parents had subsided, but empowerment set in. But, unfortunately, the wedding was a few weeks away, and life was going to turn Carly on her heel again.

The next time Joanie saw Matt was on New Year's Eve. Joanie noticed the motion sensor in the driveway kick on, and a spotlight shined on Matt's truck. Joanie approached the truck and saw Matt in the driver's seat with his eyes closed. She saw a case of beer nestled against him. She gently rapped on the window, concerned that he had been drinking and driving. Matt rolled down the window and shivered.

"What are you doing here?" Joanie hissed. She inhaled deeply. The familiar scent of his aftershave wafted through the window. An intense longing encased her, and Joanie fought back the urge to kiss him.

"I needed to see you. I brought beer. Do you want to talk? I don't have to come in. You can sit in the car with me, or I can sit outside in the cold with you. It's been too long since we last talked." Matt waited, and Joanie contemplated her choices.

She opened the passenger door and climbed inside. "I have guests inside."

She didn't say another word and looked ahead out the windshield, which accumulated tiny snowflakes. She patted her pockets with her cold hands and searched for her mittens.

"I'm sorry for not telling you earlier," Matt said. "It was years and years ago. I was young and stupid, and I didn't take it seriously. I regret marrying her, but it happened."

"Why didn't you tell me sooner?" The question shot out like an arrow, her voice stiff and straight.

"It didn't seem important. We were dating and having fun. I didn't want to complicate things."

"Wait," Joanie stopped him. "We were dating and having fun? That's it? You got married, Matt. Till death do you part. It hurt me. I loved you, and I was in love with you! You should have told me from the beginning. What else are you not telling me?" Matt winced at the word *was*.

"I do love you!" he exclaimed. "I AM in love with you! That's why I told you! We started as fun and turned into something serious, Joanie!" He turned to face her and held her eyes. "I am in love with you," he repeated. "I told you because I want to marry you. I want you by my side for the rest of my life. Don't you get that? I am madly in love with you!"

Joanie turned her head, breaking his gaze. Her whole body stiffened, and she couldn't think. Every emotion poured from her limbs to her heart: anger, joy, excitement, lust, and love. They met in the middle of her body, and butterflies rose from her abdomen to her chest. Somehow his apology turned into a hypothetical proposal.

Joanie focused on her breathing and calmed her mind. A magnetic force took over her movements, and suddenly she pressed her lips against him. The heat between them burned her. She hadn't kissed him in weeks, and her desire for his closeness pulled her to him like a magnet. She aggressively kissed his relaxed lips and warmed them against hers. She continued onto his temple, eyes, nose, and chin. The yearning for him was so intense, she felt like her heart was going to burst through her chest, and she couldn't stop.

Somehow, they ended up in her apartment. They pulled off each other's clothes as soon as the door closed. It was frantic and passionate and powerful, and Joanie never felt so much like a desired, wanted woman. That night they reconnected and healed old wounds. It was a night that Joanie had been dreaming about for weeks. She loved him, and more importantly, was in love with him. She wanted to be his wife. She always dreamed of falling head over heels in love but never thought she truly deserved that kind of passion. Finally, Matt taught her that she did deserve it.

She deserved a good man who would do anything for her. She wanted to love Matt for the rest of their lives. Joanie fell asleep with a smile on her face feeling protected from the pain her past caused.

Chapter 33

Carly sat at the restaurant table alone, despite the three table settings. She discreetly watched the people enter from behind the top of her menu. She wore oversized sunglasses that hid her eyes and her edginess. Her knee shook and bumped below the table like a metronome, causing her water to jiggle. Despite the high-eighties and pure sunshine today, goosebumps rose on her forearms.

She waited almost twenty minutes and so far, nothing.

"Excuse me, ma'am, would you like to order?" Carly retreated into herself at the word *ma'am*. Did she look that old?

"Sure, I will start with the garden salad." She couldn't imagine eating but knew she had to order. People were starting to stare. She thought meeting at a restaurant would be a good idea, being on neutral territory, but occupying the table alone increased her nervousness.

The waiter rushed away, grabbed a salad, and quickly placed it in front of her with a smile.

Carly wondered if she had the wrong restaurant or the wrong time. She rechecked her messages. Nothing.

Regret set in, and feelings of stupidity and inadequacy started to press into her mind like a tightening anvil. There was so much at stake this weekend.

Carly slowly ate her salad, trying to extend her time in the restaurant as naturally as possible. Eventually, the waiter came over to retrieve her plate, and Carly rechecked her watch. She had been sitting there for around twenty-five minutes. She felt hot tears prick her eyes but knew no one could see because of her sunglasses. She looked ridiculous wearing the oversized shades inside, but that was the arrangement she and Rick made to identify her.

She looked at her dimmed phone and wondered if Rick and Delilah would show.

Instead of ordering a meal, Carly ordered dessert. She felt sick to her stomach. Her brain told her to get up and leave and go home to Rhode Island. She didn't need a mother or a brother. She needed to be home, where she felt safe.

Her legs stayed firmly rooted to the wooden seat, despite her willingness to leave.

Jackie's wedding was the next day, and Carly wondered if her entire trip was a farce. Great expectations haunted her at night. She imagined Delilah swooping in, apologizing, and showing gratitude. Carly fought back the tears of foolishness from forming.

This meal was the first step, but there was either a miscommunication or an unwavering reluctance to come. Carly wondered what Rick told Delilah and how she responded. Why wouldn't he text Carly and let her know, instead of having her sit at the restaurant alone, waiting and hoping for nothing?

Carly ate the cheesecake without tasting it.She downed the rest of her water and picked up the check at the end of the table. She doubled the tip to make up for holding the server's table for almost an hour.

With her head hung low, she exited the restaurant and sat in her rental car, wondering what she was doing in Florida. All the confidence she carried moments before their dinner reservations blew out of her like a leaky balloon. She took off her sunglasses and let the frustrated tears fall. Hope disintegrated, and she felt her soul harden.

Next time, she wasn't going to allow herself to get hurt.

Carly navigated back to the hotel and lay in bed, letting the monotonous sounds of television fill the background. She didn't understand what happened or why no one showed up or texted to cancel. She was upset with Delilah but also upset with Rick. He was supposed to be on her side.

Carly texted Rick two question marks and nothing else to symbolize her frustration. She threw her phone in her bag and changed into her bathing suit. Florida was still hot in the middle of January. Carly refused to allow Delilah or Rick to ruin her mini-vacation. The hotel was right on the beach, and Carly pulled her beach bag over her shoulder and walked out into the sand.

The sand was warm and soft. It was nothing like the rocky beaches in New England. She could sleep on this sand and be comfortable. She leaned back in the striped beach chair and felt the silky, velvety exfoliation rub against her toes.

Carly checked her phone to find two unread texts. The first was from Sandra: **Call me! I hope your trip is going okay.**

The second was from Rick: **Sorry! I thought we were meeting tomorrow, before the wedding.**

Carly rolled her eyes. She wanted to accept his excuse but felt the wall around her heart thicken. She wrote back to Rick: **Nope. Today. No problem. Will I see you tomorrow?** She didn't want to make her maybe-brother mad and cause him to shut down.

He replied: **Yes—5:30 at the Country Club. We will be there. Chris knows.**

Carly smiled smugly and reminded herself not to get too excited because they might not show again.

She spent the rest of the evening trying to keep her mind clear. She called Sandra, checked in with Joanie, took a nap, and went into town to do last-minute shopping. She wanted to look fantastic tomorrow.

Carly wanted to wow Delilah and make her feel terrible for giving up such an incredible human. She wanted Delilah to feel shame for abandoning her and feel inadequate when she realized just how well-rounded, kind, caring, and put-together Carly was. Carly wanted to know the truth.

The next afternoon, Carly took twice as long to get ready. Every hair was securely in place, her makeup was perfect, and the jewelry she purchased made her shine and sparkle. She selected a floral dress that cascaded down to her ankles. The form-fitting bodice and wide skirt reminded her of Cinderella. The silver pendant necklace she found hit right in the middle of her breastplate, accentuating the cut of her neckline. She wore an equally sparkly bracelet. Her black, strappy sandals were not the most comfortable, but the pain was worth it to complete her look.

She felt in control, confident, and strong. She was a Davis. A survivor. A problem solver. She could feel Peter's strength and support run through her veins. She heard Ruth ask if she knew what she was doing. Carly snuffed out the hesitancy from Ruth and focused on Peter. She was Peter's daughter.

Carly grabbed her black sequined clutch and walked through the hotel lobby with her head held high. Dread draped over her as Carly believed people were staring, and she somehow mustered up the confidence to keep walking. She was going to meet her mother.

Chapter 34

The perfectly cut green grass and vast rolling hills overlooked the ocean. Bundles of flowers decorated the pavilion. Soft elevator music filled the air from the loudspeakers in the back. Despite the high humidity and eighty-degree temperature, people dressed in long and short dresses, tuxes, and suits. It was a fancy occasion, and no one seemed bothered by the weather.

Joanie's parents had money, and they certainly wanted to flaunt it for all the guests to see. The landscape of the country club far surpassed the meadow behind the inn.

There was an air of elegance and arrogance as Carly approached Sheila to say hello. Sheila gave her a curt smile, kissed her once on each cheek, and squeezed her hand, thanking her for coming. Carly wasn't sure if Sheila recognized her without Joanie by her side.

The wedding would begin in thirty minutes, and guests slowly filled the empty seats set up on the pavilion. Carly sat alone and immediately felt out of place. She haphazardly maneuvered between guests and employees of the country club to quickly find a new seat where she could watch people without being noticed.

Carly grabbed a glass of wine from one of the server's trays and took a quick sip, hoping to relax her nerves. She saw Charlene in the distance but wasn't confident that Charlene would remember her. Carly sank lower in her seat, pulled her hat over her eyes, and looked ahead.

The constant movement of guests made her dizzy. Carly rose from her seat and removed a freshly poured wine glass from a serving tray. She emptied the glass in three sips, and hints of apple exploded in her mouth. Carly grabbed another drink and walked back to her seat.

Carly blinked back tears when she saw Rick. He sat next to an older woman who looked like Rhonda Swanson. Carly squeezed the stem of her wine glass, her fingers turning white. Her breath caught in her throat, her shoulders tensed, and her body stiffened. Delilah.

Rick appeared anxious as well, squeezing the chair's seat and darting his eyes impulsively around the pavilion. Carly noticed the bottle of beer that quickly drained into his belly. He looked in her direction but scanned over her amongst the crowd.

Rick and Delilah sat a few rows ahead on the other side of the aisle. Carly still wore her oversized sunglasses and sun hat, but this time didn't look quite so out of place. The sun shined brightly overhead. Rick continued to scan the crowd repetitively-back and forth-back and forth-while maintaining small talk with those sitting near him. It was evident he was looking for Carly but had not yet found her.

The organ music started, and everyone ooh'd and aah'd and shifted in their seats. For a last-minute wedding, it appeared that most of the guests showed up. At first, Carly was unsure if she was making a mistake. Now, Carly was grateful that the large crowd of people could disguise her. She wasn't quite ready to be approached or found.

Chris stood up front, standing next to the officiant, looking down past the guests. The groomsmen and groomswoman stood next to him in a straight line. Charlene looked beautiful in her fitted tux with a single rose affixed in her hair.

Then, one by one, the flower girl, bridesmaids, and maid of honor moved toward the front of the altar to the beat of the music. Bright red smiles pulled across their faces, and flowers covered their bodies. The red heart-shaped necklines accentuated their collar bones, and the flowing, long skirts gave Carly the impression that they were floating toward the altar.

Carly scanned the wedding party and imagined Joanie there. Jackie was right. With an uneven number of groomsmen and bridesmaids, the wedding party looked off-kilter. Carly wondered how Jackie felt knowing her sister was home on her big day.

The music changed, and Jackie stood, arm linked through her father's arm. Her dress was long, flowy, and beautiful. Her face glowed with radiance. Tiny, white pearls cascaded and sparkled against her fiery locks. Carly knew how complex the wedding planning was for Jackie to manage, and it was evident that she was pleased with the results. She got her beach wedding after all.

As soon as Chris saw Jackie, he stood like a statue, smiled wide, body tensed, and eyes filled with wonder. The officiant made his remarks, Jackie and Chris said their vows, and Chris kissed his bride passionately, throwing her body backward. Carly saw the outline of a slight bump as Jackie twisted back unexpectedly. Jackie pulled herself to a standing position, grabbed Chris's hand, and held it over her head like she won the first-place trophy.

After the wedding, Jackie and Chris climbed onto a white horse with elegant legs and flowing white hair. On its head stood an erect horn that glittered in the sun. Jewels glistened under and above its eyes and around the crown of its head. Gemstone barrettes decorated the horse's tail and mane.

Jackie sat tall in front of Chris on the unicorn's back. She held onto the bedazzled reins, and Chris wrapped his arms around Jackie's torso, his fingers barely touching due to the excess material of her dress. They both smiled, their white teeth flashing to the audience, and waved upon their departure. Shiela beamed, pride springing from her eyes.

Carly laughed to herself, knowing how badly Jackie wanted to ride away into the sunset on a unicorn. The wedding guests clapped, cheered, and blew bubbles as the couple exited the ceremony. The sun started its descent, and the sky became dotted with purple and pink hues. Chris and Jackie rode off into the horizon, just as she had dreamed.

The guests filed into the country club for the reception. Carly saw Rick stalling outside the water fountain, with Delilah by his side. Then, like energy that swooped inside her and carried her beside him, she found herself staring face to face with her maybe-brother and maybe-mother.

Carly pulled off her glasses and made eye contact with Rick. "Hello, Rick," Carly said, biting her lower lip. Her fingers tingled, and she felt faint. Delilah looked at her curiously, but Carly paid no attention.

"Carly!" he exclaimed. "Good to see you!" He gave her a big hug and a tight squeeze. Carly's heart soared and exploded.

"Hello," Delilah said in a deep, raspy voice. She gave a slight wave, unable to shake hands due to a cigarette in one hand and a glass of wine in the other.

"Mom, this is Carly. Carly Davis. She and I met over the internet. She's from Block Island."

Ah, so this is how we are going to do it.

If Delilah recognized the name or the location, she didn't react.

"Mom," Rick continued, "Isn't that where Aunt Rhonda and Uncle Doug lived?"

"Yeah, small world," she responded

"Carly, how do you know the bride and groom?" Rick asked innocently.

"Oh, Chris is my cousin, and Jackie is my best friend's sister."

"Small world!" Rick replied. "Chris is my cousin too!"

Delilah was now picking up on the connection between her son and his new friend. Her eyes darted back and forth to Rick and Carly as they casually talked about family, Block Island, and the weather. Then, suddenly, Delilah's color drained from her face, and Carly gazed at a sheet of a person. "What did you say your last name was?" she asked suspiciously.

"Davis. My mom was Ruth, and my father was Peter." Carly watched Delilah stumble backward, the heel of her shoe catching on a rock. "Hi, Mom," she said snidely.

Delilah immediately turned and walked away at a quick clip.

"Mom!" Rick called, running after her.

Carly stood alone at the water fountain, stunned by the chain of events that just occurred. Delilah's response solidified her hypothesis that she was Carly's mother. Carly wondered if anyone milling around heard them or if their interaction appeared out of place. She felt like the crowd was staring at her, and she smiled sadly. Carly brushed her hands down her dress and walked toward her car with her head held high.

At the country club exit, she bumped into Rhonda and Doug, mingling by the coatroom.

"Carly!" Rhonda exclaimed. "Chris told us you were coming! It's so nice to see you. It's been, what, twenty years?"

Carly shot her a look of ice, hoping to pierce her heart. "Yeah, twenty years. Just enough time for me to figure out that I was adopted and Delilah is my mother." She pushed past Rhonda with a slight hip bump and hurried to her car.

Carly closed the door of her rental, and as the click of the door sounded, the floodgates opened. She cried tears that turned from anger to sadness to disbelief. She was rejected a second time by her mother. She looked at the ceiling of her car, apologized to Ruth and Peter for being so inconsiderate, and thanked them for everything they did.

She thought it would be a good idea to meet Delilah, but abandonment filled her again. Her birth mother didn't want her. The unfairness, the hypocrisy, and the rejection sat on her like an elephant.

She couldn't speak but needed to talk to someone. She texted Sandra: **I met her. She ran away as fast as she could. This was a huge mistake.**

Carly maneuvered the rental back to the hotel through blurry eyes. She stripped out of her clothes slowly, angrily tossing the beautiful dress and jewelry she so carefully selected for the big night on the perfectly made bed. Carly scolded herself for being such an optimist and, as a result, such an idiot. Finally, she climbed into bed and hid under the heavy blankets, wondering what she did that made Delilah hate her so much.

Chapter 35

The following day, Carly woke to warm sunshine penetrating her face. It was only seven, and the warmth from the sun was causing her to sweat from her hairline. She groaned, realizing that she forgot to turn on the air last night.

She checked her phone and found three apologetic texts from Sandra. Reading them made Carly cry again because it reinforced how stupid she was by thinking Delilah would reciprocate. Carly didn't reply. She also had two texts from Rick. The first text apologized for how the night unfolded, and the second one asked if she wanted to go out for lunch to talk. Carly had to get to the airport around noontime, and even if she stayed in Florida, she didn't have it in her. Her heart broke in two.

She showered in scalding hot water, hoping to burn her skin so severely that it prevented her from feeling. The superheated water was so hot, she cried out in pain until her insides were hollow, and her heart cried. She threw on jeans and a t-shirt, pressed a baseball cap over her wet head, and went to the lobby to grab some coffee and breakfast.

The breakfast tasted like cardboard, stiff and chalky in her mouth. Carly returned to her room to pack and leave for the airport early. All Carly wanted to do was get home to The Willowside Inn and be in a place where she felt most comfortable.

The airport bustled with people, probably returning home from their winter escape. "Ma'am," the woman behind the counter said, "you are four hours early for your flight."

"Yes, I know. If you have anything earlier, I would appreciate it." Carly wore her oversized sunglasses, hiding the cotton candy pink circles around her blue irises. She knew she would have to remove them eventually but wasn't ready to do that until requested.

The woman behind the counter clicked on keys and stared ahead at the screen for a few moments. "We do have room on our 10:40 flight. Boarding starts in twenty minutes. I can move you if you think you will make it. The terminal is about six gates from security."

Carly weighed her options. She wanted to get home but didn't know if she had the motivation or strength to hustle through the airport to arrive on time. It was like her body was stuck in slow motion, moving at the same speed as a 45 vinyl. She took off her sunglasses, revealing eyes that couldn't deny constant crying. The woman pulled her head back, trying not to react. "Ma'am, if you need to get home as soon as possible, I think you should take that flight."

Carly nodded, wiping at her eyes. Leaving Florida symbolized another door from her past that closed before it opened. "Thank you. Yes, I would like that."

The ticket transferred smoothly. The woman handed Carly the boarding pass and whispered, "Ma'am, I don't know what your story is, but I will be praying for you."

Carly smiled, took the ticket, and walked away, pulling the sunglasses back down over her eyes.

Carly thought about all the people that recently upturned her life. Rick, Delilah, Sandra, and John. By the time she got home, Carly was exhausted from the mental gymnastics of wondering where she went wrong and why she couldn't just be satisfied with what she had in front of her.

That night, around eight pm, Carly settled down in her bed. She snuggled up against her favorite pillow and wrapped herself in blankets like a burrito. The inn looked the same as she left it. A fresh dusting of snow blanketed the landscape, and the chilly air numbed the pain.

The following day, Carly walked over to the inn to help Joanie cook and clean for breakfast. She found Matt standing against Joanie, with his legs straddling hers, leaning against the stove. "Ahem! Morning!" Carly called out cheerfully, hoping her eyes didn't deceive her.

Matt abruptly turned around with a spatula in his hand. "Good morning!" he sang. "Welcome home!"

"Morning, Carly!" Joanie exclaimed, equally jubilant.

"Wow, good morning to you too! I see you both are very chipper at six in the morning!"

Joanie smiled, mixing the pancake batter. "Yes, we are!" She turned to face Carly with a wide grin spread across her face. "So how was the wedding? How was Bridezilla and Bridezilla's mother?" She snickered at her joke.

"Good! They got married! It was a beautiful ceremony. We missed you." Carly wasn't sure if Jackie missed Joanie, but she assumed that was the case.

"Ah, it was probably better that I wasn't there." She hummed quietly to herself and continued to stir the batter.

"How was Delilah?" Matt asked. Unease settled into the kitchen, and Carly wondered if either of them noticed. She paused, fully knowing this question was going to come up but still unprepared to answer.

"She was there with Rick. I met her briefly after the ceremony with Rick. She put two and two together and ran out of there quicker than I could say 'Mom,' but you know....it's fine." It wasn't acceptable, and Carly knew it.

"Oh, Car," Matt said, walking over with his arm outstretched. "I'm so sorry." He embraced her, and she held tight, refusing to let more tears form.

"It's okay. It just wasn't meant to be." Carly shrugged as if it was no big deal and headed into the dining room to escape their stares. She busied herself with table settings. "Hey, Joanie! How many people today?" she called into the kitchen.

"Just four. I think the snow scared everyone off," Joanie hollered back.

When Carly re-entered the kitchen, Matt and Joanie stood with their backs to Carly, their arms wrapped around each other in an embrace. "Ahem," Carly fake coughed. "I must have a tickle." The couple disengaged from each other and smiled sheepishly. "Okay, what's up," Carly asked, but it came out as a statement. "You guys have been weird ever since I walked in."

Joanie galloped over to Carly in four quick strides. "We have to tell you something! I don't know if the timing is right, with everything going on."

Carly eyed them for a few moments, back and forth, trying to read their body language. All that came to mind were weddings and babies, and she hoped that neither was true. "What's up?"

"Matt and I are moving in together!" Joanie exclaimed. "You get your house back!"

"Wow," Carly muttered.

"Yeah, we decided that we like each other," Matt winked at Joanie, and Joanie blushed. "Joanie is going to move in with me on the farm. We're going to see what happens."

Joanie interrupted, rapidly speaking, "But don't worry! We're still here to run the inn. We know that we still have a job to do and will do it."

"But, if you are living on the other side of the island, how are you going to take care of the inn?" Carly asked slowly.She wasn't sure if she was ready to put her problems aside and jump back into working twenty-four hours a day.

"Well," Joanie started, backtracking with her eyes, "I can be on call. If anything happens, just call, and I will get over here as soon as possible."

"You don't have a car," Carly rebutted. "What about when Matt is at work?"

"I have a bike," Joanie protested. "When it's summer, I will have Matt drop me off before his shift, and if he can't, I will ride my bike over."

"We'll make it work, Car, don't worry!" Matt said, flipping bacon.

Carly poured herself a cup of coffee and let the news simmer in her mind. Joanie was moving out. Carly would be on the clock day and night. It didn't feel fair, but there was nothing Carly could do.

"Sure," she smiled. "It'll work out."

Chapter 36

J oanie threw her clothes into her duffle bag and tossed in a few extra pairs of shoes to maximize her packing. She slowly transferred her mountain of personal belongings from the inn to Matt's.

She felt inconsiderate for breaking the news the way they did. Carly appeared upset from her recent trip, and all Joanie and Matt did were complicate things. They were both excited and madly in love. It just spilled out.

Joanie thought about her relationship with Matt and how their story organically unfolded and weaved together every passing day. Of course, there were snags in the woven tapestry they created, but weren't the imperfections within the fabric what made the final design so beautiful? Joanie never expected to move in with him. She was happy living at the inn and dating in her spare time. Everything changed one random night when Sheila's constant barrage of suggestions and demands pushed Joanie to her breaking point.

While Jackie was planning her Florida wedding, Joanie fielded phone call after phone call from Sheila, who heavily coated her messages with guilt. "She's your only sister," she said. **She was counting on you**, she texted. **You are so selfish. Your sister asked you to be in her wedding, and you don't even have the decency to uphold your commitment**, she emailed. The constant bombardment of accusations weighed Joanie down and caused her to question her ability to be a good sister and daughter.

She and Matt sat down to dinner one night when the last phone message was too much. Joanie threw the phone in anger, and it bounced off the cushioned rocker in the living room. "Why is she making my life hell?" Joanie screamed at her phone, which wedged itself between the arm and the cushion of the couch.

Matt walked over, still unsure of where they stood, and gave her a big hug. "You are amazing," he whispered in her ear. "Don't let her affect you."

Shivers ran down Joanie's back, and she scowled at herself for allowing him to affect her. She was still upset but knew she was acting irrationally.

Joanie immediately pulled away from him and tensed her fists. "I hate how she always makes me feel inferior. My entire life, I have been second to Jackie. So maybe I don't want to be at her wedding because I don't like her!"

"Don't like who?" Matt asked.

Joanie chuckled. "Both of them."

"I like you," Matt said, brushing the front of her hair back with his forefinger and tucking it behind her ear.

Joanie sighed. "I like you too. I like you too much. You make me so mad, but I still keep loving you." She tried to glare at him but instead looked like a child playing house.

"I love you too," Matt said.

He pulled her down to the couch and sat next to her with their bodies apart but knees touching. He grabbed her hands and held them together against his thighs.

"I've been thinking," he said, rubbing her fingers. "I like you. I love you. I am in love with you."

Joanie gulped, her heart fluttered, and her fingertips lost all temperature. She smiled in response.

"I want more. For us. For you and me."

Joanie nodded, the words not quite forming in her mouth. She wondered if he was going to propose, and butterflies flapped within her midsection.

"I want to wake up with you next to me. I want to go to sleep every night, looking at you. I want to share all my days near you. Joanie, will you move in with me?"

Joanie started giggling uncontrollably. She had never been proposed to and thought this was it! But then, she felt a wave of relief that he didn't ask to marry her because she didn't know if she was ready. But would she move in with him? Absolutely!

"Yes!" she screamed, throwing her arms around him. "When do I move in?"

"Whenever you want!" he replied.

They spent the next two days inseparable. Joanie started moving her belongings in, one car trip at a time, dropping everything in front of the television in his home. She felt like a queen and couldn't wait to spend the first night in her castle with her king.

Now, she stood in front of the tiny closet in her apartment, trying to cram one more pair of shorts into her bag. Matt was outside, rearranging the bed of his truck to prevent anything from flying away. Joanie still needed to pack books, blankets, and jackets that she somehow accumulated over the past year and a half.

Joanie threw the duffle over her shoulder and strode outside, giving him a tender kiss in thanks. She wasn't sure what she was thankful for exactly but felt like he rescued her. Matt wanted her, and that desire filled her heart, soul, and mind.

"Are you ready to go?" he asked, pulling the cover over the back of the truck.

"Yeah," she smiled, "I think I have everything."

He climbed into the passenger seat. "Now the fun starts!" he said, rubbing his gloved hands together. "Unpacking."

Joanie laughed, picturing the overflowing piles of bags and boxes in front of his television. "Hey man, you want me in your house. I come as a package deal with all my stuff."

He grabbed her bare fingers and warmed them in his cupped gloved hands. "I can make room for whatever you bring."

Joanie blushed, knowing that he wasn't just talking about material things. He meant her baggage, her past, and her future. She didn't respond because she was speechless.

They rode in silence to his farm. Joanie thought about Carly and how they broke the news, still feeling guilty for not considering her feelings.

Since that morning, she and Carly talked about the inn and the logistics of how they would manage. Ultimately, Joanie was an employee and nothing more. People quit all the time from jobs, and the owners figured it out. Joanie and Matt planned to remain involved, so the day-to-day operation ran smoothly. Joanie wasn't sure why she felt so guilty.

Matt and Joanie walked into the kitchen, smelling the cookies that had recently come out of the oven. A tray of cookies sat on the table with a sign that said, "EAT ME."

"Matt!" Joanie exclaimed. "Did you make these?"

He nodded, eyeing her closely. Joanie grabbed a cookie and took a bite. The warm chocolate chips oozed out of the corner of her lip and dripped onto the table.

Matt approached and kissed the remnants off her lip. "Follow me," he said, grabbing her hand.

He led her into the living room, where a large bouquet of roses sat in the center of the coffee table.

Joanie ran over to the flowers, picked up the vase, and inhaled deeply. "Are these for me?" she asked, with a wide grin on her face. Her eyes sparkled.

Matt nodded. He grabbed her hand again and led her to the staircase. Loose rose petals fluttered on every step, fragile yet beautiful at the same time.

"Wow!" Joanie exclaimed. "This is so romantic!"

Matt beamed. He kissed her lips, grabbed her hands, and led her upstairs to his room.

In the bedroom, Joanie found the closet door swung wide open and empty. In the corner, she saw a tall, empty armoire. Next to the bed, she found a second nightstand. "This room is amazing!" Joanie said. "Are those for me?"

Matt nodded. "I couldn't ask you to move in and not make room for you. I wanted you to feel comfortable here. This is your home too." He kissed her again, this time deeply, and slowly navigated his way to the bed.

Joanie felt full of life. She lay next to him and embraced his hands, running them up and down her body as if they had never touched her before. She sank into the new down comforter and felt her body relax. She was with a man who loved her and respected her. She squeezed him close and pressed herself into him.

She finally felt like she was home.

Chapter 37

C arly settled into the apartment attached to the inn. Between all the moves, the furnishings had changed too many times to count. To make it feel hers again, she moved the bed opposite the door so that the sunrise could wake her every morning. She switched the dinette table and purchased new curtains, towels, and bathroom furnishings. She felt silly for making minor adjustments to the décor, but she needed a visual reminder that she was in control of her life.

She was still angry about Rick and Delilah and her naivety about what would happen when they reunited. She should have known better, but she let hope get the best of her. Rick texted a few times over the past three weeks, but Carly deleted them before she could read them. She didn't want to open her heart just to have it stepped on again. Life was better when there was no disappointment.

Carly felt angry at Joanie for moving out, but she couldn't blame her for moving on with her life. The inn was Carly's responsibility. The business was in her name and her name only. Matt was only helping, and Joanie was helping through Matt.

Unresolved uncertainty regarding Ruth and Peter's involvement with her life haunted her. Did they know? Did they not? And if they did, shouldn't they have been truthful with her?

She needed someone to blame for her frustration and unhappiness. She wasn't ready to take ownership of her involvement in her current situation. Meeting Delilah at the wedding was Carly's idea. Rick told her he wasn't sure if Delilah would show up, and they stood her up at lunch. Why would she think things would end well? And what exactly did Carly envision in her perfect world when she told Delilah who she was? A hug? An embrace? Tears of gratitude?

Carly was an idiot for thinking things could work out.

The only person she spoke to after the wedding was Sandra. Carly believed her life would have been just fine if Sandra hadn't encouraged her to take that stupid DNA test. She partly blamed Sandra for her fate but needed a sounding board to process all her feelings. Sandra knew how Carly felt and understood the magnitude of emotions funneling like a tornado inside her.

Carly missed Peter. He always knew what to say to keep her smiling. When she was a little girl, Peter took her to a carnival on the mainland, and Carly desperately wanted to win a stuffed animal from the fishing game. Ruth, the practical one, refused to spend one more dime on the game, knowing that the money would not result in a win. Ruth and Peter argued back and forth about money and joy, and childhood dreams. Carly desperately wanted that stuffed horse with the purple tail and golden crown.

Ruth abruptly turned, huffed about the cost of food, and agreed to buy Carly fried dough with powdered sugar. Peter watched her walk away until she was out of sight and turned to Carly, who was already silently pouting about the horse she couldn't take home.

"Carly," he hissed. "Come here, quick." He walked over to the opposite side of the fishing game and gave the man a ten-dollar bill. Carly's eyes widened with anticipation. "I'm not going to stop until the money is gone or I have a horse in my hand." He winked in secrecy.

Peter knew the clock was ticking. He knew Ruth would be back, with her sour face and her narrowed eyes. The man gave Peter a nod, fully understanding the wrath of an unhappy wife, and handed him the fishing pole. Peter anticipated six minutes of action before she returned.

Peter rushed, throwing the fishing pole in and out of the water, hoping one of those throws would result in a bite. Instead, the man whispered, "Mister, you have four more shots."

Carly's heart dropped. He tried so hard, but she was going to leave the carnival alone.

215

"Yes!" Peter hollered, pumping his fist into the air. The man asked Carly which animal she wanted.

"The horse!" she giddily cried.

The man gave Carly the horse, and Peter grabbed it out of Carly's hands. "Tonight," he said, winking at her and stuffed the horse into the inside of his oversized raincoat. He zipped it up, and puffiness filled out his chest from the awkward animal.

Carly didn't have to say a word. She knew what he was saying. He would sneak the horse to her tonight. This was their little secret.

Back at the apartment, Carly found the stuffed horse in a box under the bed. Carly's heart filled with love and gratitude. She wished Peter was there so she could ask him about Delilah and the baby.

Somehow, winter turned to spring, and the calendar filled with reservations for the summer. Carly blocked Charlie and Rick from calling or texting, and life slowly returned to normal. Carly refused to waste time and energy thinking about the family that denied her.

Carly slowly turned resentful. Anything related to the inn became a nuisance, whether changing the sheets, making breakfast, or paying the bills. The mundane responsibilities seemed to overpower the joy she had in her life before receiving the DNA test results.

Matt and Joanie kept their word and helped at the inn almost as often as before the move. Carly sensed that some of the reasons why Joanie was so eager to please were because she didn't want to rock the boat and make Carly's life any harder than she already had.

Sometimes, the tension was so thick and the negativity so strong that Carly just wanted to run away and hide in her bed, never returning.

Carly was at the kitchen table, reviewing the upcoming months' reservations. Every day was booked. "Hey, Joanie!" Carly called into the other room. "Are you going away this summer? I need to make sure it's on the calendar."

Joanie walked in, holding an overflowing laundry basket of white linens. "No, I should be here all summer." She wiped her brow and pushed her bangs out of her eyes.

The sun was warm and inviting. The daffodils dotted the perimeter of the drive, and the grass was almost ready for its first mow. The change in season elevated Carly's mood slightly. Carly had a mile-long list of things she needed to do to prepare for the opening season, and she started to believe that her type-A personality was re-emerging.

She wanted to paint the house, get new patio furniture, purchase fresh linens, and redecorate the sitting room. It was enough to keep her mind occupied until the people started flowing in and out the front door.

"Okay, great," she replied. "I'm not going anywhere this summer either. I think we can coordinate, so each of us gets at least two or three days off a week."

"Yeah, that would be great," Joanie replied, continuing into the other room with the basket.

Carly continued to make her list of things she would like to accomplish before Memorial Day weekend. She had less than a month, and that pressure was enough to focus her mind. She didn't have time to think of anything else.

The following weekend, Joanie and Matt invited Carly over for dinner. She didn't want to go because their happiness irritated her. She preferred to wallow in her room, lay on the sheets that she neglected to wash, and listen to the hum of the refrigerator. Her moods varied from manic to depressed and back again. When dealing with the inn, she was constantly in motion. When dealing with all other areas of her life, she huddled in the fetal position under her blankets, wondering what she had done to make the universe so mad.

Carly looked outside her window, debating on whether or not to cancel her plans.

"Should I go?" Carly asked Sandra.

"Yes, you need to go," Sandra replied into the phone.

"I don't want to," Carly protested.

"Just go. You need to get out of the house, Carly."

Carly knew she was right and knew Sandra's advice was the same as Carly would give if the roles were reversed. "Fine."

"Carly, you have to get out of this funk."

"I tried, Sandra. I did. But Joanie and Matt seem so happy, and they left me alone at the inn. This whole year, we were a team. When she moved out, I was isolated again, running this place solo. I can't do it. Between that and the rejection from Delilah and the lack of contact with my brothers, I feel hopeless. I feel like life should be more than this."

"Carly, you need to figure it out. You can't let other people's actions define you or control you. Yes, what happened with Delilah was unfair, but it happened. Put yourself in her shoes. If a random woman approached you and told you she is your daughter, how would you react? I'm not saying it's right, but you shouldn't have been wearing rose-colored glasses. You shouldn't have been so hopeful. Life is messy and complicated. There are so many layers that influence the actions people make. You need to be okay with your choices. No one else's opinions of you matter."

Carly said nothing for a few moments. She held the phone to her ear, frustration building.

"Carly?" Sandra asked.

"I said I would go. Mom," she said sarcastically. "I will go. I will be kind and gracious and happy. Are you happy now?"

"Call me later. Enjoy yourself. Have a drink. Relax. You will be okay."

Carly hung up the phone and showered. It had been at least two days, and her hair was a greasy ball of dirty straw. She threw on a pair of leggings and a comfortable tunic and drove over to the old farmhouse.

"Hi, Matt. Hi, Joanie," Carly said, looking around the kitchen. Nothing looked different, but it appeared more orderly and complete. She pulled her hair into a ponytail, feeling their sympathetic stares run up and down her wrinkled, mismatched outfit.

"Hi, Carly! Do you want a drink?" Joanie asked.

"Water is fine. Thanks."

Random silences between statements and questions interfered with the flow of conversation. Each conversational shift was labored and intentional. "I'm sorry if I'm not the best conversationalist. I have a lot on my mind," Carly apologized.

"No problem! We get it. We're worried about you, though," Matt replied.

Joanie placed her hand on Carly's arm. "If you ever want to talk, you know we're here for you."

Carly winced at the word 'we.' She didn't have another person to make her 'me' into a 'we.' It was another reminder that she was alone.

"Thanks." Carly drank her water and watched the couple, wondering how long she had to wait before she could leave.

"How's your sister?" Carly asked, changing the subject.

"Good! She's due in a month and freaking out, as usual. She'll be fine, though. Have you talked to Chris?"

Carly shook her head. She hadn't talked to Chris about her situation since the wedding. She called and texted a few times, but he never responded. Carly assumed he was too wrapped up with baby things.

"Are you looking forward to this summer?" Joanie changed the subject again.

"Not really. I don't want the inn anymore. I'm tired of it. I just want to have the option of leaving and starting over again without any repercussions, but you know. Ruth— -"

"We'll buy the inn from you." Everyone turned to look at Matt. Joanie's eyes bulged. Carly scrunched her eyebrows, squinting her eyes.

"What?" Carly thought she misheard.

"Joanie and I haven't talked yet, but I wouldn't be opposed to buying the inn off of you. I will completely take it off your hands, so you have the freedom to figure out who you are and what you want."

Carly winced at his words, not realizing that her unhappiness coated everyone and everything around her. "We're still family, right?" she smiled for the first time that day.

"Yes, we're family. Ruth's will says you must keep it in the family, or you won't make any money on the sale. Guess what? We are still family, and we have DNA results to prove it. I'll buy it off you, and you will be free and clear."

"Matt, are you sure?" Joanie asked, not entirely understanding what he proposed. "We don't have money for that."

"We do. I just received the final settlement from my parent's accident. We can talk about it," Matt said to both women.

Carly mulled the words over in her head, shocked at his offer. It seemed too good to be true.

"But what about your home? And the farm? And the land your parents left you?" Carly asked in rapid succession.

Matt shrugged. "This place has too many memories. We can keep it and continue renting it out or sell it and pocket the money. Joanie and I need to talk about it, but we have options."

"What about your job?" Carly asked.

Matt shrugged again. "I can still work on the force. Joanie and I have a good routine right now. She's the front of the house, and I am the back. If it doesn't work out, I can sell my house, quit my job, and use the house money to compensate until we figure it out."

Joanie stood next to Matt, silent.

Carly couldn't tell if Joanie was excited, shocked, or annoyed. Joanie looked around the kitchen, bit her bottom lip, and tapped her fingers against the countertop. A small smile spread across her face, and she leaned against the counter with her chin resting in her hand.

"Sure, we can talk about it, figure out a plan, and see if it would work for you," Carly agreed, hoping her enthusiasm didn't influence Joanie and Matt's decision. She played it cool, but her muscles were dancing excitedly inside her statuesque body. Her heart thumped, her toes scrunched, and her weight shifted from side to side as she thought about getting away from the island for one final time.

***

The following weekend, Carly climbed off the ferry ramp and found Sandra waving rapidly. Carly ran up to her friend and embraced her tightly. "Hey! I am so glad to see you!"

The wounds from the wedding still sprang from Carly's mind, heart, and soul, but the anticipation of being free from the inn slightly healed them. She needed to get away from all the dead-ends in her life. Carly told Joanie she needed a break from the island to think for a few days. Portland was the place Carly craved.

"I missed you so much!" Sandra exclaimed, grabbing Carly's overnight bag. "I am so sorry." Sandra grabbed Carly's shoulders and pulled her back, their eyes inches from each other. Carly audibly swallowed and nodded.

They drove the three hours north, talking about summer plans, the hiking club, and changes in the city.

"Do you ever think about moving back to Portland?" Sandra asked.

Carly shrugged. "Kind of. I think about moving away from the inn all the time, but I don't know where I would go. I do love Portland, but I don't know if it's right for me. Plus, the inn. If Matt doesn't buy it, I am stuck with it until I die." She laughed, even though it wasn't funny.

"Do you feel like Block Island is dragging you down?" Sandra asked.

"Sometimes. I like my life, but I still feel trapped."

"What are your dreams?" Sandra asked.

Carly smiled sadly. "I don't have any anymore."

"When you think about your future, who do you see standing with you in five years?"

Carly hesitated, unsure if she was ready to speak the truth. "Delilah. Rick. Charlie. You. Joanie. Matt. I guess Chris and Jackie."

Sandra nodded. "Where do you see yourself?"

Carly shrugged. "I don't know. Not on Block Island, but close enough to visit."

They pulled up to Sandra's apartment, the front walkway decorated with irises and tulips. "Beautiful flowers," Carly commented. Sandra's apartment looked the same. Carly dropped her bag next to the couch and sat in the oversized armchair.

"So, I have to tell you something," Sandra said.

Carly stared at her, waiting. "I don't like the sound of that!" she exclaimed.

"I saw John. He looked like shit. I guess not working for months caught up with him. I think he said lobster season kicks off in a few weeks."

"That's too bad," Carly replied blankly.

"Yeah, and I felt bad for him. And I told him you were coming. Sorry." Sandra stood and broke eye contact.

"Why, Sandra?" Carly thought John was gone from her life. "That chapter of my life is over. Please don't make me reopen it."

"Sorry," she said again. "He started asking about you. It's none of his business what's going on in your life, so I told him to ask you if he wanted to know. He told me he misses you. And I felt bad. So, I invited him over in the morning. Tomorrow. Sorry."

Carly stared at her friend, unable to respond. Her life was falling apart, and Sandra thought it would be a good idea to re-enter John? The first time Sandra omitted information from Carly and John showed up at the ferry, Carly forgave her. Carly told herself it was an honest mistake. The second time she omitted information from Carly was one mistake away from being a pattern. "Sandra!" Carly cried.

"I know! I now realize that it was a bad idea, but it's too late."

"No, it's not! Uninvite him! Tell him I need space. If he doesn't get it, that's his problem!"

Sandra slowly crept into the kitchen. "Okay, you're right! I'm texting him now. I should never have done that. I'm sorry."

Carly rubbed her temples, feeling blindsided. "Wait," she called out. "Don't."

Sandra stuck her head into the living room. "Don't?"

"Yeah, don't. I'll talk to him, but no promises! And it might get uncomfortable, but you arranged this meeting, so you have to be there. I don't want him here, though. We have to meet somewhere neutral, so I can leave if he angers me."

"Okay. I'll text him that we'll meet him for coffee at the diner."

The following morning, Carly showered extra-long, breathing in the hot steam clouding her vision and choking her chest. She thought about John and why he wanted to meet with her.

"Hey, Sandra?" Carly called through the bathroom door, squeezing her hair in a towel. "I want to see John alone. Can you drop me off?"

"Sure," a voice echoed through the door.

Carly pulled on her jeggings and slid on a pair of sandals. She placed her jean jacket over her green t-shirt and pulled on her sunglasses. "I'm ready," Carly grunted. Her heart beat against her chest, and she stuffed her hands in her pockets.

Carly was the first to arrive at the diner. She sidled into the red vinyl booth and asked the waitress for two cups of coffee. The coffee cup warmed her hands, and the scent of java calmed her mind. She inhaled deeply before taking a sip.

"Hey." She heard a deep voice behind her. John slid into the booth seat across from her, and their knees bumped under the table.

Carly smiled. "Hi. I ordered you a coffee. I hope it's not too cold."

"Thanks. You look great," John said. He spoke with a slower rate of speech, carefully analyzing Carly's facial features. Carly took in his shaggy hair, just covering his ears and almost covering his eyes. His beard needed trimming, and his eyes needed sleep. He wore a red and black checkered flannel, the sleeves covering his knuckles.

"How have you been?" Carly asked noncommittally. "How was your winter?"

"Good." John took a sip of coffee. "It was lonely. I spent a lot of time alone."

Carly rubbed her thumb up and down the coffee mug handle. She waited for him to continue.

"I have a lot of time to think. I hate thinking." He took another sip of coffee, and Carly waited again. "I miss you. I miss us."

Carly swallowed the lump in her throat. "John," she began.

He looked up and interrupted. "I know the timing isn't great, but I want to start over. We have something special, Carly. I want to try again."

Carly looked into his eyes and saw years of hurt that she caused. They had a history that ran deep, and both of them shaped their choices around the pain.

"John, you deserve someone who accepts you and your decisions. That person isn't me. I thought it was, but this past year proved me wrong. I need someone who will be around when I need them, and you need someone who will let you pursue your dreams without placing blame or guilt on you. That person isn't me." Carly didn't know how, but her heart was speaking through her mouth.

John nodded. "I miss you," he repeated, his voice cracking.

Carly touched his hand. "You don't miss me. You miss having a girlfriend." She was blunt but kind. She couldn't believe how much calmness and serenity she felt. It was like she needed Delilah's rejection to forgive John and forgive herself.

"That's not true!" John retorted.

"It is, and it's fine. My life is in shambles right now, but if there is one thing that I know, I will never forget you and all you have done for me, but I am in no position to be in a relationship. Not just with you, but with anyone. I need to find myself and learn to love myself. I can't do that unless I am alone. I hope you understand."

John half-shrugged, his shoulders slumped.

"I want you to be happy, John, but I also need me to be happy. I hope you understand," she repeated.

John shrugged again. Carly stood up, tossed five dollars on the table, and pulled on her coat. "I have to go. Thanks for reaching out to me. You've helped me more than you realize. Good luck, John." Carly turned on her heel and walked out the door. Instead of calling Sandra, she walked back to the apartment, holding her head high. She didn't know what she needed, but she felt courage fill her spirit.

Chapter 38

Memorial Day weekend came in a blink of an eye. The weather was beautiful, the sky was blue, and a gentle breeze rolled off the ocean. People filled the island, and the hustle and bustle of tourists reignited a fire under the little town. Carly spoke with other business owners, and excitement for a new season and the potential to make money filled the space between them.

"Matt?" she called as she dumped brown paper bags filled with food onto the counter. "Can you help me?" Her voice disappeared against the loud hum of the vacuum.

"Matt?" she called again, walking toward the front entryway.

Matt turned off the vacuum and smiled. "Hey!" he said.

"Hi! I need your help. The first set of guests told me they are arriving tonight instead of tomorrow, and I need to make sure the back bedroom is ready. Can you vacuum that room first? It needs to be available when they arrive."

"Aye aye, Captain!" Matt saluted.

Carly continued unpacking. She went out in the yard and cut fresh flowers from her garden to decorate the bedrooms and dining room. She snipped pink peonies and purple irises and placed them in the skinny glass vases filled halfway with water. Carly placed them on each dresser in each bedroom. It looked and smelled beautiful.

Joanie wandered around the house with a bottle of window cleaner and a balled-up newspaper. "Thank you," Carly said as she passed her in the hallway. "I want to make sure that there are no streaks on any of the windows or mirrors."

Joanie nodded.

Carly headed back down to the kitchen and checked the stock of complimentary drinks and snacks. She took out a few more soda cans and transported them to the mini-fridge in the guest dining room. Floral tablecloths draped over the tables.

Everything looked perfect.

That night, the doorbell rang. Carly always found it interesting when guests who never experienced bed and breakfast life showed up at the door. She always imagined an argumentative conversation outside about the etiquette upon entering. Do you walk in or ring the bell? Is this like a hotel or more like a house? The rules were never clearly defined.

Carly walked over to the front door, put on her cheeriest face, and opened the door quickly and widely. "Hello!" She stopped. Her face dropped. "Welcome to the Willowside Inn," she said, her tone void of enthusiasm and replaced with trepidation. She hoped they didn't notice.

A party of three adults stood in her doorway, ready to upheave her life again.

"Hi, Carly," Rick said. "Can we come in? We made a reservation."

Carly motioned for them to come in without saying a word. She was fuming inside. She spent the past few months pushing away the wedding and forgetting about Delilah. Carly finally readjusted to her new reality. She told herself that trying to find her mother was a glitch in her life. She needed to forget the wedding.

"Excuse me," she said, leaving them alone in the entryway.

She made her way upstairs and found Matt and Joanie in the back bedroom. She closed the door behind her so her voice would not carry. Her face drained of all color, and she leaned against the door for support, eventually sliding down to the ground.

"Are you okay?" Matt asked. "It looks like you've seen a ghost."

Carly nodded and whispered, "Delilah is down there. And Rick, and someone else. I think it might be Charlie. Can you guys take care of them? I need a few minutes." She stepped behind the door so that they could get through the narrow opening.

Joanie and Matt left her alone in the bedroom, where Carly sat, numb. She felt blindsided and betrayed that she had no warning of their arrival. She wasn't ready to see them, even if it was her job to be friendly to all guests booked at the Willowside Inn.

She had to get out of that bedroom before they made their way up the stairs. Somehow, Carly exited the room and hid in another bedroom until they were situated. She didn't know what Matt and Joanie said to them, and she didn't care. She wasn't ready.

Carly checked the reservations in her email and found them under the name Richard Parker. They weren't even sneaky about the reservation. Carly recalled answering the phone and solidifying the booking a few weeks back. She didn't make the connection because she only knew her brother as Rick. According to their reservation, they were staying until Sunday. Sunday, Carly thought, was too long for her to avoid them. Eventually, she would cross their path and force them to reveal whatever motivated them to come.

Carly jumped into businesswoman mode and became hyper-focused on her list. She had work to do, and there was no way Carly would allow Delilah to screw up opening weekend.

***

"Knock-knock," Joanie whispered as she tapped on Carly's apartment door. She opened the door even though Carly did not respond. Joanie saw lights off, curtains drawn, and a gentle hum of music emanating from the kitchen. "Carly?" Joanie called, slowly walking through the apartment.

The apartment was untouched. Besides the music playing, there was no semblance of someone living there. Joanie thumbed through a drawer to find paper and pen and scribbled a note: **Hi. We need you in the kitchen. -Joanie**.

Carly was still in charge, and Joanie and Matt needed direction about handling the unexpected relatives. Rick asked to speak to Carly numerous times. The trio appeared relaxed and seemed to enjoy their time, but Joanie knew the real reason they arrived. She needed the tension to clear up before the remaining guests checked in.

Joanie meandered around the property, house, and carriage house, and still no sign of Carly. She checked her watch because precious time was flying by, and nothing was getting done. She walked outside and found Matt laying down new gravel on the walkway.

"Hi," she said, out of breath. "I can't find her. Maybe she went to the beach, or in town, or something. What do we do about, you know?" Joanie threw her head up and back toward the house, just in case someone was listening.

"Nothing. We continue like we don't know who they are. It's none of our business, and we have a business to run. We continue on and do our job. If Carly left the island for a few days, we would be fine. We know what we're doing."

Joanie nodded, not quite as confident as Matt.

When they arrived back inside, Rick stood in the front entryway, waiting.

"Hello!" Joanie called out cheerfully. "Can I help you with something?"

Rick looked just like Carly. Joanie was stunned by the similarities in bone structure, ivory skin, and sandy-colored hair. They were definitely siblings, Joanie thought.

"Uh, yes." Rick walked around the room, looking at the artwork on the wall for longer than any other guest Joanie previously observed. "I was wondering if I could speak to Ms. Davis?"

Joanie shook her head. "Sorry, she stepped out a while ago. She should be back soon."

Rick nodded and retreated up the stairs. "Thank you. I think we will head out and walk around the shops." He disappeared around the turn at the top of the stairs, and Joanie hurried into the kitchen.

Matt was right. It wasn't her problem, and it wasn't her problem to solve. Carly was fine. She would figure it out.

The rest of the guests arrived, and Joanie and Matt greeted them, showed them to their room, and explained how breakfast worked. Without Carly there to help, it would be a busy weekend with no sleep, sore muscles, and lots of coffee. *Happy Opening Season*, Joanie thought.

***

Carly snuck home late that evening. After she saw Rick and Delilah standing on her doorstep, she had to get away. Carly didn't know where she was going, but she needed to sort her mind. She walked along the island, checked out the tourists pouring off the ferry, and noticed all the newly opened shops for the summer season.

Carly continued walking. Her legs were tired, but she refused to stop. She stood in front of the Historical Society, wondering how she got there.

"Welcome," Mrs. Jackson said with a smile on her face.

"Hello," Carly mumbled. "I don't know if you remember me."

Mrs. Jackson looked at Carly quizzically.

"Carly. Davis," Carly muttered.

"Ah, yes, what can I do for you?" Mrs. Jackson asked.

"I wanted to ask you about your son and his co-worker. The sibling of the Swanson's. Do you remember her?" Carly eyed Mrs. Jackson curiously, not quite sure if she could trust her response.

"I don't remember her name. She was in her early twenties and a student at the Culinary and Hospitality college. She worked with my son."

"David?" Carly asked.

"No, my son Billy. How do you know David?"

Carly faintly nodded. She felt foolish for assuming David was lying to her when he said he didn't know anything. " I met him here when you were on vacation." Carly redirected her attention back to Mrs. Jackson.

"Oh. Yes, the niece interned for the summer. I think she was with your parents for a while."

Carly cringed at the word *parents*. "What happened after she left?" Carly questioned.

"Well, she went back to college. I don't believe she ever came back. At least, I never saw her again."

Carly sighed and took out the newspaper article. "Mrs. Jackson, do you know this woman?" The crease distorted the woman's face.

"Yes. I believe this is her. Where did you find this?"

"In my parent's basement." Carly wanted to ask more questions but didn't have the energy to prompt and probe Mrs. Jackson for information. "Mrs. Jackson, is her name Delilah? I know all about her."

Mrs. Jackson sighed and turned her back to Carly. She stood still as a statue.

"Oh. Yes, dear. Delilah."

"Thank you," Carly said. Validation consumed her. "Do you know anything about my adoption? Or how I came to the island?"

Mrs. Jackson looked uneasy. Her eyes narrowed, and she pursed her thin lips so tightly they disappeared into the darkness of her closed mouth.

"All I know is that your parents found you on their doorstep in a basket. You had a blanket and a note. Your parents kept it quiet. They took a few years off from the inn to raise you and reopened it again when you were four. They didn't want people to ask questions, and they didn't want to answer any suspicions or accusations. Eventually, people stopped caring to know the details."

Carly choked back the lump in her throat. It sounded so tragic and surreal.

"So you don't know anything else?" Carly asked.

"No."

"Why did you lie to me?" Carly's voice quaked at asking such a personal question to someone old enough to be her grandmother.

Mrs. Jackson smiled sadly. "Dear, we all have our secrets. The families who live on the island have been on the island for generations. All of the secrets from the island are buried deep in the sand. I couldn't be the one to tell you because I gave your parents my word." Her voice softened and gently wrapped around Carly.

The jigsaw puzzle pieces started to fall into place, and the haziness around her past cleared. She needed to clear her head from all this new information swirling in front of her. She tried to organize the pieces, but the details were just out of reach. She knew she had to face Delilah before the weekend was over.

The following day, Carly reluctantly shuffled into the kitchen. Joanie said she would be over at sunrise, and Carly hoped she hadn't overslept. She didn't want to go, but her feet guided her into the all too familiar kitchen.

Matt and Joanie stumbled around the kitchen, trying to get their breakfast groove on. It had been half a year since the inn was packed, and managing multiple families of vacationers was different than juggling one or two at a time.

230

"Morning," Carly said.

"Hi!" Joanie turned to Carly. "I didn't expect you—Matt, can you get the coffee ready? I need to go cut the fruit."

"I'm here to help," Carly announced. "It's opening weekend. I'm not going to let one unwanted reservation throw me off my game." She smiled at the others.

"Sure thing," Matt said to Joanie, pulling out the coffee filters.

"Great," Joanie responded to Matt or Carly. Carly was unsure because her eye gaze was focused on the knife slicing through the strawberries.

Carly knew the kitchen was not big enough for three adults who hadn't yet learned the breakfast dance, so she headed into the dining room to finish setting the tables. She stopped mid-step, halfway between the kitchen and the dining room.

Sitting with her back to the kitchen was the petite woman with the same features as Carly. She hadn't turned when the door swung open, and Carly fought the urge to turn around and hide. Instead, she inwardly sighed and slowly approached.

"Good morning," she said, with as much authority as she could muster.

Delilah turned, her face made up with mascara and lipstick, and Carly saw her own blue eyes staring back at her. "Carly," Delilah said. "Come sit." She patted the hard, wooden chair next to her.

Carly didn't want to sit. Her heart was mending from the Florida fracture. Delilah didn't entirely break her heart, but the fissure was widening. She walked over to Delilah and stood next to her in protest. From this angle, she could see Delilah's graying roots and perfectly manicured nails. "I'm good," Carly said coldly, standing with authority.

Delilah looked up at her with sympathetic eyes. Perhaps it was sadness or maybe regret, Carly wasn't sure, but the intensity of her stare forced Carly down into the chair next to her. She felt her heart softening, seeing that this moment was not easy for Delilah.

"Your father was a great man," Delilah said, looking out the window.

Carly didn't say a word.

"I'm sorry for causing you heartache. At the time, I felt like I had no choice.

231

I was overwhelmed. I was jobless, homeless, and scared. My priorities were all mixed up, and I wasn't giving you the life you deserved. I had to take care of myself before I could take care of you. By the time I got myself clean, it was too late. I couldn't go and disrupt your life again."

Carly nodded, the knot in her throat preventing her from speaking.

Delilah continued. "I felt betrayed at the wedding. That was why I ran. All of my children blindsided me. You included. And I couldn't be there anymore. I have been thinking over the past few months, praying over what to do. I knew I had to apologize because my choices directly impacted you, and it was unfair. You had no choice in the matter."

Delilah didn't make eye contact with Carly. Carly saw a single tear roll down her cheek.

"Can I ask you something?" Carly asked after a few moments of silence.

Delilah nodded.

"Did my mom and dad know that my dad was my dad?"

Delilah nodded. "Your dad knew. I don't know if your mom knew, but I assume she did. I went to my sister, who knew I had a baby and knew it was someone from here because of the timing but didn't know who. Peter and I had to sneak around, and I swore him to secrecy about our affair."

Carly shivered, hating that her father was an adulterer and hating that she was the result of that.

"After my mother kicked me out of the house, I contacted my sister and confessed. I told her I was going to leave the baby at a fire station. She convinced me to tell the father before denying both of us. I had to tell her who it was. She was furious at me. I told her to contact Peter for me and tell him I needed to speak to him. She hated doing my dirty work, but I couldn't have Ruth asking questions."

Carly nodded again, swallowing loudly. Her mouth felt like sandpaper.

"I told Peter about you. You were probably six months old by then. I told him I needed to get clean, and he understood. So we concocted a plan about getting you to him. My sister met me at the ferry in Connecticut and took you here. All I had was a diaper bag with a handful of diapers, one bottle, and a blanket. I handed you over, and that was the last I saw of you. Chris's parents placed you on your parents' doorstep. They never said a word about what they did. I never talked to my sister again. I tried to contact her, but all my mail returned to me, and they ignored my calls. I don't blame them. I was a coward and foolish and put them in a terrible situation." Delilah cried silent tears that fell in rapid succession.

Carly wanted to reach out to her, but she couldn't drop her guard and be vulnerable.

"Did I have a birth certificate?" Carly asked, never having found her birth certificate.

"You did. I gave it to Peter. He was named on the birth certificate, even though any evidence of my relationship with Peter was dangerous. When Peter pursued adoption, the state contacted me because I was the listed mother. I was deemed unfit due to my drug addiction, so they never questioned giving you to Peter. I assumed your parents hired a lawyer and handled the adoption without me."

"What was my name?" Carly asked.

"On your birth certificate? Your name was Hope Hanna Murphy. Murphy was my maiden name."

Carly nodded. Her name was Hope. It felt appropriate considering her mother's sad story.

"I forgive you." Carly gave Delilah a quick, awkward hug. Then, she stood up quickly and exited the dining room to assist with breakfast.

Her mind was spinning with all the information. So much of her childhood made sense now that she was older and could look at things objectively. Life was messy and complicated and full of good and bad choices. Carly thought she would feel relieved after meeting Delilah, but she felt emptier than she did when she woke up that morning.

She got through breakfast on autopilot and kept the small talk to a minimum. Joanie and Matt knew not to press for additional information. They could see Delilah, Rick, and Charlie in the dining room. They appeared happy, chatted about the weather, and asked what activities they should do to fill their day.

After breakfast, Rick excused himself from the table and made his way to the drink station. Carly stood behind the table, filling the sugar bowl. "We're going to check out the lighthouses later. Would you like to come?"

Carly smiled and nodded at Rick. Her first response was to decline the offer graciously, but she knew that this opportunity would probably never cross her path again. So instead of feeling angry for her circumstances, she forced herself to feel curious instead. "Sure, that would be great."

As she entered the kitchen, she felt a lightness in her step. Excitement was building at the possibility of having a relationship with her siblings. Hope grew as she thought about the opportunities to start again.

That day, Carly learned the story of her past and experienced the healing power of forgiveness. Carly was ready.

Hope, Carly thought. *What a perfect name.*

Epilogue-Six Months Later

"A re you sure you want to do this?" Carly asked Matt and Joanie. They sat across from each other at a large conference table in the lawyer's office, a stack of documents in front of them.

"Absolutely," Matt replied, grinning.

Joanie looked at her left hand and noticed the tiny prisms of color flash across the beige wall. She angled her hand and watched the rainbow arc dance, livening up the atmosphere.

"Okay," the lawyer said. "We are going to sign here," he pointed, "and here."

After some tough negotiations with Carly, Matt agreed to a reasonable price for the inn. He could be the inn's new owner with one stipulation: the carriage house was Carly's for as long as she lived or as long as they owned the inn. Matt and Joanie agreed, and the purchase and sale began.

Once they signed the papers, the three friends celebrated with hot chocolate down near the shore. The December air was chilly and brisk, but the excitement combined with the hot cocoa overpowered the chill. They sat on a bench facing the ocean waves. The sun was shining and warm, despite the snow on the ground.

"So, what are you going to do now, Miss Freedom?" Joanie teased, whipped cream sitting above her upper lip. She smiled and wiped the foam with her gloveless hand.

"I'm going to Florida," Carly said. "I'm leaving this weekend."

"Tell Rick I said hi," Matt said.

"I will. I'm going for a month and will be back after New Year's."

"Are you spending Christmas with Delilah?" Joanie asked.

"Yes. It'll be our first holiday together. I'm nervous but ready. I'm hoping for the best but expecting the worst. I won't allow my expectations to crush my spirit again." Carly put her arm around Joanie. "Thank you for everything."

"Of course! That's what friends are for."

"And don't worry, I will be back to help you plan for the wedding."

Matt smiled, and Joanie squeezed Carly's shoulders. "I can't wait."

"Are you happy?" Joanie asked.

Carly smiled. "I am finally free to love myself enough to learn about who I am. I have hope and faith that I will be better off because of this year. I'm ready to go on a new adventure in Florida and find more of me."

The three of them sat in silence, lost in their thoughts.

Carly's phone buzzed in her pocket. She fumbled with her coat and checked to see who was calling. "Oh!" she jumped up from the bench. "I'm going to grab that. It's Delilah."

Carly moved away from the bench and spoke with her mother. Joanie couldn't hear Carly's words, but her smile, tall posture, and the smile lines around her eyes told her that Carly would be okay.

Joanie looked at her ring again and squeezed Matt's arm. "She's going to be okay."

Matt leaned against Joanie, looking at Carly laugh into the phone. "She's going to be okay," he agreed.

They sat in silence for a few moments, watching joy and enthusiasm spill out of Carly's eyes and upturned lips.

"Matt?" Joanie asked quietly.

Matt turned to Joanie, her eager eyes sparkling. "Hmm?" he asked.

"I want to have a baby."

Matt pulled her close. He didn't respond at first, but Joanie didn't mind. This was the first time she ever mentioned starting a family, and she wanted to feel him out. She knew she was planting the seed and didn't expect a response right then. Joanie snuggled into his jacket, smelling his cologne faintly through his clothes. She felt at home next to him.

Lost in her thoughts and dreaming about their life together, Matt faintly whispered, "Me too."

Joanie knew they were going to be okay.

About the Author

E.D. Hackett lives with her husband, two children, and three fur babies in Massachusetts. She always enjoyed writing short stories and journaling when she was a child. She majored in Journalism for a hot second in college and eventually graduated with a Master's degree in Speech-language pathology. E.D. Hackett is an SLP by day and a writer by night.

For most of her adult years, her writing was placed on the back burner due to the chaos of full-time parenting and full-time work. With a little encouragement, she decided to write a novel, write it well, and write it scared. Hope Hanna Murphy is her third novel.

She hopes to convey themes that are relatable to all women and hopes they are enjoyed by all readers. She can be found on Facebook, Instagram, and Goodreads, as well as her website www.edhackettwrites.com

You can connect with me on:

🌐 https://www.edhackettwrites.com

📘 https://www.facebook.com/edhackettwrites

🔗 https://www.instagram.com/e.d_hackettwrites

🔗 https://linktr.ee/Edhackett

Subscribe to my newsletter:

✉ https://www.edhackettwrites.com/contact

Also by E.D. Hackett

E.D. Hackett writes Women's Fiction novels that address self-discovery, friendship, family, and finding happiness.

An Unfinished Story

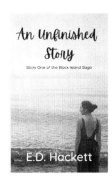

This is the prequel to <u>Hope Hanna Murphy</u>.

Every decision we make sets us up on a new trajectory of what our life will look like.

Meet Joanie.

Her life has been one predictable decision after predictable decision because the fear of change was never strong enough to break the comfort of consistency. Now, her house of cards is falling down because the company she has dedicated her life to is on the brink of collapse. When given an opportunity to save her job and start fresh, Joanie dives in head first hoping for the best. What she doesn't realize is that her expectations and desire for the future are put in question when Matt, a local police officer, who may or may not be looking for love walks into her life.

Meet Carly.

She used to live her life according to her dreams, goals, and desires. A family crisis pulled her back to the place where she grew up and ran away from as soon as she could. Now, she is caught between living the life her parents dreamed of and wanting to drop everything to run back to the life she built for herself. She left her love to help her family, and she wonders if it was worth it.

Two strangers meet.

A random encounter through a mutual friend sets up Joanie and Carly on an adventure of self-discovery and finding happiness. Will it be happiness for forever or happiness just for now?

Jump into the summer that changed their lives and taught them what it means to make decisions that may or may not be right, but will change the trajectory of their lives forever.

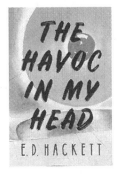

The Havoc in My Head

An inspirational pseudo-memoir about survival, finding joy, and throwing away life's expectations.

Ashley Martin has the perfect life and her need to control was the reason why her life was unfolding just as she expected. When people looked at her, they wanted to be in her shoes, with the supportive husband, well-behaved kids, beautiful home, and highly respected job. Unexpectedly, a terrifying medical diagnosis shatters Ashley's perfect life and she wonders how she will pick up the broken pieces.

After a plethora of symptoms led Ashley to the ER, her life is turned upside down in an instant, and her definition of happiness and success crumbles between her fingers. As Ashley stumbles through the medical maze she is forced to travel, she struggles with isolation and loneliness as her identity is slowly stripped away. Ashley simmers with her thoughts, realizing that her marriage is broken, she doesn't know her children, and she was replaceable and disposable at work.

Can Ashley accept the path that is before her and find the strength to battle and survive while learning how to redefine what a happy, successful life means?

Made in the USA
Middletown, DE
29 January 2022

59133004R00139